THE BETA AND THE FOX
LYNN BRANCH

ISBN 9798993794020

For the misfits, the dreamers, and the ones who've always felt a little out of place.

CONTENTS

Prologue

Kat

"Look, Mom, I finally finished it!" I yelled, holding my picture over my head as I walked into our kitchen.

She was stirring miso soup at the stove, still in her business suit. Mom tossed a glance over her shoulder.

"It's nice," she said, not even looking at it.

I glanced down at the drawing in my hand. It was our orange cat, Chico, in the window, looking out into the back garden. The drawing had taken me weeks; hours of my time in art class.

My dad walked in, staring down at his fancy new phone. He leaned over and kissed Mom, commenting about how good dinner looked.

As he shuffled past me, I held up my drawing. "Look, Dad, I drew Chico. Mr. Withers, the art teacher, says it's my best work so far. He says I'm better than anyone else my age."

Dad grunted, not looking up, and pushed around me, heading towards his office without another word. My shoulders dropped, and I stared down at my drawing. It must not be very good. I never did anything that they liked.

Mom pulled the kitchen curtain aside, looking out at the sidewalk. "Where's Celia? I thought she was walking with you today."

"She was, but she was taking forever talking to Kelsey, so I just came the rest of the way by myself."

Mom didn't reply, but as if on cue, my sister walked through the door. She was fourteen, four years older than me, and was old enough to try out for the cheerleading squad this year.

As soon as the door opened, my mom dropped her spoon and turned to Celia. "So? Tell me! How'd it go?"

Celia squealed, jumping up and down. "I made it, Mom! I made the squad!"

Mom rushed to hug her, gushing, "Of course you did. I never had a doubt!"

Dad poked his head around the corner, grinning. "So it's good news, I'm guessing?"

"Yes!" Celia said, digging in her bag and producing a cheerleading skirt.

"That's great! As long as it doesn't affect your grades, like we talked about."

"It won't, Dad! I promise!"

He walked over and hugged her, making my heart feel sick. I didn't think he'd ever hugged me like that. Not even once.

My parents were saying things like, "Congratulations! We knew you could do it. We're so proud."

I looked down at the drawing in my hands, but it blurred as tears filled my eyes. I placed it in the trash next to me and retreated to the room Celia and I shared. No one noticed I was gone. They never did.

Later that night, I clutched Chico and sobbed into my pillow, trying to understand why they didn't love me. I just wished I knew what I'd done. Then maybe I could fix it. Ms. Brienne, my teacher, explained that if we made a mistake, we could apologize and try to make it better. But I didn't even know what I should be sorry for.

My mattress dipped as Celia climbed into my bed with me, wrapping her arms around me.

She stroked my hair. "What's wrong, sissy?"

"Mom and Dad hate me, and I don't even know why!" I sobbed, burying my face deeper in the pillow so they wouldn't hear.

Celia sighed, tightening her hug around me. She didn't argue about it, and that only made me feel worse.

"Why can't I just be like you?" I whispered, my heart aching like I'd been hit in the chest.

"I know it's hard, Kat. But someday you'll get it. You're just too little right now."

I shook my head, not understanding what she meant by that.

"What did I do?"

"You did nothing. I promise."

"Then why?"

"Ask Mom. But I want you to know that I love you and I always will."

I snuggled closer to her, finding some comfort in her embrace. Finally, my sniffles quieted, and I felt the soft pull of sleep.

CHAPTER 1

FINN

Sixteen Years Later

I UNBUTTONED MY CUFFS and rolled them up, still in my suit from Gideon and Eris' wedding. It was a beautiful ceremony, and I wanted to vomit. After downing a shot of whiskey, I tapped the bar, telling Pike I needed a refill. He obliged, once again attempting to engage me in a conversation about my mood. I ignored his questions. Usually, I was the life of the party, but now I felt like I could barely breathe.

'That's because we need our mate. Why are we sitting here, idiot?' my wolf, Shaw, asked.

I pulled the note out of my pocket and read it for the millionth time.

> *Finn,*
> *I know we have to do something about this, but I can't stay. I don't understand where my mind is. Please don't follow me. It'll just complicate everything. I'll be back.*
> *-Kat*

This referred to our mate bond. She'd stayed for a week after her liberation from the dragon's keep. During that time, she'd championed the sport of avoiding me, and I'd championed the sport of stalking her.

We'd barely had a conversation. Then she'd disappeared and left me with nothing but a hole in my chest and this shitty note.

'She doesn't want us to follow her. I'm trying to respect that.'

'That's stupid. You're so stupid,' Shaw snapped, rushing me with a wave of possessive desire. *'Someone could be with her now! What if it's another man?'*

The glass in my hand shattered, and I barely felt the cut in my palm. I sighed and opened my hand, taking the rag Pike handed me. *'Will you shut up? She's not doing that!'*

'What if she is? She could be with him now. And you're sitting here! What if he marks her? Steals her?'

I swallowed and rubbed my temples, trying to find a buoy of rationality in the ocean of his jealousy.

'Do her emotions feel like she's enjoying a man right now?' I asked him, knowing that arguing with the stubborn brute was pointless.

She was so fucking sad. Her aching sorrow in our partially formed bond had been drowning me since the wedding started.

'That's because she needs us. Let's go!'

'Go where? We don't even know where she is!'

'Don't give me that! Your brother can find anyone with his fancy computer.'

I jumped because a hand landed on my shoulder.

"Finn! Look, Finn's here!"

A girl I'd partied with. Slept with.

I mumbled, "Just go," and shrugged her off, trying to temper my guilt so Kat wasn't affected by it.

"What? Come on—" she started, pulling on my jacket.

I erupted. "Just go! Get away from me!"

The bar quieted, everyone looking our way, and she spat, "Fine, asshole. What the fuck is your problem?"

I didn't answer, slumping in my seat and tapping the bar again. "Just bring the bottle, Pike."

I would've gone if Kat had asked. It didn't matter where we were going; I just wanted to be with her. I had a detailed daydream of meeting her parents and convincing them that wolf shifters weren't so bad. Showing them I could make Kat happy. We were fated to be together, and the Goddess never made mistakes. Blah, blah, blah; all of that rhetoric fed to every wolf shifter from the moment they could toddle. It wasn't supposed to be this way. The mate bond was presumed to be the easiest choice a shifter ever made.

Kat had suggested meeting her parents was a terrible idea, assuring me they would never accept me. In the same conversation, she'd hinted she might never accept me either.

My kind and your kind, Finn... we just don't agree.

Shaw was relentless. *'It's the fox in her that hates us, but her wolf is mine! We can win her heart. You shouldn't have let her go without us. Feel her pain. She needs us. We need her.'*

'I didn't let her go! She left!'

He growled at me, not bothering with a response, and finally, thankfully, resorted to the silent treatment.

A hand fell on my shoulder, and I was shouting, "Does it look like I want company?" only to find Gideon. And Eris. Fucking awesome. Just the people I wanted to see. I took one look at their interlaced fingers and drank the rest of my whiskey in one gulp.

"Did you call him?" I asked Pike, and the wince on the bartender's face answered when he didn't.

My brother grabbed under my arm. "Let's go home, Finn."

He tried to pull me to my feet, but I didn't budge. "I'm good where I am. Thanks."

Before he could say anything else, Kat's despair ripped through the bond, making my chest roll into itself. I grabbed the front of my shirt, closing my eyes and hissing at the pain. "Fuck. What is that?"

"What's wrong?" Gideon asked.

"I don't know," I gritted through my clenched teeth. "She's in so much despair, it's painful."

Involuntary tears formed in my eyes as waves of her sorrow crashed through me. I blocked the bond so I could compose myself and stood, making a decision.

"I have to go. I have to find her," I said, searching my brother's eyes for disappointment.

We had a lot going on right now with the dragons, the end of the world, and the artifacts, but nothing mattered to me except Kat. I didn't know where to start, but I was going to find her. Katarina Kimura. I was sure I could dig something up.

He clapped me on the shoulder and smiled. "Be careful out there. Call me if you need anything. Try to hurry if you can."

I turned, jogging to the exit, but Eris spoke up. "Hey, Finn?" I turned back to her. "Kat told me she grew up in a little town called Ontario. It's just outside Los Angeles. If that helps."

I nodded and threw the door open. "Yes, it does. Thank you!"

I left my car. A jog to the pack house would sober me up, and I needed to buy a plane ticket.

'It's about time,' Shaw grumbled.

Chapter 2

Finn

I SAT IN MY rental at a small gas station in Ontario, California, and watched as dawn crested the horizon in the east. After driving stupidly fast to Seattle, I'd taken an overnight flight and driven straight here from the airport in Los Angeles. Besides some fitful dozing on the plane, I hadn't slept. Every time I cracked the bond open to check on Kat, the same drowning sorrow overwhelmed me.

It's not like I had her address, so I had scoured my phone. Her last name was Kimura, and I had found a local insurance agency with an associate by that name. They opened in thirty minutes, so I sat out front and waited, drinking a coffee.

Gideon and I spent some time in the human world when business in the stock market called for attention, so I wasn't completely unversed in the ways of humans. We had the internet too, which was dominated by their content.

The clock counted down the minutes like it was clogged with molasses, but a lady finally came to the glass door and flipped the sign to open.

"Good morning, sir. What can we do for you today?" she asked when I entered, giving me a Colgate smile.

"Yeah, hi," I said, glancing around. "Is Mr. Kimura here? I'd like to see him."

She stood. "Of course! He's always early! He is in his office. Follow me, please."

We walked down a hallway to a windowed door. Looking in, I recognized the man seated at the desk inside from his business picture on their website. He had reading glasses on and was typing on a laptop. The woman knocked and opened the door, sidestepping so I could walk in.

He smiled at us. "Cindy, who—" He stopped short when his eyes fell on me.

His kitsune could certainly sense what I was.

Cindy hesitated, glancing between us. "This gentleman asked to see you."

When a human could pick up on the tension in the room, it was thick.

His smile was gone, and his dark eyes were frigid. "Yes, come in. Thank you, Cindy."

She nodded and hurried out, probably glad to be anywhere else.

"Why are you here, wolf?" he hissed, and I noticed his hands moving under his desk. I could smell silver, and my brows lifted. He'd retrieved a weapon.

"Woah, woah, woah. That's unnecessary. I'm Finn Greenwood," I said, holding my hands out in front of me. "I'm not here to cause trouble for you. I just want to find Kat."

His face darkened, and he walked around the desk, going to the door and opening it again. "Leave. Never return."

I frowned. "Not until I get some answers. I promise I won't harm her, but I must see her."

He was shorter than I was and leaned up into my face, sneering at me. "Katarina is dead to me. She has been for years. I don't know where she is, and I don't care. Now get out of my office or I'll call the police."

Inclining my head, I did as he asked. The door slammed shut behind me, causing Cindy to jump at her desk by the door. She turned, looking concerned as I walked by.

"Is everything okay, sir?"

"Yep," I said, forcing a smile. "Thank you for your help."

I stepped out onto the sidewalk, intent on sitting in my car until Kat's father went home and then tailing him. There was something going on with this family dynamic that I didn't understand.

'He meant those things he said,' Shaw muttered. *'There was no lie in his convictions.'*

I glanced to my right and noticed a man in a business suit smoking a cigarette. Recognizing his picture as another sales associate, I walked over to him.

"Hey, man. Left mine at home," I said, indicating the cigarettes. "Can I bum one off of you?"

"Oh. Yeah, of course."

He held the pack out to me. I took one and put it in my mouth, accepting the lighter he offered. I rarely smoked, but I did occasionally have a cigar when I was drinking, and I lit the cigarette, trying not to choke on the rancid smoke.

"So, you work here?" I asked, indicating the building.

He glanced up from his phone. "Yeah, man. Selling insurance, living the dream, you know? Why? You need a policy?"

"I'm good," I said, chuckling. "So are you around Mr. Kimura much?"

"Who, Ken?" He shrugged. "Yeah, he's alright. He's not really been himself these last couple of months since his daughter passed away."

I shook my head. "No, actually, Kat isn't dead. She got back yesterday. She's alive."

His eyebrows shot up. "They found Kat? That's crazy! But I was talking about Celia. That whole thing was so sad, man, I can't even imagine. To have one of your daughters murdered and the other missing. It was nuts. I can't believe Kat's alive. I thought she was dead for sure. Not sure it'll make Ken any happier, though. He's a private man, but I always got the vibe they had issues."

"Kat's sister is dead?" I asked, realization dawning.

"Yeah, man. Awful. Some psycho." He lowered his voice, leaning into me. "I heard that all the blood was drained from her body. Can you believe that? Some creepy shit, right?"

That must be where all the despair in the bond was coming from. When the dragon and his vampires took Kat, they must've killed her sister as well. If Kat had already been drugged, she wouldn't even have known. During our brief conversations, she had talked about her sister in the present tense, not the past tense, so she didn't know that Celia was dead.

"Wow, that is crazy," I said, pushing my barely smoked cigarette into the sidewalk and then throwing it in the bin next to us.

He eyed me with a glint of suspicion. "How do you know the Kimuras?"

"I'm a friend of Kat's."

He nodded slowly, and I started walking to my car, but an idea struck me.

"Hey, one more thing," I called to the guy as he was walking towards the front door. "Do you know where Celia is buried?"

He arched an eyebrow at me, but said, "Yeah, we all went to the funeral. Bellevue Memorial."

"Thanks!"

CHAPTER 3

FINN

MY WINDOW WAS DOWN. I sat in my car in the parking lot outside the cemetery, tapping my fingers on the steering wheel. She was here. I could smell her sweet scent drifting lightly on the breeze. It was soft and floral, with an undertone of sandalwood.

'What are you doing?' Shaw demanded. *'Go find her. She needs us.'*

'You're a real grump-ass lately, you know that?'

'That's because the Moon Goddess paired me with an idiot who's scared to talk to his own mate.'

'I'm not scared! I'm trying to figure out what to say. What we did today could be seen as super creepy to people that aren't used to wolf shifters. I don't want to freak her out.'

'Coward,' he taunted me, making me bristle.

'Asshole,' I countered, and threw my door open. I saw his wolfish smirk in my head and growled as I stepped out onto the pavement. *'I am not a coward.'*

'Prove it.'

I slammed the door louder than I should have at a cemetery and winced. Using her scent as a guide, I walked the rows of headstones until I found her.

My heart clenched. She was lying on the ground next to a large marble headstone and clutching a backpack to her chest. Her black hair was spilled out on the surrounding ground, and she was more inked than I was, the entirety of her arms and what was showing of her back covered. Many of the designs were feminine, but macabre. A fractured skull with flowers growing out of it. An orb weaver with a web in the shape of a heart.

As I got closer, I realized the headstone was made for three plots. The middle read Celia Ann and had the dates of her birth and death filled in. Kat's parents had already purchased their own plots on either side of Celia's, their names and birthdates filled in as well. The surname Kimura was at the top of the stone. They'd left Kat out of the family plot.

Grass hadn't had time to grow over the grave yet, and Kat was lying parallel to it on her right side. Her back was to me, so I didn't know if she sensed me.

'Okay, I found her. Now what? Since you're so smart,' I said to Shaw. He conveniently chose to stay quiet.

'Yeah, who's the coward now?'

KAT

'Our mate is here,' Rieka, my wolf, purred to me.

'Yeah. I know. I can smell him.'

Hana, my fox, hissed, *'He reeks of filthy wet dog.'*

'You wish that were true,' Rieka barked back, bristling.

I'd noticed his scent a while ago. Pine trees and coffee. And cigarettes. I didn't realize he smoked.

'Make him leave. Reject him so this can be done,' Hana insisted.

Rieka whined. *'No! No, Kat, don't listen to her. The Moon Goddess chose him for us.'*

'Oh, who cares?' Hana said. *'He's a wolf. A disgusting brute. I want nothing to do with him, and neither does Kat. Right, Kat?'*

Rieka ignored her. *'We should go home with him.'*

'Over my dead body!' Hana shrieked.

Rieka growled, *'That can be arranged,'* and they started squabbling like they often did, their yips, growls, and barks echoing in my head.

I groaned, pressing the heels of my hands to my eyes. *'Just shut up! Both of you. Please.'*

The groan worried Finn. I felt it in this weird, icky bond we shared that stole all of my privacy, and I heard him walk closer.

"Kat? Are you okay?"

A high-pitched cackle cracked through my lips. "Okay" was not the word I would use to describe my current state of mind.

"Why are you here, Finn? I asked you not to follow me."

"I felt your pain, you know, through the bond. I was worried about you."

I closed my eyes, and new tears formed, pushing past my lashes. "Sorry about that. No one deserves to feel this shitty."

"It's okay. I'm good. I promise." There was a pause and then he added, "I'm so sorry about your sister. I know that means little, but I am, truly."

Tears spilled over, and I started crying again, telling him through the sobs, "Those fucking vampires killed her."

Celia had been at my apartment with me that day. I knew it was the vamps who did it, and that they didn't tell the dragon. If Xeron had known, he would've tormented me with the information daily in that stone prison.

I couldn't stop the blubbering. "They murdered her, and I didn't even know it. They didn't need to do that, but they did. I thought he was done torturing me when we got out of that stupid castle. Little did I know, the worst was yet to come. My parents blame me. They disowned me last night when I showed up. For real this time."

They hadn't been fans of my life choices these last three years and often told me I was dead to them. But Celia would convince me to show up for dinner, and they'd let me share an awkward meal until it inevitably turned into another lecture of how much I shamed the family. Celia always defended me, but it didn't matter. Nothing I ever did would erase the pain I caused them just by existing. Add in the fact Celia had been killed because she was visiting me, and I knew for sure they never wanted to see me or speak to me again.

I sobbed, holding my little duffle bag to my chest. They'd let me go into our old room and grab a few things, at least. I had mostly taken pictures and other little keepsakes of Celia. A sketchbook and some pencils. That was it—everything I had left in the world.

"She was the only person who ever loved me, Finn!" I wailed, sobbing into my duffle bag.

His distress riddled the bond, and I felt awful for him. This poor guy was mated to a basket case. A born loser. The abomination that ruined my family's lives. I should reject him and get it over with for his sake, but I figured he would reject me soon enough. When he realized how messed up I was, he'd be gone. Just like everyone else.

"Come back to the pack with me. Eris is there. We can help you, Kat. You're not alone."

Hana gasped. *'Live with the wolves? He must be joking!'*

'You like Eris, Hana,' Rieka reasoned.

'Our time together in the dragon's keep surpasses her heritage. But we don't know this man!'

'Where else can we go?' Rieka asked.

My apartment was gone. I'd stopped there first when I got to Los Angeles. After I'd disappeared and the cops were done with it, all my stuff, including my stash of saved cash, had been taken, sold, or thrown away by my landlord. My old place was already occupied by a new tenant.

'We can hang out with Eris for a few days to get a handle on things, and then we'll be on our way,' I said. *'Start over. Seattle maybe? I'm sure we can find work there.'*

Hana grumbled but didn't argue. I really didn't have anywhere else to go, and Eris was a good friend. My only friend. I knew she would have a place for me.

That meant I had to say goodbye to the only person who'd ever loved me.

I looked over my shoulder at Finn. "I'll be right there."

He got the gist and nodded, meandering back toward the parking lot.

I laid my hand on the dirt next to me, and the sobs started again. "Goodbye, Celia. I love you and miss you forever. I'm so, so sorry."

I had already told her a million times since I'd been lying here. If it weren't for me, she would be alive and getting ready to start her last semester at the university for her doctorate.

Finn was waiting and held the door open for me. He grabbed my arm to help me get in, but when I felt those strange tingles dancing between us, I yanked away. I didn't feel the bond now, so I couldn't know his feelings. It did that, went away and came back without reason.

We rode in silence back to Los Angeles.

CHAPTER 4

FINN

I FOUND A HOTEL near the airport, and Kat and I both walked up to the check-in counter. The guy was scrolling on his computer and obnoxiously chewing a piece of spearmint gum.

With limited enthusiasm, he asked, "Can I help you?"

"Yeah. I need a room for one night."

He went to type something, but Kat said, "Two rooms."

I looked at her, and she held my gaze, her face flat. When she'd pushed me away at the cemetery, I'd blocked the bond to hide how much it bothered me. Now, I let it drop and felt she was anxious beneath the deep sorrow that still dominated her feelings.

'She'll run again,' Shaw said, and I worried the same.

"One room," I repeated. "But two beds."

The guy lifted his brows and looked at Kat, gnawing on his gum like a rat.

"That's fine," she mumbled, and pretended to be looking at the generic art in the lobby.

The guy took my credit card and scanned it, clicking keys on his computer for a few seconds. "Kay, room three fifty-one. Thanks."

He handed me a little envelope with keycards, and I gave one to Kat. We shuffled back to the car without speaking.

I grabbed my bag and reached for her duffle, but she snatched it, holding it close to her chest. "I've got it."

I nodded and closed the trunk, wishing I knew the right thing to say.

'She is traumatized. She might never trust us,' Shaw said.

'Yes, she will. It's been two hours. We just need more time. I'll never give up on her.'

He grunted his agreement.

Later, I sat on my bed with my laptop while Kat showered. I was arranging our flight home the next day when she came out of the bathroom. She wore a tank top and running shorts, showing off more skin than I'd seen so far.

Oh, gods.

I daydreamed about inspecting each of her tattoos thoroughly, and I slammed the bond shut to hide the reaction that thought elicited in my pants. Cursing myself, I took a deep breath and tried to focus on the computer screen. I failed. My eyes almost immediately trailed back over to her while she brushed her waist-length black hair. It was quite a task, and hair that long obviously took time and patience to maintain. I could see her reflection in the mirror, and I stared at her, unable to help myself. Her skin was flawless except for two beauty marks, one on her jawline and one just a few inches below that on her neck. Her oval-shaped face was elegant in its classic beauty, like a Hollywood movie star. My stare lingered on her soft red lips that contrasted against her pale skin. I thought about kissing them and wondered how they'd feel against mine.

When I got to her eyes, which were a sweet golden-brown color, they were glaring at me, and she scrunched her nose, as if to say, *can I help you?*

My gaze snapped back to my computer, and my face warmed. Since when did I blush?

"Okay," I said, clearing my throat. "We have a flight tomorrow morning at nine."

She came over and stood right next to me, bending to look at the screen. My eyes drifted to her cleavage, but I forced them back to the laptop before she noticed.

"I hope you didn't book Southwest," she said, reading. "They're like, my least favorite to fly with. Long story."

A soft smile lifted the corner of her mouth, and I was struck by her beauty. My hand itched with how badly I wanted to grab her waist and pull her into me.

"Delta," I mumbled, distracted by how sweet she looked. It was the first smile I'd really seen from her since we met. Albeit, a small smile, but I was happy to see it.

"First class? I've never flown first class," she said, turning to me with raised brows.

I said, "Yes," but her breath caught when she realized for the first time how close we were. Her hair had fallen over her face, and I couldn't stop myself from reaching up and tucking the renegade strand back behind her ear.

I thought it was a sweet moment until she smacked my hand. "What do you think you're doing?"

"Uh—" I searched the bond and felt she was annoyed, but that desire burned beneath it. Unsure what to do with the contradiction, I mumbled, "Sorry."

My phone chimed a text, saving us from the tension, and I picked it up, scanning the message. I sighed and scrubbed my hand down my face.

KAT

I was trying to compose myself while he read the text on his phone. Gods, help me. I didn't realize how intense this mate bond thing was going to be. His scent filled the entire room, and I loved it. Gross. When he'd argued for one room, I'd been both horrified and secretly glad. It calmed me to be close to him, as much as I hated to admit it.

'Of course he calms you. He is our mate,' Rieka said, and her happiness filled my heart.

'You need to cool your jets,' I snapped at her, pinpointing her as the source of all this confusion.

'Remember what Eris told us? The mate bond between wolf shifters is the most powerful bond out of all supernaturals.'

Having not been raised in a wolf pack, I was realizing there were a lot of things I didn't understand about that part of myself.

Hana huffed. *'If this mate bond is so special, then why was he so promiscuous before us? Eris also told us he is a womanizer, remember?'*

Cue all the bad feelings. Doubt, anxiety, and, most of all, distrust. I waited for Rieka's answer, but she only whined.

He sighed, and I looked up at him. "What's wrong?"

"Do you think you can fly back without me tomorrow?"

"Why?"

"Gideon just texted me. Diamond Moon is already making a move on the Giza artifact. He knows I'm... busy. But he wants me to go after the one in the Amazon as soon as possible. Now that I know you're safe, I can."

I picked at my cuticles, digesting the information. That Alpha dick from Diamond Moon—Lyric? Leroy? Lyle?—whatever his stupid name was. He was making things really difficult for everyone after what they discovered at Xeron's keep. Eris had explained everything to me.

"So, like, the Amazon rainforest?" I asked, looking up at Finn.

He nodded, already typing on his laptop again.

"Like Brazil?"

"Yeah. It looks like I'm going to Rio."

My thumb drifted up to my mouth and chewed the nail, thinking. I wanted a reset. I had to find myself in this new world that I had been forced into—with no Celia and no family—and I needed to figure out who Kat really was, because I honestly didn't know.

Seattle was cool, but Rio? I could go have an adventure and see if I liked it. If I did, maybe I'd just stay.

"Can I come with you?"

He stopped typing, and his head snapped up. "What?"

"To find the artifact. I want to come with you. I think I would like to... get away from everything," I explained, shrugging at the end. "Please? I won't get in your way."

"You're serious? You want me to get two tickets?"

I nodded.

Joy burst through the bond from his end, and I hoped my face wasn't as red as it felt. No one had ever wanted to be around me with this intensity. Obviously, he didn't realize the truth yet. Somehow, I always ruined everything.

My brows lifted when he said, "Don't be sad, Kat. I can't stand the thought of ever making you unhappy."

Stupid mate bond.

"It's not you."

He cleared his throat. "Well, do you have a passport?"

My heart sank. "No."

"That's okay. Gideon can get one lined out."

"So fast?"

"Money talks."

"So, that's a yes?"

"It might be dangerous."

"I can take care of myself," I said, crossing my arms.

"Then it's an absolute yes."

"Oh. Cool," I said, tapping my toes on the floor. I expected more of a fight.

For something to do, I grabbed my bag. I loved this old bag, but it had a bad habit of falling open when you held it wrong, which, of course, I did. Everything spilled out, and I jumped for the sketchbook first to hide my art.

"Here, I'll help," he said, putting his laptop aside.

"No, it's good. I've got it."

He helped anyway, and we gathered the pictures that were splayed out over the floor. When he went to hand me the last one, he said, "I like this one."

In the picture, Celia and I stood next to each other, her arm slung over my shoulder. I was six or seven years old. We were covered head to toe in mud, our smiles and eyes popping brightly in contrast.

My throat tightened as I looked at my sister, remembering. "A water line in our neighborhood had burst that day, flooding an empty dirt lot. All the kids went out there and played in the mud. It was awesome."

I'd grabbed a photo album, and I dug it out so I could put the picture in there for safekeeping. When I opened it, a fresh wave of emotion hit me. Almost every picture had Celia in it. They were usually taken of her accomplishments, with me squeezing into some shots, too, at the annoyance of Mom and Dad.

"Who's that?" he asked, pointing at a picture of me and another young girl with honey skin and curly brown hair.

"That's Mara. We were best friends in grade school, but she moved away. My teacher took this one. We won first prize for our science fair project in fourth grade. Mara was a freakin' whiz at science. I think she's some fancy lab person now who does research for a university. My parents were proud for once because we won, but I was just along for the ride, honestly." I pointed to the poster board behind us in the picture, complete with bubble letters, of course. "That was my job. I'm the artsier type, you know? Celia is the smart one."

I turned to the final page, and the last sketch I'd done just before they kidnapped me fell out into my lap. It was done with colored pencils. Celia was sitting on the garden swing at our parents' house. She wore a white dress and smiled, waving at me. Lavender plants bloomed all around her. *Was* the smart one, I reminded myself.

My heart clenched, and I snatched it, but he asked, "Holy shit, did you draw that? That's amazing."

"Yeah, I did."

"Wow. I could never have the patience to do something like that."

We sat in silence while I shuffled things in my bag, and I could feel him staring at me. Again. My face heated, and I turned to him.

"Can you stop staring at me?" I spat, but my thoughts were betraying me.

Gods, it should be illegal to be that attractive. He had brown hair with strong red undertones that he kept shaved close on the sides and longer on top. I'd always been a sucker for beards, and he had one, of course. It was significantly redder than his hair and kept neat. His eyes were hazel, something I noticed he shared with both of his brothers.

Like me, he had two full sleeves of tattoos. His weren't colorful like mine, all gray scale. A wolf's head, pine trees, and ravens dominated the one I was staring at. My stupid brain wondered briefly if he had anymore elsewhere on his body, and my mouth went dry at the thought.

My blush deepened when he said, "No, I'm sorry, but I can't seem to stop staring at you."

Rieka swooned, while a thick wave of disgust washed over me from Hana.

"Look, Finn. You're a really nice guy; I can tell. I think it would be better for you if you just, you know, rejected me? Eris said that's a thing. Then maybe the Moon Goddess can give you a chance with someone who deserves it."

His eyebrows went up, but his jaw set in stubborn determination. He grabbed my chin and leaned so close to my face I thought he might kiss me. My heart thundered.

"Not a chance. I've waited a long time for you. Besides, I can tell that you're amazing, Kat. You just need someone to prove it to you."

CHAPTER 5

KAT

W E'D GONE LATE NIGHT shopping at a supermarket, buying anything we might need for our trip. I was kind of at a loss. What
does one bring on a fantastic adventure to search for a mysterious
ancient artifact? Did Indiana Jones have a packing list?

Finn walked with the cart, throwing random things in. His newest
acquisition was bug spray, extra strength. Yeah, probably a good move.
I'd seen enough episodes of *Naked and Afraid* to know we didn't want
to mess around with the bugs down there.

'Well, we're certainly not going to be naked!' Hana said, and I imagined her clutching her pearls in horror.

My eyes widened. *'No! No, that's not—'*

'I am certainly NOT afraid to be naked with him!' Rieka sang,
practically panting in my head.

Hana made a gagging sound, and my face caught fire as my wolf
conjured some R-rated images of what that might look like for all of
our viewing pleasure.

'Gods! Rieka!' I shouted, turning my face away when he looked at
me.

Hana was appalled. *'She is disgusting! Disgusting! Can we exorcise
her?'*

My wolf hee-hawed her braying laugh while I tried to focus on
shopping, hoping he didn't feel any of what had just happened through
the bond.

We'd already grabbed a suitcase for each of us and then picked several sets of clothes. I had to watch myself because if I even laid a hand on anything he threw it in the cart.

Finn was deep in thought, reading the back of some emergency food packet. The art supply aisle was close by, and I wandered to it. It was comforting to stand among the familiar pencils, brushes, paints, and sketch pads.

While I was absentmindedly looking at the options, I felt his presence at the end of the aisle. He was watching me. Again. I set the art set I had in my hand back down and joined him.

I looked at the full cart. "Is that everything?"

"Yeah, I think so. We can probably buy anything else we need when we get to Rio."

I nodded, and we walked up to the checkout area. I eyed the in-store McDonalds, drool collecting in my mouth. It'd been a while since I had anything to eat.

"Wow, if you stalk that Mickey D's any harder, it might take out a restraining order."

He grinned sheepishly, most likely embarrassed by that corny joke. I liked corny jokes. I wanted to laugh, but I wasn't about to let him know that.

Instead, I rolled my eyes. "Well, you would know a thing or two about stalking, wouldn't you, wolf?"

"Uh... you got me there," he said, and took out his wallet, handing me a crisp hundred-dollar bill.

I couldn't help but notice about twenty more in there. I knew from the house that they lived in that these guys were loaded, but gods.

"You can get yourself anything you want. And just get me the same."

"Finn... I can't really accept all of this," I said, holding up the bill and indicating the cart.

He held his hand up to stop me, shaking his head. "Don't worry about it. You're on a special mission for our pack, all expenses paid."

I eyed him for a second and then put the money in my pocket.

"It's not *our* pack," I said, unwilling to let it slide.

Nonchalantly, he said, "Oh, yeah."

"I'm paying this back."

Even if I had to send money from Seattle or Rio or wherever I ended up, I'd pay it back.

He shrugged as if he didn't believe me. "Of course, whatever you want."

His flippancy annoyed me, and I said, "Shut up, Finn."

His brows lifted, but I turned on my heel, stomping over to the restaurant. I waited for him at the doors. It took longer than I expected, but I finally saw him heading towards me.

FINN

I lay in my bed, watching her back quiver. I knew she was crying even though she hid her sobs in her pillow. The bond was rocking with tumultuous sorrow.

My heart ached for her. The thought of losing either of my brothers was unimaginable. Plus, I had grown up with loving parents, something I'd taken for granted until now. Dad could be stern sometimes, but he loved us dearly.

Looking through Kat's pictures, I'd noticed they were almost all centered on her sister. None featured Kat's accomplishments, like her high school graduation or something. The ones with the entire family were weird; it looked like a loving family of three, with Kat thrown awkwardly to the side.

I didn't understand what the problem was with her parents. Something just didn't make sense. I had sensed her dad was purely a kitsune, and I assumed her mom was, too. So, how was Kat part wolf? Did her mom have an affair, and they both resented Kat for being a reminder?

There was so much I didn't know about her, but I was determined to find out. My hands itched right now to hold her. Shaw was pushing me, wanting me to climb into bed with her. I didn't, though. I doubted she was ready for that. At random times today, I had felt her desire for me through the bond, so I knew there was hope for me yet. But each time it was accompanied by just as much, or more, disgust.

I dozed off at some point, and when I woke, she wasn't in bed. When I sat up, the first thing I realized was that my dagger that had been on the nightstand was gone.

The bond was open, and she was in one of the darkest waves of sorrow I'd felt so far, making me clutch my chest.

"Kat?" I called, panicked.

There was no answer, but light streamed under the bathroom door.

Afraid of what I'd find, I jumped across her bed and threw the door open just in time to see her finish the cut.

"Kat!"

Her long black braid fell into a pile on the floor. She sobbed at herself in the mirror, her face blotchy and red. Her hair now hung just below her chin.

I said, "Kat. Gods, are you..."

I stopped myself, remembering her reaction when I'd asked that stupid question at the cemetery.

Instead, I said, "I'm going to take that, okay?"

She didn't argue and let me gently slide the dagger from her hand.

"Kat?"

Her sorrow was still rolling into me, but it was like a switch flipped, and she said, "I'm fine."

"What?"

She pushed past me and climbed back into her bed. I stared at her form under the covers, trying to understand.

CHAPTER 6

KAT

THE FLIGHT ALTOGETHER WAS about twenty hours, and we were finally on the last leg of the trip. Next stop: Rio de Janeiro. It had been a long trip, but I had zero complaints because we were flying first class. It was my first time, and it was pretty awesome. Good food, better drinks, and the nice bathroom at the front of the plane. The seats were leather, cushy, and reclined all the way back.

Finn was sleeping, leaned back and snoring quietly in the seat on my left. He'd insisted I take the window seat.

We hadn't talked about the bathroom incident at the hotel. We had just woken up and gone on like it had never happened, even though I knew he was flabbergasted.

I'd been in a dark place, trying to accept that my sister was dead because of me. And what girl hasn't chopped their hair off during a crisis? Admittedly, most probably didn't use a dagger that had killed people, but I made do with what I had. I reached up and touched the short bob for the thousandth time, marveling at how light it felt to move my head.

I wasn't even sad, which was odd because Kat before the dragon's keep would've died at the thought of cutting it. Now, it felt like I'd shed a heavy layer of my old self.

Finn's mouth was hanging open, and he had one of those little eye covers on. I snickered, wanting to take a picture, and reached for my phone only to realize that I didn't have one anymore. Duh.

Finn's phone was sitting in the cup holder, and I grinned, leaning across him to grab it. I flipped up the menu to access the camera. Trying to control my giggling, I snapped a couple of pictures. I set the funniest picture as his lock screen and went to his messages, sending it to Gideon, too.

My heart dropped when I clicked out of it and saw three alerts displaying texts from different women.

Sarah:

> **Hey babe... miss you. Text me.**

Bailey:

> **Sorry about the bar. Where've you been? I've been thinking of you.**

Candice:

> **It's been too long... we need to hang out ;)**

To add salt to the wound, I clicked on one conversation, scrolling back through the texts. My gut grew heavier reading through a handful of sexually charged messages between Finn and the other girl. Feeling sick, and pissed at myself for feeling that way, I clicked out of it and put his phone back.

'See, I told you!' Hana hissed. *'We can't trust a wolf.'*

I thought Rieka would defend him, but to my surprise, she just whined. My heart ached, sorry for her.

'The only reason he likes you is because of this bond! Don't you see?' Hana continued. *'Otherwise, Sarah, or Bailey, or Candice would be in this seat. Maybe all three! Who knows the depths of his depravity?'*

I tried to mitigate the jealousy rolling in my gut. *'Hana, it's not like we can judge.'*

'That was different. It was a job.'

'It doesn't even matter. This was never going to be a thing. We're just using him to get to Rio.' It felt like I was trying to convince myself as much as them. *'I thought I could just wait for him to reject me. I can't believe he didn't after last night. But I'll just do it.'*

'He won't accept it!' Rieka said, whining.

'I know what will convince him.'

My fox was thrilled to hear it, but my wolf was overcome with sadness, turning away in my mind and retreating into herself. Their emotions always conflicted, like oil and water, and pulled me in too many directions. I pressed my heels to my eyes, trying to find some sanity.

FINN

The engine of the plane shifted, stirring me from my sleep. I peeked out from under my eye cover to find Kat was watching the movie available and had the headphones on. She had her knees pulled up to her chest and rested her chin on them.

"What're you watching?" I asked, leaning over closer to her.

She recoiled and reached up to turn the movie off. "Nothing."

My eyebrows knit as I studied the side of her face, noticing that she refused to look at me. The bond was weird. Kind of nothing. A cool numbness.

'What happened?' I asked Shaw, confused.

Things had been going well. Kat was perfect; she was sassy and funny and adventurous. She even laughed at some of my stupid jokes, and I had thought we were making progress.

Her icy demeanor continued until we got to where we were staying. She barely spoke to me, offering only one-word answers to any questions I asked.

Our reservation was for a smaller hotel chain that offered ground-level condos right on the beach. Kat and I walked up to the check in, and the concierge greeted us in English.

I smiled at her. "Hi. I reserved one unit under Finn Greenwood."

She started typing, but Kat spoke up. "Is there any way we can get another unit? I need my own room."

My eyebrows shot up, and I looked at her, confused. The concierge glanced awkwardly between us and then started typing on her computer again. I was still trying to get Kat to look at me when the concierge cleared her throat.

"I'm sorry, ma'am. We're booked. But the units have three separate bedrooms."

Kat nodded. "Thank you for checking."

My heart sank, and I sighed. The woman typed some more and then handed me keycards for the unit, calling over a young man to carry our bags.

He showed us to the unit and left our bags inside the door. I was thanking him and offering him a tip while Kat hurried past me. She walked straight into a bedroom, and the door slammed, followed by the determined click of the lock.

The bag boy offered me a sympathetic look. "Have a good night, sir."

"Not likely," I muttered, shutting the door.

My mind was reeling. What happened? Was it the incident in the bathroom at the other hotel? I still had no idea what that was, and we hadn't talked about it. Was it because I didn't bring it up? Should I?

'Why is she so confusing?' I asked Shaw, and to my surprise, he agreed.

'It's that fox. If she were just a wolf, these issues would be moot because we'd have mated with her and marked her the first day.'

I dug in my suitcase and pulled out the sketchbook and pencils. She'd fancied them at the store—I could tell by the way she looked at them—so I had gone back for them while she bought us food. I set them on the table, a peace offering in hopes she might talk to me at least.

Scrubbing my hand down my face, I retrieved my bag and carried it to the master bedroom. My phone dinged, and I grabbed it out of my pocket.

Gideon:

> **Very flattering.**

My brow furrowed, and I clicked into our conversation, chuckling when I saw the picture she'd sent him. When I returned to my messages, my heart dropped into my gut. Two conversations with girls I'd been with before Kat with new messages. And a third open with a text I knew I hadn't read.

It felt like I swallowed a lead weight as I scrolled back through the conversation and saw what she might've read.

Shaw growled in my head. *'You idiot! Fool. I told you all these years to just wait for our mate—'*

'I know!' I snapped.

I barely stopped myself from throwing the stupid phone through the plate-glass window, tossing it on the pillows instead, and sitting with my head in my hands.

CHAPTER 7

KAT

I was marching to the master bedroom when I noticed the art set on the kitchen table. The one I'd been looking at in the store.

'Ignore it,' Hana said. *'A meaningless gift meant to cajole you into a lifetime sealed to this horrible man!'*

I strode past it and burst into the master bedroom. Finn—okay, had his shirt off—but that wasn't the point. He was standing by the bed, and looked up, obviously not expecting me.

"Kat, I know you saw—"

"Saw what? That you have a tendency to share your penis with everyone? I don't care."

His mouth dropped open, and he started stuttering an answer, but I blurted, "I'm a dancer."

"What?"

"A dancer. Like, I danced to make money before the dragon took me."

"Okay. Dancing... is nice. Ballet?"

My mouth fell open, and I scoffed when I realized he was serious. "Why do you all say that? No! No, not ballet, you stupid wolf!"

He looked around like someone else might pop out from behind the curtains and explain this to him.

Hana said, *'Well, he's certainly not an intellectual.'*

"Exotic dancing, Finn!" I snapped, putting my fingers on my temples. "Stripping!"

The bond wasn't registering his emotions again, but I didn't need it. It was like watching the stages of grief play out in fast-forward on his face. Denial, anger, depression, acceptance.

"And you're pissed at me? When were you going to tell me about that?" he asked, his voice rising in volume.

"I wasn't! You know why?"

"Why?"

I straightened my shoulders, repeating exactly what Eris told me she'd said to Gideon when she tried to reject him.

"Because, I, Katarina Kimura, reject you, Finn Greenwood, as my mate! So there! Just accept it so I can get on with my life and you can call SarahBaileyCandice and go find your stupid artifact!"

Gods, I didn't expect it to actually hurt, but it did. My chest tightened like I'd been punched in the heart.

I turned to leave, and he was on my heels. "I will not! I will not accept it! Where are you going?"

The pain disappeared at his words, but I knew if he marinated with that information for a while, he'd change his mind.

"Out!"

"Out? Kat! It could be dangerous! You can't—"

I slammed the door behind me, and looked both ways, choosing my path at random and running so he couldn't catch me.

Kitsune were faster than wolves. At least in the short distance. Wolves had better endurance. Luckily for me, I was both.

FINN

'How fast is she? Gods! Fuck!' I shouted at Shaw, my anger roiling.

I opened the bond again, and it was a mess of her emotions. A little sorrow, a little anger, a little guilt, and a lot of happiness. Happiness? How dare she? I'm out here worried sick, running around Rio without a shirt on, and she's happy.

'She must be drinking alcohol,' Shaw said. *'Your emotions are stupid like that when you drink.'*

We followed her scent, going in circles for over an hour before it ended at a club. At least it was early enough in the evening that there wasn't a horrible line.

A bouncer boasting a heavy Portuguese accent stepped in front of me, blocking the door. "No shirt, no entry."

"What?" I looked behind me at a woman wearing a bra for a top. "She doesn't have a shirt!"

"Yeah, but no one wants to see your tits, Americano," he said with a deep laugh, and let her squeeze past me through the door.

'Rip his head off,' Shaw said, pushing me with a shot of his aggression.

The guy was human, so I could do it. I definitely could. But rational thought told me: bad idea. Gideon would not be happy with the cleanup.

"For fuck's sake!" I shouted, and spun on my heel, jogging down the sidewalk.

A booth was selling shirts that had a big white heart with Rio written in the center. I didn't care. Whatever. It was a shirt.

When I got back, the line was way longer. I tried to cut, but a group of American women with shirts that said "Divorce Support Group" shamed me. However, their drunk, horny friend, whose shirt read "ivorced and looking for the D" was the real reason I moved to the back of the line.

'Humans are awful,' Shaw said, and I agreed while both of us fumed, watching the stupid sunset as the line moved at a snail's pace.

When I got to the door, the bouncer put up the little velvet rope. "We're full."

"Full of shit," I snapped, digging in my pocket.

His smug smirk almost ensured his head was no longer attached, but I got out my wallet and pulled out five hundred bucks, slamming it into his waiting hand as he stepped out of the way.

CHAPTER 8

KAT

T HIS CLUB WAS INCREDIBLE. I stuck out like a sore thumb in my red plaid skirt and black t-shirt, but it didn't matter. Everyone was so nice, and the broad smiles and colored ribbons danced around me in a whirl. I could almost forget about my shitty life. Alcohol helped, and I slid some more of Finn's money across the bar. A shot called a lemon drop was returned in its place, and I downed it, barely tasting the alcohol.

The bartender winked when I tipped him generously, and I said, "Thank you!"

The dance floor was packed now; upbeat, sweaty fun. Finn's emotions in the bond were fluctuating between worry and annoyance, but I ignored them and the pangs of guilt I was feeling. I danced my little heart out, having such a good time that one of the platform dancers in her beautiful feather headdress grabbed my hands and pulled me up with her.

She said, "You move your body so well! Dance with me!" and I loved her thick accent.

And we danced. It wasn't sexual between her and I, but it was definitely sexually charged, and we got quite a bit of attention. I finally jumped down, pushing through the crowd and riding my buzz back to the bar. Another lemon drop down the hatch. I had enough money for one more, but the bartender was busy, so I sat and waited.

'I'm a piece of shit for having this much fun,' I said to my mental companions.

'Yes. You broke our mate's heart!' Rieka said, whining.

'Not him. Well, kind of him. But, I meant Celia. I only found out she was dead two days ago.'

'Everyone reacts differently to grief,' Hana said.

'But still...'

A hand fell on my shoulder, and the scent of hair gel overwhelmed my nose. "Hey beautiful, you're too pretty to be sitting here frowning. How 'bout a smile?"

I could tell he was American. Not only from his accent but also because he was wearing a powder blue Vineyard Vines polo with all the buttons open and khaki shorts. I bet if I checked out his shoes, I'd find a brand-new pair of Sperrys. Not my type. Not even close. Rolling my eyes, I scooted away and looked for my bartender.

"Hey," he huffed. "I said you're beautiful. Didn't you hear me?"

He grabbed my arm, and I turned to him, glaring daggers. I assumed Mr. Too Much Hair Gel must not receive a lot of rejections based on the dull anger burning in his eyes.

"I heard your lame-ass pickup line, and I'm not interested. Move on."

He frowned. "That's not very nice. I bet I can change your mind. Come dance with me."

He pulled on me and I didn't move, trying to get my arm out of his grasp. What a freakin' creep. I didn't panic, though. Being a dancer, I'd handled similar situations.

'It would be in his best interest to leave,' Rieka said.

'I would love for him to leave,' I answered, not understanding her amused tone.

Finn appeared and ripped Mr. Hair Gel's hand away from my arm. It was so loud and busy, only a few people noticed when the guy shrieked, falling to his knees while the bones in his hand popped.

"Gods!" I yelled, grabbing Finn by his sleeve. "What are you doing?" The bond was white-hot with his jealousy and clouded with dark rage. "Let him go!"

He didn't, but I knew how to get him to. I walked away. A side exit was close by, and I pushed my way toward it, stepping out into the fresh ocean breeze.

The door slammed open behind me, and I winced when I heard the brick crack from the force.

"Oh, no. No way. You're not running again."

"I'll do what I—"

I screamed as his arm wrapped around my waist, yanking me to a stop.

The next thing I knew, my back was against the cool brick of the club wall, and he was looming in front of me. His eyes were a different color, yellow to show his wolf was riled, and his pupils were blown.

"Let me go, Finn."

"No."

"Excuse me?"

I tried to push him, but he grabbed my wrists and pinned them above my head.

"Excuse you, Kat? Excuse me! Do you know how worried I've been? Only to find you in there... dancing and talking to some—"

"He was talking to me!"

"It doesn't matter! You are..."

"What? I'm what, Finn?"

"*Mine*. You are mine. I reject your rejection. I want you."

"No. You want a mate. Not me."

"That doesn't even make sense. You are so confusing!"

"It absolutely does make sense. You only want me because you don't have a choice."

"That's such bullshit. You have no idea what you're talking about or how special this is. We are made for each other!"

"You don't even know me, Finn."

"But I want to."

I shouted, "Why?" and felt a sardonic smile spreading across my face. "Seriously! What have you seen so far that suggests I could form anything close to a healthy relationship?"

He chose not to answer and totally shifted gears. "I know I need to apologize. For sleeping with those other women. I'm so sorry. I was pissed at the world because I had to wait for my mate while it felt like everyone else found theirs the day that they turned nineteen. When I thought I wouldn't find you at all... it spiraled. It's not an excuse. I should've waited."

I looked away, glancing up the alley at the busy street. No one had noticed this interaction in the shadows.

"I don't care who you've fucked, Finn. It doesn't matter."

"It matters to me. You're hurt by it. And I know you are because you've been so transparent and so kind, always leaving the bond open."

The brakes squealed in my head. "What? Leaving it open?"

His brow furrowed. "Yeah. You can block it. Didn't your wolf tell you?"

'Rieka!'

'Did I forget to mention it?'

'You... bitch!' I said, sure I'd never been so angry with her.

'See! You can't trust them!' Hana crowed. *'We can't even trust our own wolf!'*

It was so easy. With Rieka's help, I slammed up a wall in my mind and he was gone. Peace from his invading emotions.

Finn looked like he regretted mentioning it, but said, "I'm never letting you reject me, and I'll never reject you."

"Maybe you didn't hear me before. I danced. Naked. In clubs. For men to give me money."

As I expected, his face pinched like he wanted to vomit, but he muttered, "I don't care."

"Oh, please. Yeah, you do!"

"Fine I do!" We stared at each other until he asked, "Was there... a lot of touching?"

I stared at him, wondering how to answer. Touching the dancers was a big no-no, so really, there hadn't been. The girls waiting on the tables were groped more often than the performers.

When I understood what he was really asking, my voice rose an octave. "I didn't sleep with all of them! Unlike you!"

"Why'd you do it?"

"Because I needed money, and my parents obviously weren't going to help."

"What is their problem with you?" he asked, and I backtracked, never willing to talk about that.

"I wanted money because I was apprenticing to be a tattoo artist by day, but it doesn't pay anything, okay? I needed my own apartment, in LA, and waitressing doesn't make enough."

He stopped and looked at our shoes, taking a deep breath. "It really doesn't matter what you did or why. It's in the past, Kat. All that shit is behind us. Can't we look forward?"

"You don't want a future with me, Finn," I whispered, struck by a sudden chord of sadness. "I'm unlovable. It's the story of my life."

"I do want it. I'll do anything for a chance."

"Shut up," I said, rolling my eyes. "You're stupid and you're stubborn and you don't know what you're talking about."

"I'll prove it."

"Nothing you ever do will convince me—"

Finn swallowed the rest of the words, leaning down and pressing his lips to mine. His hands still held my wrists, and they tightened their grip, instructing me to stay where I was. Rieka and Hana were squabbling in my head, trying to tell me what to do, and, for once, I tuned them out. He was demanding. A tug from his teeth on my lower lip, telling me to open for him. I did, lost to him and his pine and coffee scent. And to these tingles between our lips. My stupid, noisy mind quieted, and I thought of nothing but the kiss.

His voice was rough. "Put the block down."

Mine was a whisper. "Why?"

"Then you'll see. You'll know how much I want to just... devour you."

The kiss deepened with the words; his tongue warm as it slid over mine. When I opened the bond, his desire rushed into me, so smoky hot I couldn't tamper a shaky gasp. My entire body trembled as if he'd run his hands over my bare skin.

He paused, saying, "Fuck, I like that. I liked that sound a lot."

I was burning up, the ache in my stomach and thighs more powerful than I'd ever known it to be—ever known it could be.

"Don't you want to hear it again?" I asked, encouraging him when I knew it was foolish.

His hands dropped my wrists, one flattening on my cheek and the other holding my nape, pulling me closer, cradling my face to his. I could feel how he wanted me, not only in the bond, but from his electric touch. The alleyway was sizzling with the heat between us.

My hands floated to his shoulders, and as hot as I felt, he was warmer. Maybe I should be more concerned with my sudden mental pivot, any apprehension disappearing as I molded my body to fit his. I'd never made good choices, so why start now? Consequences didn't matter. What only mattered was that he stepped closer, his large frame pushing me back against the wall. The heat of his skin easily passed through our shirts, warming me, and when I gasped, a deep rumbling sound vibrated in his chest.

The primal noise rippled over my lips, over my skin, and tightened that ache in my core. His hand slid from my cheek, traveling down so it brushed the side of my breast. I arched my back, allowing a moan to break free. A soft, whispery one that begged him to keep going, but his hand stopped to rest on my hip.

When he broke the kiss, my eyelids fluttered open, and our eyes crashed into each other.

"Am I convincing you?" he asked, his thumb sliding up and down my hip bone.

"Maybe."

He laughed, the sound rich and husky. "Only maybe? I need to try harder."

"Yeah, you do."

But it was I who kissed him. My hands drifted from his shoulders to his nape, pulling him to meet my waiting lips.

His breath was rough, a sharp exhale as his hand drifted lower, finding the hem of my skirt. The skin of his palm was warm and rough on my bare thigh, sliding under the red plaid while the ache settled between my legs, unbearably heavy and throbbing.

I shifted my leg, silently begging him to continue higher. He stilled, his hand stopping only inches from where I needed it to be.

"I'll make you come right now, right here in this alley. Do you want it?" he asked, and my fox and wolf both reacted with fervor, each pushing to have their way.

Hana was saying, *'He isn't interested in you aside from his primal need to finish this bond!'*

While Rieka argued, *'The bond is perfection. He wants you, Kat! We're the other half of his soul! You can't deny how right this feels.'*

In my head, I screamed, *'Quiet! Both of you!'* and aloud, I stuttered, "I-I don't know what I want."

His disappointment was sharp, but he asked, "Are you sure? That kiss tells me otherwise."

I closed my eyes, trying to take a deep breath. It only overwhelmed my senses with more of him and his dizzying scent. "This mate bond is so intense. I'm not ready to decide."

His hand on my thigh flexed. "I'm not asking about the bond. I'm asking about right now. Do you want me to make you come?"

I opened my eyes, and his features were sharpened in the low glow of the neon lights. There was a hunger in his gaze that made me swallow. He looked like a predator showcasing the word he'd used earlier. *Devour.*

"If I said yes, would you be able to stop with just that?"

His shock splashed cold in the bond. "Stop? Are you asking if I would force myself—" His eyes widened before he could finish his answer.

"Finn?"

"Shh."

I didn't need to ask again, because I smelled it, too. Rot and decay, drifting upwind on the soft ocean breeze.

Vampires.

CHAPTER 9

FINN

"KAT. GO WAIT FOR me at the front of the club."

"What? No way!"

"I'll be right back. Go wait!"

"Okay, sure," she said.

I started jogging, heading into the darker inner city. Only seconds later, I heard footsteps padding next to me and looked over. She was running with me and smiled like we were on a pleasant evening jog together.

"Kat!"

"What? Haven't you ever watched a scary movie in your life? You never split up!"

"This is not a movie. You're gonna get yourself killed!"

A woman screamed somewhere up ahead, and Kat started running again, shouting over her shoulder, "No, you're gonna get someone else killed while you're trying to act like my daddy!"

"Kat, wait! You're—"

My pride couldn't bear to finish with, *too fast*, and I took off after her as she already rounded the corner ahead.

It was like running through a dark, unfamiliar maze, but I knew she was tracking them by their rotting smell, and I followed her sweet floral scent. Sweeter still because of that kiss. She desired me, I didn't care what she said.

I could hear a disturbance ahead, and Shaw and I both panicked, so I let him loose, shifting as we rounded the next bend in the maze. There were three vampires, a dead human man, and a woman cowering in the corner.

The vamps were trying to get their hands on a little white fox, who hopped around on the piles of trash, narrowly avoiding them and snapping her teeth. One grabbed her, and she yelped, but she was so fast. The fox contorted in his grip and bit his finger off. The vampire howled with pain, throwing her against the wall with a sick thud.

Shaw was seeing red, and he caught the vampire, jaws locking on his neck and ripping his head free in one swift yank. The other two bloodsuckers elected for survival, and climbed up the walls like insects, making their escape to the roof.

Worried about Kat, Shaw loped over. Her leg was hurt, but the little fox panicked when he nudged her, and she bit him. On the nose. He yelped, and I'd never felt the brute so stunned. The fox growled, pulling her lips back over her teeth.

Something hard smashed over Shaw's head and he whirled, only to find the human woman with a broken chair leg. Her neck was bleeding, so she'd been bitten, but Kat arrived in time to save her life. She shuffled over to the little fox and started talking in Portuguese, holding her chair leg out defensively.

Shaw was so flustered, he shifted, leaving me to deal with the situation.

Now naked, I held up my hands, trying to calm the woman. "I'm not going to hurt anyone. It's okay." I put my hand on my chest then pointed to Kat. "Amigo... and, uh, amiga."

The lady looked over her shoulder, where the white fox had disappeared behind a dumpster. Her eyes widened, and she took off her shoulder shawl, handing it over.

I heard Kat say, "Thank you. It's okay."

She emerged from behind the dumpster with the shawl barely covering her body, and I turned around, not willing to risk a boner at the worst possible time. My shorts were destroyed, but the Rio shirt had ripped perfectly at the seams, so I grabbed the pieces, tying them around my waist.

The woman was saying, "Obrigado. Obrigado," and hugging Kat.

"We need to go," I said. "Before someone shows up."

The vampire was a pile of ash, but there was still a dead human here, and that could complicate things.

Kat grabbed the woman's shoulders. "Run. Understand? Run."

The woman nodded and skirted around me, her sandals slapping as she fled.

We stared at each other, and I made an intense effort to focus on her face. "Is your arm okay?"

"Oh. Yeah. It's fine."

"Well, you almost got killed," I scolded her, and she put her hand on her hip, the other holding the shawl closed.

"Well, if you weren't so slow."

I frowned, my eyes narrowing. "If you could work as a team, that'd be great."

"Oh," she scoffed, rolling her eyes and brushing past me, "that's rich coming from the guy that was going to leave me behind!"

I followed, stopping to grab my wallet from my shorts pocket. "If you hadn't rushed in, we could've captured one of those vamps and questioned them."

"If I hadn't rushed in, that lady would be a raisin of her former self!"

Okay, true.

"Besides, you're the one who killed him, wolf! What was that all about?"

He hurt you.

I didn't say it and changed the subject. "You bit me!"

"Hana doesn't like you. I told you, Finn. Your kind and mine—we don't play well together."

"You are my kind! You're so..." I trailed off, clenching my jaw.

"Wonderful? Lovely? Fierce? Brave?" she offered, knowing I wasn't going to say any of those things.

I decided to throw her off and agree. "Yes. All of the above."

She sighed, but said nothing, and I smirked.

I was behind her, and the shawl was so short I could see the bottom curves of her ass. She had tattoos that wrapped around both her thighs, a black wolf and the moon on one and a white fox and the sun on the other.

My eyebrow lifted, and I watched her walk until she said, "You're staring again."

"I'm looking at your tattoos. Promise."

"You're a shit liar, Finn Greenwood."

"Don't act like you wouldn't be staring if the roles were reversed."

"At your ass? Not interested."

"Oh, who's the shit liar now? What about that kiss?"

"What about it?"

"I enjoyed it."

She shrugged, and the shawl lifted, making my heart stop. "It was okay."

"We both know you thought it was better than okay. I would, personally, like to finish it—finish you—I mean." She snorted, but I saw gooseflesh break out over her skin. "I know you want it."

"I think you have a highly inflated sense of self-worth. It's never happening again, I promise you that."

I said nothing, wondering how I could get back to where we were in that alley. Me, inches away from touching her. From feeling how slick I knew she was, and tasting her, and slipping my fingers into her wet...

I growled in frustration and stopped myself, adjusting the shirt on my waist. We were on the beach, which was thankfully, mostly empty.

Unable to let the conversation drop, I said, "You won't think my ego is highly inflated once my tongue is on you."

She scoffed, but I saw the blush rise up her neck. "That will never happen!"

I'd been on eggshells with Kat, and I was done with that. I could charm women. It wasn't like I didn't know how to seduce a woman, and I was giving a full effort from now on. She wasn't responding well to polite, sweet Finn, and she already wanted to reject me. It's not like I had anything else to lose.

"I promise it will happen."

At the balcony door, she had to stop and wait for my key. Glaring up at me, she said, "Just let me reject you."

"Uh. Let me think about that. Oh... how about no?"

"I hate you."

"You'd like to. But you don't. I'm going to win that fox over."

"Shut up. Are you going to open this door or what?"

I slipped the key card in the slot but never stopped looking at her. She glared up at me, her arms crossed over her chest.

We entered the kitchen, and she hurried toward her room, but stopped, looking at the art set.

"It's yours. Take it."

"Don't tell me what to do," she snapped, turning to face me. Her eyes dropped for just a blink to the loincloth I wore, her pupils dilating.

"You like my new shirt that much?"

She rolled her eyes. "Gods, shut up, Finn," and spun on her heel, snatching the art set on her way to her room.

I watched her slam the door and heard the lock click. Under my breath, I muttered, "What's in that mini bar?" and retreated to my own room.

CHAPTER 10

FINN

K AT AND I SPENT the next twenty hours taking turns driving farther inland while the other slept. Well, Kat slept. I mostly prayed to the Moon Goddess for mercy because my mate was hands-down the most terrifying driver I had ever been in a vehicle with.

Stop signs and speed limit suggestions meant nothing to her. She just did her own thing. I really didn't want to be that stereotypical "women can't drive guy," but my hand was sore from gripping the "oh shit" handle at the top of the door. Even during battle, I had never feared so greatly for my life.

After a particularly terrifying incident involving heavy rainfall and a logging truck, Shaw had whined in my head, *'She wants us to reject her so badly that she's homicidal.'*

I mentioned this to her, and she laughed like it was no big deal, saying, "Oh, I know I'm a terrible driver, but I'm really good at it."

As if that was supposed to provide me some comfort—it certainly did not.

We arrived at our destination miraculously unscathed. Gideon had called ahead to a town midway between Rio and Porto Velho and arranged for a guide to drive us the rest of the way in an off-road style jeep. Civilization had been rapidly swallowed by jungle as we'd traveled inland, and an average vehicle would not cut it anymore.

When we arrived in Porto Velho, our tour guide, Paulo, offered to take us as far into the jungle as he could. He asked some villagers about the coordinates we were headed to, and they'd looked at us like we were crazy.

"What did he say?" Kat asked after the last man had fervently delivered a monologue and walked away with a scoff.

"He says there are ruins there. Something old and evil. He says we'll all die if we venture too close."

I said, "Sounds like the right place. And you're still taking us?"

"Your brother pays well."

Now, we were driving on the "road," which was hardly a road, edged up against a steep mountain on one side and overlooking a sheer drop-off on the other. It was still pouring rain, and I decided I would probably never ride in a car again after this trip, gripping tightly to my new best friend, the "oh shit" handle.

Kat and I both sat in the back seat, and she was dead asleep, her head lolling against my shoulder with every bump and jerk of the vehicle.

Paulo started shouting in a panic and slammed on the brakes.

"What? What is it?" I asked, leaning forward to look out the front window while Kat snorted awake. My heart stopped. "Oh, you've got to be kidding me!"

He threw it in reverse, but we were in big trouble. A giant mudslide was washing down the side of the mountain, taking massive trees and the road with it. It would reach us in seconds. I couldn't believe how loud it was, rumbling as if we were sitting inside a thunderclap.

Kat's hand squeezed my leg, and I looked over. Her eyes were wide, and she was hyperventilating. Our fear mixed in the bond, overwhelming me.

"Kat!"

I unbuckled myself and jumped over her, straddling her and clinging to the seat around her. It felt like the only thing I could do to protect her.

It was slow motion and the fastest thing that ever happened at the same time. My stomach bottomed out, tumbling with the vertigo of the vehicle being pushed and then falling. Metal creaked and whined as the jeep bounced down the embankment.

Glass flew in a blizzard around us. I shut my eyes, and my claws dug into the fabric of the seat, not willing to let go of my mate.

KAT

I didn't know how many times we'd rolled, but it felt like it lasted hours. The jeep finally came to a stop, tires down. Finn had jumped over me, holding onto my seat and protecting me with his body. A normal human wouldn't have been able to fight the momentum, but he certainly wasn't a normal human.

The quiet was unnatural after the deafening noise of the crash. I could hear Finn breathing hard next to my ear and the patter of heavy rain on the metal roof. My sense of smell recovered next, and I was overcome by the scent of iron. Fresh blood.

I cracked my eyelids open. "Finn?"

He groaned and leaned back to look at me. His face was a mask of pain, riddled with concern.

"Are you okay?" he panted.

"Yeah, I think so." I tried to take inventory of my shaking body. I didn't think I had any serious injuries, but my adrenaline sang so loudly I might not realize if I did.

Hissing through his teeth, he leaned back, and I looked down.

"Oh, shit, Finn!"

A tree branch, maybe an inch and a half in diameter, had impaled him through his back and stuck out of his abdomen. If he hadn't been there, it would've pierced my chest.

"I'll be okay, love," he said, but his words slurred like he was drunk.

Love?

Finn groaned and reached around, trying to pull it out. He couldn't and relaxed against me, breathing hard.

"Can you get it?" he whispered in my ear.

"Oh, shit. Oh, my gods. Okay, okay. Hold on."

My hands were shaking so badly I didn't know if I could.

'Breathe Kat. He needs us,' Hana said, pushing her confidence to me.

Rieka whined.

Taking a deep breath, I reached around behind him and gripped the branch with both of my hands. I pulled, but the resistance was greater than I expected. I grunted with effort, and it slowly started to slide out of his body. It sounded so gross. I gagged multiple times listening to the flesh squelching as it moved.

"Oh, gods."

He groaned and took big, deep breaths, fighting the pain.

"I'm sorry. I'm so sorry," I repeated, tears sliding down my cheeks.

The branch gave way so suddenly I gasped, yanking it free. He sighed, relieved, but I could feel that my shirt was soaked. I looked down. With the branch gone, the wound gushed blood into my lap.

My mind was back on its heels at the sight of so much red, and I gagged again. "Oh, no! Stop that."

His lips were by my ear again, and he snickered. "Glad... you didn't barf."

"Shut up," I snapped, unable to believe he was joking around.

I held my hands on the wound, trying to keep pressure on it, but blood rushed through my fingers, hot and sticky. I looked up at his face, shocked to find him smiling down at me.

He was so pale, though, and I whined, "Finn?"

"You did... so good. Don't worry, my wolf... says it'll be okay. I might... pass out, though, for a minute."

He slumped against me, his weight pinning me. I attempted to push him back towards the other side of the seat, but with the way the roof had caved in, I couldn't move him.

My arms were the only things I could use, so I ripped his shirt off of him and pressed it to both sides of the wound as best I could. He was right, though. The blood flow was already significantly slower. His wolf was healing him.

"Oh, Finn," I said, a sob choking me. I rested my head against his shoulder and held him, tears streaming down my cheeks. All I could think was that he'd called me love.

CHAPTER 11

FINN

I STIRRED, WINCING AT the stitch of pain in my gut. My poor liver. It was dark, and the chirps and whirrs of night insects filled my ears. My night vision kicked in, and I looked down. I was still sitting over Kat. Her head was slumped back, and she snored louder than I expected from someone so dainty, her mouth hanging open.

While she was passed out, I could stare at her all I wished, and I marveled at how she was still beautiful—even snoring and drooling a little.

Alright, that's a new level of creepiness, I thought, tearing my eyes away to check my wound.

My heart clenched when I saw that she'd fallen asleep with her hands on either side of it, trying to keep pressure on it. It was mostly healed now, sore but manageable.

I reached behind me to the driver's seat, not harboring much hope, and felt for Paulo's neck. I didn't even look for a pulse because his skin was ice cold.

"Kat?" I whispered, running my knuckles over her cheekbone.

Her eyelids fluttered, and then she startled awake.

"Finn! Are you okay?"

"Yeah. I'm okay."

"Can you move?"

I lifted my brows twice. "Maybe I don't want to."

She was unimpressed, wrinkling her nose. "Finn. I'm pretty sure there's a dead guy in the front seat."

"Yeah, you're right. Let's get out of here."

Trying the handle, I discovered the door was jammed shut. I kicked at it the best I could, finally busting it open. My muscles were so stiff I had to roll off of her, barely able to stay on my feet by leaning on the door.

She was stiff too, sliding out and rubbing her thighs. "Wow, you're really heavy. My legs are so numb."

I arched an eyebrow. "Well, thanks a lot."

"No! I didn't mean it like that. I-I mean, you are heavy, but it's muscle. You're, uh, very muscular." I grinned, and she blurted, "You have no idea how bad I have to pee."

I laughed, wincing at the pain in my side.

When she returned from her potty break, Kat said, "You didn't have to do that."

"Do what?"

"Jump on me and shield my body with yours. Like, what the fuck was that? I mean, you just don't have to be so extra."

I turned to look at her. This woman. I was keeping her, that I knew. She probably thought she was playing it cool with her sass, but she was wringing her flannel shirt in her hands, and I heard that tremor in her voice.

"You were worried for me," I said, grinning. "You like me."

She crossed her arms over her chest and walked toward me. "I was not, and I do not. And even if I was, it was just because I don't want to be in the middle of the rainforest alone."

I stood and smiled down at her. "I definitely don't believe you."

"Do you ever shut up?" she asked, stepping around me to dig in the wreckage.

We salvaged what we could from the car. Kat's duffle bag was thankfully unharmed, and the pre-programmed GPS was also intact. My backpack and our camping gear were crushed, most of it unusable.

I discovered a fresh shirt, and Kat changed her clothes that were crisp with my dried blood. We ate some squished jerky I found, and yanked the seats out of the jeep, breaking them until we could form two makeshift cots.

I didn't think either of us was sleeping, though. We dozed, both of us tensing at every little sound. I had grown up in the woods, but this jungle was unsettling. The GPS showed that we still had a ten-mile hike to get to our coordinates. It may not seem like much, but the foliage was so dense I had a feeling it was going to suck big time.

After a particularly weird sound startled us both awake, Kat abandoned her cot and squeezed in next to me without saying anything. To accommodate, we had to spoon, and I pushed my happiness through the bond. I rested my hand on her upper arm and then couldn't help but slide it down to her waist.

"Don't get handsy," she said, but I swore she pushed her hips back into me on purpose.

"You're grinding on me."

"I'm getting comfortable," she said, wiggling against me. "Is that okay with you?"

"That is more than okay with me. Keep doing it, and this jungle will get even louder with the way you'll scream my name."

"Oh, please. Scream?" she said, laughing. "As if I couldn't take whatever you're dishing out."

I scoffed at the challenge. "Let's find out if you're so sure." My fingers curled under the hem of her t-shirt.

"I already told you that was never happening," she said, and her hand fell on mine, her sharp little nails digging into my skin. "So, that better be a flashlight I'm feeling in your pocket."

I grinned. "More like a Maglite."

My smile broadened when she tossed her head back and cackled. "Gods! Shut up, Finn."

I could certainly push this further considering her mood, and that she'd crawled into bed with me. I should push it. Kiss her again. The blood I'd lost was taking its toll, though, and with her next to me, I relaxed. The pull of sleep burdened my eyelids, and they drifted shut.

The next morning, I let Kat sleep and shifted to my wolf, using him to dig a small grave for Paulo right next to the wreck so he could be recovered by his family. When I finished burying him, I shifted back and dressed, calibrating the GPS and planning our best route through the jungle.

KAT

We were pushing through the thick brush at an agonizingly slow rate. The sun was high in the sky, and it was so hot and humid I thought I might throw up. Not to mention the bugs, biting us mercilessly despite the extra strength spray. Finn stopped hacking with the machete and turned to me.

"We should just shift. This sucks," he said, sweat dripping down his face.

"What about our stuff?" I asked, clutching my duffle to my chest.

"I'll shift first and you can tie it to my back, and then you shift. We're never going to make it at this rate."

"Okay."

He took his shirt off and then started unbuckling his belt. I turned away, my face hot, and he said, "Nothing you haven't seen before."

Yes. He'd been naked in that trashy alley. His ridiculous Herculean muscles with the finest dusting of chest hair on display for the world to see. And everything else, too.

"Tell that fox not to bite me again," he said.

'Or what?' Hana snapped.

"She says 'or what'?"

"I'll bite her back."

They were threatening words, but the way he said it made my thighs ache.

Rieka sighed. *'Oh, my.'*

'He's a bold man,' Hana said, and my brows shot up.

'That's the second time you've spoken of him without adding some kind of insult,' I pointed out.

'So?'

'You like him,' Rieka teased in a singsong voice.

'I do not!' she barked, and added a half-hearted, *'That's disgusting.'* Rieka and I giggled at her, and she huffed, ignoring us.

I heard the telltale sounds of a shift behind me and turned to find Finn was now his large black wolf.

I tied the bags onto his back with some difficulty. His wolf was giant, and my shoulders were level with his, so I could barely reach. When I finally got it done, my clothes were damp with sweat. He stared expectantly at me, and I blushed, ducking behind a tree to undress.

He pushed his disappointment to me through the bond, and I laughed, my heart beating fast at the thought of being naked in front of him.

I almost shifted to Hana, like always, but said, *'Rieka... would you like to, you know, come out today?'*

She perked up. *'Really?'*

I'd only shifted to her once since I turned nineteen. I wanted to be kitsune, so I always kept her hidden, blaming her even while knowing it wasn't her fault. She was proof of my mother's pain. She was my shame.

'Yeah.'

'Yes! Oh, thank you, Kat!'

The magic took control and soon I stared down at black paws. My sweaty, torn, dirty clothes sat in a pile, and with no way to pack them, we just left them there.

Rieka shook her head and bounded around the corner, yipping at Finn's wolf. I felt a ripple of surprise in the bond, and his wolf slapped both paws on the ground, wagging his tail before pouncing.

Both of them danced around the clearing, nipping each other's necks. They were playing, and it was so freakin' cute. Shaw, whose name I just inherently knew now, as if he'd told Rieka, licked her muzzle. I'd never felt such joy pulsing from my wolf, and I was hit by a surprising amount of emotion.

'Focus, wolf, we're on a mission,' Hana said, but I sensed even my serious fox was slightly enamored by the sweetness of the interaction.

Rieka whined and yipped, following Shaw into the brush.

Traveling in this form was a hundred times faster. We were idiots for waiting so long. We even had to cross a large river, and I certainly wouldn't have wanted to do that in human form. Finn was adorably concerned with keeping my duffle dry during the crossing, and I didn't know what to do with these feelings gathering in my chest when I thought about it.

After hiking most of the day, we broke out of the brush into a large, empty clearing. Finn shifted back and handed me a set of clothes from my bag. He was checking his GPS, his brow furrowed.

I was behind a tree dressing when he said, "I don't get it. This is where it's supposed to be."

I looked around. "There's nothing here."

"We better take a closer look. Maybe there's a secret door or something."

I walked into the clearing ready to search, but he turned and pinned me with curious eyes.

"But first, I have to know, are you aware that you're an alpha wolf, Kat?"

CHAPTER 12

FINN

S HE STARED AT ME, mouth open. Her eyes glazed over, and I knew
she was talking to her wolf.

"What do you mean, an alpha wolf?"

So, she didn't know.

"Your wolf is black. Rieka is born of an ancient alpha bloodline. It
makes her stronger and bigger than omega wolves. What do you know
about your father?"

"My sperm donor," she corrected, looking at the ground. "And I
know nothing about him."

"Nothing at all?"

Kat looked up at me, opening her mouth to speak, but then clamped
it shut. She focused on something behind me and shoved past me into
the clearing.

"Do you see that?" she asked, jogging towards the center.

On the ground, a small red light glimmered in the waning sunlight.
I hurried after her and tore away the foliage. Underneath there was a
stone circle adorned with red rubies in the shape of a dragon.

Kat gasped. "It's like the world's fanciest sewer grate!"

I snorted a laugh and worked my fingers under the edge of the stone.
With some effort it lifted a fraction, and I grunted, finally loosening it
enough to lift it and flip it back. It landed with a loud thump and my
nostrils filled with the scent of old earth.

A small tunnel, just wide enough for a single person at a time, plummeted straight down into darkness, and a primitive, rickety looking, wooden ladder appeared to be the only way to get down.

I glanced up at Kat. "You first."

Her eyes went wide, and she shook her head. "What? No way! We're actually going to climb down that thing?"

I laughed and tightened my backpack as much as I could.

"You can stay up here if you want. Chicken."

"I'm not a chicken!"

"Are too."

She crossed her arms and peered down into the darkness. "I'm just saying that this ladder can't be OSHA approved."

I didn't know what that meant, but I got on it, and, still holding the edge of the opening, bounced up and down.

The ladder clattered like a bone wind chime but held my weight.

"Come on, Katarina, where's your sense of adventure? She's solid!"

She shook her head. "Don't ever call me Katarina, Finnic."

"Who told you that?" I demanded.

"Eris."

I growled under my breath, but she crouched to climb down. "Gods, this is crazy."

"I'll catch you if you fall," I said, looking up at her. Our faces were close. I wanted to kiss her.

Her lashes dropped, and a small smile curled her lips. "You promise?"

I said the first thing that came to my mind. "I do. And if I can't save you, Kat, I'll fall with you."

KAT

My breath caught, never expecting an answer like that, and I watched Finn disappear into the darkness down the ladder of certain death.

"Holy shit, this is wild," I whispered.

'Well, you wanted to go on an adventure,' Hana said, snickering.

"How's it going?" I yelled down after Finn.

"Good! Just ignore the child-sized spiders, and it's good!"

Cool. Great. I pushed out a shaky breath and steeled myself, tightening the strap on my duffle bag. I started down the ladder, closing my eyes because I'd rather not see any of these giant spiders. The air was musty, and the wood of the ladder was slick with moisture.

"I made it down!" Finn's voice boomed in the tunnel around me. "You can do it!"

I took the steps one at a time. It felt like I climbed for years, and I wondered if I'd been transported to the twilight zone, destined to climb down this ladder for the rest of my life.

My stomach dropped, and I screamed, "Oh, shit!" when I went to take the next rung, and my foot found nothing but air.

"It's okay," Finn said, laughing. He grabbed my waist, and I opened my eyes. A couple more inches and my toes met solid ground.

'*Smooth,*' Hana said, and Rieka brayed her wolfy laugh.

"Right. Of course. I knew that," I said, laughing like it was no big deal.

He said, "Told you I'd catch you," and his eyes burned into me, even when his smile was soft. With his hands still on my waist, I suddenly found it hard to breathe.

To escape, I tore my eyes away. When they adjusted to the surrounding dark, I gasped. "Woah!"

He nodded his agreement. We'd descended into a giant cavern beneath the earth. Water dripped off of stalactites in a constant patter, like underground rain, and the air was dense and cool with moisture. It was a relief, letting us escape from the sweltering heat.

Rising before us was the most magnificent thing I'd ever seen. A stone temple or pyramid at least twenty stories tall. It was stacked so that the brick-like stones ascended up like stairs, and at the apex of the building, there was a crystal dragon holding the biggest ruby that I had ever seen in its mouth. A massive door sat halfway up, blackness waiting beyond the opening.

"It really is like Indiana Jones," I whispered.

Finn gave me a strange look, and I shrugged, tapping my temple. "It's an inside joke. Have you seen it? I know Eris is a little naïve to the outside world."

"Yes, I've seen all of those movies. Eris' original pack were traditionalists, rejecting most human related things."

"Why?"

"At one point in history, humans hunted our species with the intention to annihilate us."

"Why isn't your pack like that?"

He shrugged. "My father came to understand things could be gained by embracing human technology, and primarily, the stock market."

"What happened to your father, Finn?"

"He died."

"How?"

"Why do your parents hate you so much?"

My brows lifted at his sudden skirt of the topic. "Because I was a dancer, and I only ever aspired to be a tattoo artist. I brought shame to them and our family."

"Why did they treat you so badly before that? It's obvious in your pictures—"

"It doesn't matter," I snapped, not willing to travel that road.

We stared at each other, guarding our little secrets, until he said, "Well, let's do this."

FINN

We entered the temple, greeted by another vast room. The walls were adorned with various gems; rubies, emeralds, amethysts, diamonds, and sapphires were intricately woven into a giant mural depicting five dragons, each one represented by a different gem. The mural repeated, covering every inch of wall and ending at an enormous double door with a stone lock.

Crystal-clear water flowed from ports in the walls, snaking across the floor in winding channels.

Our footsteps echoed on the stone as we walked with our mouths hanging half-open, both of us lost to the beauty of the chamber.

Kat's hand hit mine, and she glanced over. "Are you trying to hold my hand?"

I would hold her hand in a heartbeat, but I said, "No, why would I do that?"

"I thought maybe you were scared."

"Oh, please." After some consideration, I asked, "If I pretend to be scared, will you hold my hand?"

She shrugged, grinning, but we'd arrived at a door at the back of the room.

It was secured by some kind of combination lock with five stone buttons that could be pressed. Each stone had one of the five jeweled dragons on it.

"What's the sequence?" Kat asked, studying the tiles. "What order should we push them in?"

I looked at the mural. It was always the ruby dragon, the emerald dragon, the amethyst dragon, the sapphire dragon, and then the diamond dragon. I smirked—too easy—and pushed the buttons in that pattern, each one giving way with a soft swish. To my surprise, nothing happened. The door stood silently, and the buttons all reset to their original positions.

"I guess that wasn't it," I said, my brow furrowing.

A loud groan echoed through the room behind us, and we spun around. I grimaced, watching a giant stone door drop from the top of the door frame and slam shut over the opening we'd just entered through.

Kat looked over at me, wide-eyed. "You don't just start pushing buttons! I thought you said you watched the movies?"

"My bad," I said, looking around the chamber for another way out.

CHAPTER 13

W E SEARCHED EVERY INCH of wall in the room looking for the answer to the puzzle on the door. It could honestly be any combination depending on how you looked at the mural.

During our search, we found the shoulder-high dragon statues that lined the walls were actually torches, and we lit them. The flames created quite a spectacle, dancing off of all the gems in the room like a light show. Our beautiful tomb.

Finn was up at the door, putting in random combinations and muttering to himself. He had a pen and was writing each combination he tried down on the bare skin of his hands.

I heard him mumble, "Emerald, ruby, sapphire, amethyst, diamond... gods, I'm going to run out of skin." Louder he said, "Kat, can I write on you?"

"Isn't that pointless? I mean, how many combinations could there be?"

"A hundred and twenty. As long as the colors aren't allowed to repeat in the sequence."

"How do you know that?"

"It's just like math class. If I assign a digit to each color—one for ruby, two for emerald, three for sapphire, four for amethyst, five for diamond—and treat it like a number sequence, calculating the possible arrangements of the five numbers, there are a hundred and twenty permutations of the digits."

'Not an intellectual, huh, Hana? What do you say now?' Rieka asked, and Hana ignored her.

My brows lifted, and my stupid heart fluttered. "Did you just say permutations?"

He turned over his shoulder and waggled his brow. "You like that?"

"You don't seem like a permutation guy."

"I know," he said, and turned back around, going back to his muttering.

"Do you need help?"

"I may need your bare skin in a minute."

"The only bare skin I have is on my face and my unmentionables."

"Yes, I am aware," he said, and snickered.

"You want me to bend over so you can write on my ass?"

He paused, and I felt a ripple of excitement in our bond. "Are you volunteering?"

I thought of that kiss in the alley behind the club and my thighs clenched with a burst of tingles. "It's, like, life and death, isn't it?"

"Maybe."

"If we don't get the door open, we'll be trapped down here forever."

"That's true."

"Well, I don't want to die."

"Me neither," he said, and tried another combination as if he were only half listening.

'Is he being coy?' Hana asked.

I smirked because he was.

"I better clean the canvas first," I said, pushing him.

"What? Are you telling me you're gonna wash your ass?"

I snorted a laugh and dug around in my bag to see what I had left. One low-quality beauty bar leftover from the LA hotel survived the wreck. It was broken into three pieces, and it smelled like grandmas, but beggars couldn't be choosers.

Wearing my bikini, I used a water bottle to collect water from one of the spouts and dump it over me. Finn kept talking to himself like he was still working on the door, but I could feel his eyes on me. I thought of just getting naked and seeing what happened.

'Oh, please,' Rieka said. *'You know exactly what's going to happen if you get naked.'*

Yeah, I did. Sex would happen. The sex I'd imagined a thousand times since that kiss in the alleyway. Thinking about it made my thighs tight. I didn't really know what our future held—if we would actually end up being mates forever or not—but I could no longer deny the chemistry between us.

It was heartbreak. That's what would come of it. The rejected child that lived in my soul was terrified of opening up to someone.

Rieka wasn't giving up, pushing me. *'He will always love you, Kat. I know you don't understand, but he already does. That's what Shaw said.'*

Love? Oh, gods.

'Hana? Anything? Tell me to be smart. Be the voice of reason here,' I said.

'I don't know. He's kind of okay. For a wolf. He threw his body over yours in that wreck.'

'That doesn't help.'

The longer we were together, the more I wanted him. More than I'd ever wanted anyone before in my life. The thought elicited images in my mind of what it would be like to be with him. That was all it took for heat to build in my stomach, accompanied by a rapid flutter of butterflies.

Shit, the bond was open. I had to be careful, or he'd sense it.

"What are you thinking about over there, Katarina? It's very distracting."

I slammed the bond closed, blushing.

"Nothing!"

I pushed my burning face into the water, trying to cool down.

What if we had sex, and it wasn't as good as he'd hoped? All my life I had disappointed people, and I was terrified he would be next. That I would not be the mate he expected.

When I pulled my face out of the water, I sensed he was there, right behind me. He ran his finger up my spine, making me shudder at the electric tingles that sparked with his touch.

"You shouldn't lie to me."

"I wasn't!"

"You might've blocked the bond, but I do have a good sense of smell, you know?"

"Wha—"

I was halfway through the word when I understood what he meant. He could smell me, as in, that I was horny. Oh, my gods. My cheeks exploded with tingling heat, and I stared at the dragon spout in front of me.

Rieka brayed her wolfish laughter, and I said, *'You knew!'*

'It's okay. He likes it. Loves it. You'll drive him mad.'

'Oh... wow. That's so weird.'

I felt his fingers at my nape, holding the tie of my bikini.

He said, "I'm going to take this off now."

I nodded. "Okay."

Finn pulled the string, and the top of the bikini fell. The soft mist of the water danced over my bare breasts, and my skin tightened with goosebumps. A shiver ran through me, from the cool water, or from him, I couldn't say.

He unfastened the tie that rested at my mid back and the entire thing dropped around my feet. Then, making me shudder, he traced the triple moon tattoo on my back. A waxing crescent and waning crescent flanking a full moon on either side. It represented the femininity of the Moon Goddess and the phases of a woman's life: the Maiden, the Mother, and the Crone. His skin was hot on my cold back, like a flame dancing over ice.

"Open the bond for me?" he asked.

I did. Letting my desire be free and knowing it was edged by anxiety. That feeling was thrilling, though. Like it was my first time again, and it was with someone I actually wanted to be with and not some random guy I hooked up with at a party when I was too drunk.

His feelings were a rush, making my head spin. Burning, unrelenting want. For me.

He said, "What are you so anxious about? You seemed sure last night that you could handle whatever I'm dishing out."

"I'm anxious we're going to die in this stupid room," I lied. "I can certainly handle you."

"I hope so. Nothing about you inspires me toward gentleness."

My breath was shaky when his hands grabbed my waist. I yelped when he unexpectedly yanked me back into him with a husky growl. His lips were on my neck, kissing, and my eyelids fluttered with the sensation, so blissfully wicked that I couldn't help the moan that parted my lips. My neck had never been so sensitive before. I laid my head back against him, and ran my hands up my stomach, grabbing my breasts and kneading them. My skin was lit by my nerves, my nipples beaded.

His hands closed over mine, and we were touching my breasts together. The pleasure raced through me, settling between my legs with a tight twist in my core.

He nipped my ear, saying, "I want you bad, Kat."

"Damn it," I whispered, almost hating to admit he'd been right, and that I ended up like he said I would. Wanting him. Needing him. "Me too."

"You're my dream, and I don't want to wake up," he said. "I've imagined it; how you feel. I need to be inside you."

"With your tongue?" I asked, remembering he'd threatened me with that.

"My tongue and my fingers and..."

I expected him to say cock or one of the alternative monikers dubbed for it. I thought that was the obvious next step, but he gripped my hair and pulled my head to the side. I gasped as he said, "My teeth," and pressed them to my neck.

A salacious wave of heat rolled down my body, and his hand on my breast rolled my nipple between his thumb and finger, pulling a whimper from me.

The ache between my legs was too intense, and I pressed back into him, grinding. His breath was short, and his hand flattened on my stomach, encouraging me not to stop. We didn't need music to dance.

His hand drifted lower until his pinky edged under the band of my swimsuit bottoms.

Yes. Yes. I pushed my feelings through the bond, begging him not to stop. He stilled, stopping his hand in its descent, just like in the alley.

I giggled, a throaty sound. "You are so mean."

"You can call me whatever you want, and I mean that. Tell me what you want, and I'll give it to you."

I put my hand over his and pushed it down. "Touch me. Touch me here."

My hips lifted as he skimmed a finger over the slit of my core. "Here?"

My breath caught. I'd never done anything like this. It felt scandalous, but so natural at the same time. Naughty, but right.

"Yes. And here."

My middle finger was on his, and I pressed it to my clit. I could feel my own slickness, how wet I was. We moved together, his finger with mine, drawing slow circles that made my breath shallow. I was lost in it, biting my lip.

"There's more," he said, his voice a whisky drawl of smooth malt and honey. "I know there's more you need."

Together, I led his finger lower, gasping at the slow push through my folds into the heat of my core and then deeper, both of our fingers sinking inside me.

"Oh, gods," I moaned. "Like that. More. Another."

He didn't hesitate, drawing his next finger up and plunging it in to join the others. There was a pinch of discomfort, the stretch temporarily overwhelming, but it quickly evaporated into sharp pleasure.

It was like he was holding his breath, and he let it go in a slow exhale that was heavy on my neck. "That's so good. That's what I want. You feel amazing. Beautiful. So tight and wet."

I had my hand in his hair and turned over my shoulder, searching for his kiss. Our hands were moving together, and I rolled my hips, seeking for each slice of pleasure, pushing up on my toes and back down over and over.

"That's it, Kat, make yourself come. Fuck my hand and imagine it's my cock."

My blood pounded, scorched by those words, and I dropped my head against his shoulder. My hips rocked, my core coiling, and I was gasping against his lips. The kiss was frenzied, and I did just as he said, chasing down the bliss that it promised.

He caught the cry of my pleasure in his mouth, moaning with me as a wracking orgasm ripped through me. Explosive, unyielding pleasure flooded every vein and every cell of my body. I rode it for a long time, and he didn't stop until I pulled my hand away, my legs shaky.

"Oh, gods. That was beautiful," he said. "I want to taste you."

Still trying to form a rational thought, I stuttered, "I—"

I didn't expect him to actually do it. He lifted his two glistening fingers past my face and drew them into his mouth, a deep, primal sound rolling through him when he did.

I moaned. I don't even know why, but it was like I could feel his tongue on me when it wasn't. The echo of his fingers throbbed in my core.

I reached back, finding the very thick, very hard length straining the zipper of his shorts. My thighs clenched at the feel of him.

His body jerked, and he made a sound. Something like a dark, succulent laugh. "If you're going to do that, I hope you understand the consequences."

"I just want to give you what you gave me."

He brushed his lips over my ear. "So do I, but I don't want your hand, Kat. Fingers aren't enough and my tongue is not enough. I want you and that wet pussy, and if you keep that up, I'm going to pick you up and fuck you against this wall. And it won't be sweet, and it won't be gentle."

My stomach fluttered, and my voice was like silk, or some kind of rare velvet I'd never heard from myself. "Don't threaten me with a good time, Finn."

I slid his zipper down, and his lips curled into a smile against my ear. "You naughty girl."

"Am I?"

He growled in his chest, and spun me, picking me up. His mouth was on my breast, licking and sucking until my head kicked back against the wall.

Then, by chance, I saw it. My eyes snapped to some kind of chandelier hanging in the middle of the ceiling. We hadn't noticed the shape before, but at this angle I saw clearly it had five layers, the biggest at the top and the smallest at the bottom. It was covered in moss, that's why we hadn't seen it, but what drew my eyes was a diamond on the top layer, twirling in the torchlight. I searched the rest. An amethyst, a ruby, an emerald. All on different layers.

Finn, noticing my attention had drifted to other things, said, "Kat?"

I shouted. "That's it!"

His voice was thick. "What?"

"It's sapphire, emerald, ruby, amethyst, diamond!"

I wiggled free of his hold and bounded up the stairs to the door. Excited that I'd figured something out—done something right—I pushed the buttons in that order.

There was a clicking inside the mechanism, and the bars holding it shut shifted as the stone door cracked up the middle. I had to step back as it opened toward me, and I wrinkled my nose at the rush of stale air. It smelled awful.

Finn came to stand beside me. His desire was still roaring in the bond, but it was the undercurrent of pride that made me blush.

"How can you call me mean and then do that to me?"

Oh, no. It was a little rude to just leave him... like that. My heart dropped, and I looked over and then down with wide eyes. He'd fastened his zipper, but the bulge was still there.

I tried not to, but I couldn't stop a raspberry of my lips that turned into a laugh. My bikini bottoms had been soaked, and now he had a giant wet mark on the front of his shorts.

"Was it that exciting?"

"Ha. Ha. Ha," he said dryly, giving me a side eye.

I covered my mouth to hide my smile. "I'm sorry. Do you want to... continue?"

"Yes. I. Do. But, I think you've made it so we have to move on. This could be our only chance. We don't want this to close again forever."

"Whoops." I reached up and held my nose, my nasally voice asking, "What's that smell?"

It was acidic. A sour scent that wasn't exactly unbearable, but it made my nose tickle.

"Magic. The really dark kind."

"Oh. Shit."

"Yeah. I hate magic." He sighed, and his eyes drifted down. "Now put those boobies away before you drive me mad."

Having totally forgotten I was topless, I snatched my hands up, covering them with a blush and a giggle.

CHAPTER 14

KAT

H IS DISAPPOINTMENT WAS SO powerful as we packed our things, that
I mumbled, "I'm sorry. I should've waited to open it."

"Don't apologize. I'm not mad," he said, chuckling. "I just want you.
Now that I've proven that to you, I just need to get this over with so
we can pick up where we left off. I'm telling you if this was anything
except the end of the world at stake, I'd be fucking you."

Unable to stop myself from riling him up, I said, "Still? Figured you
might be done by now."

It had only been a handful of minutes since I'd opened the door.
Less than five.

His mouth dropped open. "Excuse me? Are you implying I can't
last?"

I shrugged, laughing.

He scoffed, starting, "Oh, I can fuckin—" but he stopped and nar-
rowed his eyes at me. "You'll find out soon enough. Now get up here."

I bit my lip, a twist of heat in my core at the thought of finding out.
We stood at the threshold, and I wondered if the door would close
behind us again, trapping us deeper inside the structure.

As soon as we crossed in, the lanterns that lined the walls started
lighting on their own, one by one, down a long corridor. The flame
burned green instead of red, casting everything in a strange, sickly
glow.

We took a few cautious steps in, and the door behind us creaked and slowly started closing. It slammed and the ticking of the lock mechanism echoed around us in the corridor.

The scent that Finn told me was magic was overpowering in here. I looked to my right and jumped when I saw we weren't exactly alone. Rieka and Hana whined in my head, feeling unsettled.

It was some kind of burial chamber. Dead people, completely skeletonized, were laying in individual open tombs built into the wall. Each of them was dressed in medieval-looking armor with a broadsword resting on their chest, their hands on the hilt. They were stacked three tombs high and end to end down the entire corridor. At the end, there was another door with an identical lock to the one we'd just passed through.

Finn grabbed my hand and squeezed it. We walked in silence. The only things I could hear were the strikes of our shoes against stone and my own erratic breaths. When we were about a third of the way down, my ears picked up a small shuffle. Finn stilled, stopping mid-step, so I knew he heard it, too.

We turned, and I choked on a gasp, fear climbing up my throat as a shrill scream. One of the dead warriors was climbing out of his spot, his armor clinking as he awkwardly stood. His movements were so jerky and unnatural I felt sick to my stomach watching.

"Necromancy," Finn spat. "This is why I hate magic!"

The warrior next to me stirred, shuffling awake, and I gasped, panicking. "Oh, shit!"

They all moved, and the sound of armor clinking filled the corridor.

"Run!" Finn yelled, putting his hand on my lower back and pushing me towards the locked door.

The warrior closest to me attacked, swinging his broadsword with impossible force for something with no muscles. I screamed, ducking a strike, and Finn kicked the warrior in the chest. He shattered to pieces and Finn picked up the sword, deflecting another blow with it.

"Shift!" he told me, and then he started to, his body quickly contorting as his wolf came forward.

"I can't!" I answered, clutching my duffle bag to my chest.

I couldn't leave it behind. If I tried to carry it in my mouth, I wouldn't be able to fight as my wolf or fox. Finn destroyed another dead soldier, and I picked up the broadsword he'd dropped, flailing it around and screaming like a maniac.

Luckily, the zombies were slow and uncoordinated, and I did more damage than I expected to. Total psycho mode paired with supernatural athleticism was surprisingly effective.

Finn, as Shaw, tore through them like tissue paper, his snarls rolling like thunder around us. Their numbers grew overwhelming in this tiny chamber and even when they were dispatched, they started putting themselves back together again.

I screamed, "Gods! They don't die!"

Shaw barked to show he understood and motioned his giant head toward the door.

We fought our way there, sweat beading on my forehead from the effort. When we made it, I attacked the lock, pushing in the combination that worked before. Nothing happened; the buttons slowly reset themselves while I gaped in horror at their defiance.

"Shit," I whispered, trying to think.

Finn was fighting off the horde behind us, and I tried the same combination again. Nothing. My shaking hands hovered over the buttons.

'Maybe it's reverse?' I shouted in my head, but I couldn't think of what that would be. My mind blanked.

Hana and Rieka both shrieked, *'Diamond, amethyst, ruby, emerald, sapphire!'*

I pushed the combination in, and, to my relief, the lock started clicking.

"Yes! Finn, I got—"

A sword fell across my lower right arm, and I cried out. The weapon was dull, but heavy, and easily inflicted blunt damage. I felt my bones break under the force.

Shaw growled from my other side, where he'd been overwhelmed by five or six warriors.

He pushed through them and jumped on my attacker, dispatching him while the door swung inward.

I rushed through, followed by Finn. He fought back the skeletons until the door shut with a soft slam, closing one in between the giant stone slabs with a sickening crunch.

I looked down at my arm, sucking in a breath of pain. There was a deep cut, and I could see my fractured bone inside the open flesh.

"That's gnarly," I mumbled, sidestepping and feeling a little faint.

Finn shifted, rushing to my side to catch me.

"Kat! Oh, gods, I'm so sorry."

I could feel his shame pulsing through the bond.

"It's okay. It'll heal."

Finn grabbed it, and I whined, tensing. He held it straight, though, bracing and supporting the break. We watched it, the bone growing back together as my flesh started weaving into itself and closing the open wound. It was healed in just a couple of minutes.

Finn shook his head. "Holy shit. That was fast, even for a wolf shifter."

He looked up at my face, and the side of my mouth lifted. "I guess it helps to have two supernatural spirits instead of one."

Rieka barked. *'Yes. We can be a team sometimes, right, fox?'*

'We can,' Hana agreed, and I smiled, unsure if they'd ever experienced any kind of harmony before.

Finn hugged me, holding me and taking a deep breath. I could still feel his anger and guilt in the bond.

'He wants to protect you,' Rieka said.

I ran my hand up his bare back. *'I know.'*

His bare back. I was suddenly aware he was naked and pressed up against me. A pang of desire rushed through me, and I blushed, giggling.

Finn barked out a laugh and held me away from him, looking down at me. "You really are the girl for me. We barely escaped certain death. You sustained a serious injury, and you're still thinking about sex."

"You're naked! Again!"

"So?"

"If I was naked, what would you be thinking about?"

His eyebrows waggled. "How about you get naked, and we find out?"

"That would be very irresponsible. We're on a mission."

"If my big brother were here, he might accuse me of often being irresponsible. It's part of my charm."

"Well, we should focus."

"Why?" he asked, and I snickered because he sounded so whiny about it.

I pointed across the chamber we were in. "Because look."

He pouted, refusing to look, so I grabbed his chin and turned his head that way. With his cheeks squeezed, he said through puckered lips, "Oh, yay. We found it."

A small, plain-looking dagger rested on a pedestal in the middle of a large room.

The witch's blade.

CHAPTER 15

FINN

I LOOKED AROUND, WONDERING what possible fun this room could have in store for us. The acidic scent of magic was even stronger, burning my nostrils and making my head ache. I glanced at Kat, looking at her arm again. I hadn't protected my mate like I should have. That certainly wouldn't be happening again.

I'd lost all of my stuff in the last chamber, so she rifled in her bag and handed me a pair of tiny pink sweats, giggling. I squeezed into them, sighing while she was near hysterics.

She held up a black and pink polka-dot crop top. "Would you like the shirt?"

"I'll pass. Don't want you getting too turned on."

She scoffed, laughing, and we took in the room together.

This chamber was smaller than the first one we'd been in, built of the same stone blocks. Huge floor lanterns lit the room, their green flame bright but eerie. Our goal, the athame, sat on a stone pedestal in the center.

Directly above it, a giant bronze bell hung from the ceiling. It looked like one you might find in an old clock tower. At the back of the room, I could see another ladder ascending the wall and an opening at the top. Thank the gods. An exit.

"Holy shit," Kat squeaked, pointing to our left.

I looked over and sighed. Really? The giant skeleton of a dragon lay on the floor, like it had curled up to sleep and died there.

"We should be quiet," she whispered.

My brows lifted. "Uh, after your screeching in the last chamber, I think everyone in the building is wide awake."

Her and that sword. I'd had to watch myself the way she swung it around, with her eyes *closed*, shrieking like a banshee the entire time.

"That was my battle cry!"

I snorted, choking on a laugh. "Well, I was terrified, that's for sure."

She slapped my shoulder. "Shut up. We need something of similar weight to change out for the athame, because it's probably on some sort of pressure plate or something."

I arched an eyebrow at her. "We have no idea how much it weighs, though."

"Seriously. I've seen enough movies. That's what we have to do."

"If it's not the same weight, it won't work."

She walked over to the wall and picked up a loose piece of stone, bringing it back.

"This is it," she said confidently, handing it to me.

"I doubt this weighs the same. It's too heavy."

"Well, I guess you're gonna find out," she said, grinning and giving me a little shove toward the platform. "Good luck, Finnic."

I growled, leaning at her, and to my surprise, she leaned in and growled back.

"Stop it," I said, our noses only a few inches apart.

"Or what?"

"Or there'll be a spanking in your future."

She grinned, and I noticed how pointy her little canines were when she growled again. The bond was dancing with our humor and our lust, two fun emotions that went deliciously well together.

"Gods, let's get out of here," I said, unsure how much longer I could wait to have her.

She smacked my ass, a loud slap on my right butt cheek, and said, "You've got this."

Taking baby steps, I walked to the pedestal, glancing back once to make sure she was staying put. She had selective listening, as I had learned from the vampire incident.

Kat waved me forward. I made it to the athame without incident and stared down at it. It looked so normal. The six-inch blade was dull, with barely any edge on it, and the handle was a simple leather wrap design. I was expecting something fancier.

'You feel it, though, don't you?' Shaw asked, unsettled.

'Yes.'

The blade may not look like much, but I could feel the magic radiating off of it in waves. I sighed. I didn't want to touch this thing.

But I had to. I held the rock up close to it and, taking a deep breath, I switched them as fast as I could. The blade hummed in my hand, vibrating with power.

I held my breath for several seconds, watching and listening. When nothing happened, I turned to Kat, grinning. She gave me a thumbs up and danced a jubilant little jig towards me, snapping her fingers.

The celebration may have been a little premature.

The stone beneath my feet groaned, and the pedestal descended, retracting down into the floor. At the same time, a mechanism on the wall opposite the dragon clicked loudly, and I realized a wheel was attached to a rope coming down from the bell. The wheel turned, and the bell started ringing. It tolled three times, shaking the entire room so that dust rained down from the ceiling.

KAT

I covered my ears, gritting my teeth to keep them from chattering with each toll of the bell. My whole body vibrated with the rhythm of the strikes, and dust coated my head and shoulders.

My ears were still ringing when it quit, and I glanced up at Finn. He was watching the dragon, and said, "No, no, no. You stay!" like he was talking to a dog.

Fido didn't listen. The dragon's bones rumbled as it stirred from its long rest and started to rise to its feet.

"Kat! Let's go!" Finn yelled, gesturing towards the ladder at the back of the room.

I sprinted to meet him, and he grabbed my arm. We ran together towards the ladder, but the dragon was faster than it looked, cutting us off and roaring.

'Holy Hades! How does this thing roar with no vocal cords?'

'Magic, I guess,' Rieka answered. Hana yipped in agreement.

The bony tail swung around like a whip, nearly decapitating both of us. We ducked just in time, and Finn dragged me away from the beast, handing me the athame.

"You take this and go to the ladder. I'll distract it," he said.

I was about to argue, but the dragon thrashed its tail at us again. Finn pushed me away from him and then ducked. One vertebra grazed across his back and cut into his skin.

He growled and yelled, "Kat! Please, just go. I can't focus with you here!"

I huffed, but did as he asked, unzipping my duffle and throwing the athame in. I flanked around the dragon while Finn yelled at it, trying to draw it to him. It didn't even look in his direction, though, tracking me instead.

Its giant jaws snapped at my back. I screamed, and I was barely fast enough to keep ahead of the bite, diving behind a stone pillar. Its tail followed, demolishing the pillar and raining stone down around me.

'It's tracking the artifact,' Hana said. *'But also guarding the ladder.'*

I nodded and peeked around the pillar. Finn was running this way, his face pinched with rage. It was almost comical, with him squeezed into my tiny sweats like that. I was more interested in what was behind him, though. The bell was attached with a rope to the ringing mechanism.

An idea hit me, and I ducked and ran towards Finn. I shoved the duffle into his stomach, making him grunt.

Over my shoulder, I yelled, "Stand where the pedestal was and don't move until I tell you!"

I didn't give him any time to argue and ran towards the bell mechanism, extending my claws. He realized what I was doing and turned to face the dragon, narrowly ducking another swipe of its tail.

The dragon descended towards him, opening its bony jaws for the kill. Finn bravely held his spot, throwing the strap of my duffle bag over his shoulder.

The dragon lunged, and I screamed, "Now!"

Finn jumped sideways, missing the clamping jaws by mere inches. I slashed at the rope. To my dismay, the first strike didn't completely sever it, and I had to hit it again.

In slow motion, the bell plummeted in a clanging descent from its spot on the ceiling. It landed on the dragon's hips instead of its head as I had hoped, but it did its job. The heavy bell crushed the beast, shattering and splintering bone. My ears rang from the noise, but I heard the dragon's pained screech. Even magic was incapable of mending the extensive damage.

Finn grabbed my hand, yanking me towards the ladder.

"Time to go."

He pushed me up before him, and I climbed as quickly as I could, slipping and scrambling for the hole in the ceiling. I shouldn't have looked down, but I did, and a wicked wave of vertigo swept through me. The dragon was dragging the top half of its body towards the ladder.

I climbed faster, and I was only a stretch from the top when the ladder started to convulse. The dragon was biting and pulling on it at the bottom. I screamed, clutching tightly to the rung I was on.

"Go! Go!" Finn yelled.

I had about eight rungs left and started scrambling, trying to ignore the sounds of snapping rope and wood around me. When I was about five rungs away from the top, Finn put his hand on my butt and pushed me, throwing me the rest of the way. I was still screaming as I clawed out of the opening. The ladder fell from beneath my feet.

"Finn!" I shrieked, knowing he couldn't have made it in time.

He clung to the edge of the opening with his fingertips, grunting with effort. The ladder fell away, landing on top of the dragon, who roared again. I gripped Finn's wrists and pulled as hard as I could. Gods, he was heavy.

He fell forward with a grunt, landing on top of me. I felt around his back and sighed in relief when I felt my trusty ol' duffle bag was still attached.

I cheered, "We made it! That was INCREDIBLE!"

My voice echoed inside the giant chamber, and I realized we were on top of the temple, the hole we climbed out of hidden behind the dragon statue holding the giant ruby.

Finn put back his head and howled a long, happy note. Rieka was dying of excitement, so I joined him, laughing.

He held me, our foreheads together while we giggled like idiots, both of us riding the high of facing down death and coming out victorious.

CHAPTER 16

"THE GODDESS SURE PICKED me a wildflower," I told Kat, looking down and running my thumb over her cheek. "You're very brave."

"I'm brave? That was a lot of trust you gave *me* down there."

I hated the way she said *me*, like I should never have faith in her.

"Why do you always do that?"

"What?"

"Try to convince me you're not amazing. Because I do trust you, Kat."

"You shouldn't. I'm such a dork... I just..." She put her fingers on her brows, her thumbs on her temples. "Usually I mess everything up, you know?"

"I've seen nothing that suggests that in our time together."

When she pulled her hands away, her eyes were glassy, and her lip quivered. "I ruined my entire family just by existing. They'd have been happier if I had never been born. Celia would be... not dead."

I shifted her in my arms. "Please tell me what that means. Just by existing. When I talked to your dad, he said... you were dead to him."

Her mouth dropped open. "You met my dad? How'd that go?"

"He threw me out of his office."

She laughed, but it wasn't happy, it was the saddest sound I'd ever heard. Her face pinched, and the tears formed again. "I really don't like to talk about this."

"It's just you and me. No one else ever has to know. A secret for a secret?"

She nodded and took a shaky breath. "My mom works at home most of the time. A medical transcriptionist. Once a month, she has to go into LA and deliver her files to the hospital she works for. She was there late once because of some big hospital fundraiser, and everyone was busy, so it took forever to get her work exchanged. The garage she usually used was full, so she had to park in a sketchy one down the street. She was walking through it..." Kat's voice thickened, and she had to fight to get the rest of the words up. "She tried to run, and she fought, but some guy, he got her. And he raped her. In the open, right there on the fucking concrete; some brazen monster."

"I'm so sorry, Kat," I whispered, all of it starting to come together.

"She didn't even tell my dad until she realized she was pregnant. Then six months later, I showed up. He just knew I wasn't his, you know. There's a bond between a father and his kits, or pups, I guess, for you."

I nodded, knowing there was.

"How they hated me... I think I'm lucky they didn't smother me in my crib, but sometimes I wish they had," she wept, crying harder. "They ignored me my entire life. Unless I did something to shame the family. So, I made a habit of that just to get attention. I could've been something other than a dancer, but I liked how it got to them, you know? I liked to needle them so they would have to look at me for a moment."

She paused, and by the way she stared up at me, I knew she wanted me to understand the dancing thing, so I said, "It's okay. I'm not worried about that. At all."

"The worst part is I went most of my life not understanding what was wrong with me or why they despised me like they did. Then, when I turned nineteen, surprise! I had a wolf in my head. Yesterday was only the second time I've ever shifted to Rieka." My heart dropped, and Shaw whined in horror. Kat pressed the heels of her hands into her eyes, sobbing and saying, "I'm sorry. I'm so sorry. I was ashamed." The apology was for Rieka, not for me, and Kat continued, the words coming fast. "Eris and the other captives at the dragon's keep are the only ones I ever told I'm a hybrid, besides you. But someone in my family talked about it because the dragon knew, obviously."

I sighed, sad for the little girl in all those pictures. "That's why they pushed you aside and pushed you away."

"I tried to ask her questions—my mom. She wouldn't talk about it, and I don't think she knew much, anyway. The only thing she told me was he was a wolf shifter, her fox sensed it, and that he was rich because he had gold and diamond cufflinks on, with the initials RC."

The hair on my neck perked up at that. Had I seen that somewhere? I doubted it. The probability of me knowing the exact wolf who was in that parking garage that night in California was astronomical.

"My entire life," she whispered, pulling me away from thoughts. "I've been the disappointment. The outcast. The screw-up. And I'm so terrified..." She gulped, fighting tears. "I'm so fucking scared that you'll see it. That one day you'll wake up and look through the haze of this mate bond and see me. The real Kat, and you'll be disappointed, too."

"No! No, I could never. I do see you. I see you more than anyone else ever has. I can feel your feelings and your heart, and I think you're incredible. And I need you. I'm glad we didn't do it right away, complete the bond, because this time together halfway around the world has shown me I'd choose you anyway. That you're imperfectly perfect for me."

She nodded, but didn't look convinced, and I brushed her hair back, wiping her tears from her cheek with my thumb.

"Look what we just did together! I wouldn't have chosen another to fight an undead dragon with. Never. I know it's going to take a lot to unravel all the hurt you've felt, but I'm not going to give up. I'm too stubborn, and you know it."

She leaned over and kissed my hand, my palm, and it was the sweetest thing I'd ever seen.

After a moment of silence, I whispered, "A secret for a secret. Right?"

"You don't have to tell me anything. You really don't. It's okay."

"I want to. You should know, you know? The things that shaped me. Not just the good, but the bad, too."

She nodded, and I swallowed, clearing my throat. "My father died because of me." My brows knit, and I looked at her, watching her process the words while I pried open this old wound. Guilt was strange. It could be tempered and contained, until you almost forget it's there. Then, with just a thought, it can become as raw and grating as it was the day it was born. "It was the first call for me after I turned twenty and completed the program. For warriors. Our soldiers," I explained, unsure if she knew. "And I was nervous. I wanted to do good, to be a good soldier, like Gideon. He's good at everything, and it's always the pressure to measure up. Dad was Alpha, so he ran point on the operation. A good-sized group of vampires, but nothing that should've been too much."

"I can relate, at least, to an older sibling that seems impossible to follow," Kat whispered, the side of her mouth lifting to encourage me with a sad smile.

I nodded, looking past her at the stone we laid on. "I got to lead my own group. We were supposed to rendezvous, cut them off, and basically trap, corner, and kill them. But when we were moving, I sensed the vamps had shifted. I linked Dad. Tried to tell him I thought I should push sooner, but he said, 'Just stick with the plan, it's okay. You're young. I know you're excited.'" I paused and shook my head, still shocked that it was the last I'd ever heard his voice. "I just remember being so conflicted. I knew in my gut I was right, but I didn't trust myself. I should've been more insistent. I would be today, you know? But I wanted to be a good soldier, and I listened. I went to the rendezvous, but they never showed up. When the Alpha dies, you feel it. Pain ripping your heart to pieces." Kat ran her hand down my back, and I put my hand on my chest, remembering. "I started drinking... sleeping around. To feel numb or to feel something. I don't know. It fucked me up, but what it did to Mom..." I closed my eyes and shook my head again, knowing if Eris wasn't some crazy special healer, Mom wouldn't be with us. At least not mentally. Emotions I usually kept bottled bubbled to the surface, and I toyed with the neck of her t-shirt, rolling it between my fingers. I cleared my throat. Twice.

She said, "Finn—"

I was afraid she was about to say exactly what I didn't want to hear, so I interrupted, "And no one ever blamed me. Or let me blame myself. 'No, Finn, you were just following orders.' But, like, I know whose fault it is. I blame myself, and it pisses me off that nobody else does. I know that sounds so stupid, but if I'd just listened to my gut, my dad would be alive."

"You should've listened to your gut," she said, and I looked up at her face.

"What?"

"I'm blaming you. Do you feel better?"

"No."

"I'm pretty new to this intense grief laced with guilt thing, but I don't think anything really makes it feel better. We just get better at living with it. Because if I say Celia's death is my fault, what will you tell me?"

"That it's not."

She shrugged. "It doesn't make me believe it."

"It just sucks," I whispered. "The grief is so heavy when it comes with guilt."

"Yeah, it is. One second I'm okay, and then sometimes it feels like I'm drowning."

I nodded. "Stuck in the dark."

We were quiet, and when I looked at her, I was struck by her beauty. By her honesty.

"You lit a candle for me, Kat." Her lips curled, but her eyes were glassy, and I asked, "Won't you let me throw you a life jacket?"

"What if I pull you down, too?"

"I told you. If I can't save you, I'll sink with you. And fuck it, we'll throw a party at rock bottom."

CHAPTER 17

KAT

M Y SOUL WEIGHED NOTHING as we climbed the ladder back up through the tunnel. I still couldn't decide about the future—our future—but from now on I was going to do my best to make my own contentment. I had spent my entire life waiting for my parents to manifest into the happiness I craved; to realize their love for me. Something I had never considered was that maybe it was their fault, not mine, that it would never happen.

How cliché, this epic adventure was actually achieving some self-actualization.

I needed to let the past drift away and stop defining myself by that experience. Eris liked me. Finn liked me. Maybe I wasn't totally unlikable.

I squinted in the late afternoon sun when we reached the top of the ladder. We had been down in the cave for almost an entire day and hadn't slept. I had one box of granola bars in my duffle, and Finn and I split them, eating all but two.

"Damn, this is going to suck without my wallet," Finn said, frowning.

"Hey, wait," I mumbled, digging through my pack. "I think I found it in the wreck."

He sighed and took it, kissing my hand as he did.

"We should sleep."

I nodded. My eyelids were so heavy that I could barely keep them open.

"Since we don't have our gear, we should shift. It'll be easier to sleep that way."

I nodded again.

We both shifted. Hana agreed Rieka should get another turn since I had shorted her these last years. Rieka licked Shaw's muzzle, and they curled up together.

It was one of the best nights of sleep I'd ever had, as my wolf under the Amazonian moon. We didn't wake until the morning sun was climbing high in the sky. I stretched, still in wolf form, while Finn stirred awake and did the same. He shifted and tied the duffle to my back.

"You ready to go?" he asked, patting Rieka's neck.

She licked him, and he shifted back. We made good time to the wreck with Shaw leading the way with his nose. A gentle rain soaked our fur, but we didn't stop as we passed the car. I tried not to look at poor Paulo's grave.

We ran down the road back toward the village, stopping when it came into sight and shifting back to our human forms. Finn had to once again squeeze into my pink sweats, and I felt too exhausted to even giggle.

The people wouldn't speak to us or look at us; some ran inside and closed the doors and windows.

"What is this?" Finn asked, looking at me with raised eyebrows.

"I don't know. Is it because we went into the temple and came out alive?"

Finally, a man came out and addressed us with a dark glare and broken English. "You go. Leave. You bring death to us."

Finn looked at me again, and I shrugged, asking, "What do you mean?"

"You come here, and now two are dead. No blood left," the man explained, tapping his throat.

Those poor souls. The vampires followed us here,' Hana said, and I glanced around at the dense forest, as if they might be watching me right now.

Finn held out eight one-hundred-dollar bills to the man, pleading for a ride to the halfway point towards Rio.

The man hesitated, staring at the money, and then finally took it. He came back a few minutes later with another man and a small, beat-up, white pickup truck. We went to get in, and they locked the doors, indicating the bed. Finn looked at me, and we sighed, climbing in and sitting shoulder to shoulder with our backs resting against the cab.

I nodded in and out of sleep on the bumpy drive, my head occasionally dropping onto Finn's shoulder. He didn't sleep at all that I saw, watching everything. The men switched drivers a few times, and stopped for gas once but drove well over twenty hours straight.

They dropped us on the outskirts of Brasília without a second glance, leaving us in a cloud of dust as soon as our feet hit the ground.

We walked the rest of the way in, stopping at the first hotel we could find and getting a room. Finn was able to call Gideon while I showered. It was still early evening, but I climbed into the bed, exhausted. I heard Finn in the shower and then felt the bed dip as he joined me. We were sharing beds now, and I didn't mind at all. His arms encircled me, and I sighed, drifting away to a deep sleep.

We were on the move early the next morning. When we stopped to eat, I ordered three different breakfasts for myself, scarfing them all down with gusto. The jerky and protein bars had kept us alive, but I was dying for some actual food. Finn found himself some new clothes and rented us a car. It was still fourteen more hours back to Rio.

"I didn't see your passport when I grabbed your wallet," I said. "Do you have it?"

He shook his head. "No, it was in my pack. The skeletons have it now."

"How are we going to fly home?"

He shrugged. "Now that we have the athame, Gideon isn't taking any chances. He's sending the private jet to get us."

"Wait. You guys have a jet?"

"Yeah, we never use it, though. It's a gas guzzler. One of Dad's weird purchases," he said, and chuckled.

I shook my head in disbelief. I was going to fly in a real private jet.

I noticed Finn did not ask me to do any of the driving this time. He had previously suggested I wasn't a great driver, which was ridiculous. Part of me suspected he was out for revenge when he exceeded double the speed limit most of the way, making me reach for the oh-shit handle more than once.

Thanks to his reckless driving, we arrived in Rio while the sun was still up. The jet would arrive in the morning to pick us up, so we returned to the same place we'd stayed a few days earlier.

While we were in the lobby, Finn said, "Here. Why don't you go enjoy some of that?"

I took the money he was handing me and looked at where he was indicating. A luxury salon and spa.

"Really? Why?"

"It was a rough trip. Why not?" He handed me a keycard. "We're in the farthest unit down when you're done. Try not to end up anywhere alone and be careful. Keep your nose peeled for vamps."

"Got it," I said, and wandered over.

The ladies were great, and I had my chop job of a haircut shaped into an asymmetrical bob. A little edgier and much more me. It was followed by a massage, my first one ever, and I had my fingernails and toenails done, choosing red for the color.

The black silk robe they'd given me was complimentary, and I had it on over my clothes when I returned to the room. Inside, I found a buffet of fine Brazilian cuisine waiting. There was a literal mountain of barbecued meat on a spit, coils of steam rolling off of it, and my stomach rumbled. Finn wasn't with the setup, though. I peeked my head into the master bedroom but didn't find him.

The soft scent of a cigar drew me to the lanai. I couldn't see him, but I heard him talking, so I stopped at the door, listening to his phone conversation.

"Yes. Every month, I want a bouquet delivered to the grave. Yeah, I'm serious. Lavender and roses."

My brows lifted, and when he continued, my bottom lip quivered.

"Yes. That's right. Celia Kimura. Bellevue Memorial." A pause. "For how long? Forever, I guess. As long as the credit card works. Yeah, you heard me right. A new bouquet to be delivered once a month for her... alright, awesome. Thank you so much."

I blinked, letting two silent tears roll down my cheeks, and turned my back to the door, hugging myself while a shaky breath rattled in my chest.

'That's lovely,' Hana said, and I felt my little fox was swooning. *'I think that's wonderful.'*

Rieka said, *'He is wonderful.'*

I smiled, basking in a sense of peace I hadn't felt since I woke up on my nineteenth birthday with two warring canines in my head. *'You two better be careful. You're making a habit of agreeing with each other.'*

When I was sure he was off the phone, I opened the door.

"Hey. The food looks great."

He smiled over at me and was quick with an answer. "Not even close to how good you're looking."

"The spa was nice."

"I like your hair. A lot."

I reached up and touched it. "Thank you. Actually, thank you for everything. I appreciate it. All of it."

He stood, stretching his back and saying, "I don't even know how to accept that 'thank you' when it's been my pleasure to have you here."

"Just do it and don't be stubborn. For once."

"Fine. As long as you eat dinner with me. A date."

"A date? Don't all those granola bars and the jerky count?"

"Yes, they do. But I mean, I could take you out? Would you rather?"

"No." I shook my head. "I like this better."

"I knew you would."

His self-assured tone made me chuckle. "Really? Do you think you know me now, Finn Greenwood, after a couple of nights in the Amazon jungle?"

Finn grabbed my fingers, running his thumb over my knuckles. "I may be a slow learner, but I learn. And you're the easiest subject to study. That helps."

I couldn't explain exactly what it was about the words that made my eyes well and my nose tingle. Maybe it was just the way he looked at me. When I said nothing, he asked, "Aren't you hungry?"

"Starving."

We ate so much food. It was some of the best in my life. When I was more stuffed than I'd ever been, we returned to the lanai and listened to the ocean. I sketched on the pad he'd gotten me, and we talked about his life. What it was like to grow up in a pack. I envied his ability to tell a story, and how he could make almost everything funny somehow.

"So, yeah, the cat creeps me out." He was talking about Eris' sister, Enid, and her companion Hades.

"I think he's supposed to creep people out." I giggled. "It's like his job. Her little bouncer."

A silence fell between us, but it wasn't awkward. It was nice, too. I didn't know if I'd ever experienced that. The ability to sit quietly with someone and not feel the need to fill it with empty words.

The moon was almost full, and it seemed big tonight, its white light dancing on the ripples of the water. We looked at each other and shared a smile. A coy one.

He said, "Kat..."

But I stood and hugged my sketchbook to my chest. It was a pencil sketch of him dressed as Indiana Jones. Kind of silly but fitting.

I said, "Goodnight, Finn," and his brows lifted, but he nodded. A sharp cut of disappointment sliced through the bond, but I felt him bury it.

"Goodnight, Kat."

I smiled and kissed his cheek, then walked inside.

Rieka said, *'Wait. You're going to bed?'*

'What else would I be doing?'

'Well... mating.'

'Ew. Don't call it that.'

'I just was sure that's where we were headed.'

I snickered. *'I'm definitely not going to bed.'*

CHAPTER 18

FINN

SHE WALKED INSIDE, AND I looked at my drink, swirling the ice around.

'Well, that sucks,' I told Shaw.

I had thought the tension was leading up to something there.

'Follow her,' he said, and I thought about it.

'She said goodnight.'

'I hate you. May the goddess bless me with a bolder human next time.'

'You're so dramatic,' I said, and took out the new phone I'd bought while Kat was at the spa.

Gideon answered on the second ring.

"Finn?"

"Yeah. We're settled in Rio. No sign of the vampires so far." I sniffed the air, checking again if I could smell them.

"Okay. Just be alert. I'm sending warriors on the plane. I can't believe they haven't—"

The door opened, and I stopped listening. Kat walked past me and, as far as I could tell, she wore only her silk robe. She said nothing, going out to the beach.

My mouth was hanging half open, and when she tossed a smile over her shoulder, then slid the robe down her body, I cut him off, saying, "Bye," and dropped the phone.

She was naked, and I was already tearing at the buttons on my shirt. I did a quick scan of the beach, making sure we were alone. My hand fell to the athame. I had purchased a sheath for it, and I was keeping it on my belt. Checking up and down the beach once more, I felt it was safer here. Losing it out in the ocean would be a disaster. I would watch it closely.

Never one to be shy and not wanting her to feel lonely, I took off my shorts and boxers, tossing them.

Kat was in the water up to her waist, her back to me, and she gazed up at the moon. The pale light shimmered on the waves, a glowing picture frame that illuminated her inked skin.

The beauty of the image made my breath hitch, and I called, "I thought you were going to bed?"

"Changed my mind."

"You were teasing me!"

She smiled over her shoulder, and I watched her cheeks flush when her eyes dropped down my body.

I waded into the ocean, where she waited for me. Just her being naked was plenty, and I was already hard. Our anticipation mixed in the bond, and I wrapped my arms around her.

"You want that spanking, don't you?" I asked, kissing her ear.

"Maybe I do. I can't seem to get you out of my head."

"I'll admit you've been in all my thoughts, too, and they're so inappropriate."

"It makes me happy to know you think of kissing me as much as I think of kissing you."

I sighed, pleased to hear those words. "Kissing and the rest of those lovely, dirty things."

I pressed against her, sliding my cock up and down the cleft of her ass, lubricated by the ocean. She melted into my embrace, moaning and gripping my forearms with her hands.

Feeling the scales tip in my favor, *finally*, I asked, "You want me? Do you want this?"

She put her hands on my hips and whispered, "Yes."

I turned her towards me, grabbing her chin and pulling her face to look up at me. Her breath was shallow, and she gazed up at me through her thick lashes. I pushed my lust for her through the bond and watched her pupils dilate. She ran her hands up my chest and laced her fingers around my nape, pulling herself up to my lips.

I met her halfway, kissing her. Her lips were like silk, and I relished her sweet scent mixing with the ocean breeze. Her taste was even better; my newest addiction. Kissing her was an experience that I would never recover from. She opened, inviting my tongue to slip inside, and her desire burned so hot, I couldn't focus.

Shaw was annoyingly present, pushing me to hurry. *'She said yes. Mark her.'*

'Shut up so I can.'

Kat slid her hands up my cheeks and pushed them into my hair. Her nails bit into my scalp, and I growled in my chest, reveling in her aggression as the intensity spiked. Our movements were desperate while the waves kept their constant rhythm, pushing and pulling.

KAT

When we were breathless, Finn broke the kiss. "You want me as your mate? Let me mark you tonight. Please."

I swallowed, feeling as though I'd tripped and fallen flat on my face. "I don't know. I'm sorry! I don't know." His disappointment dampened the fire in the bond, but I grabbed his cheeks. "I want tonight. I want tomorrow. I know that."

He picked me up, and I wrapped my legs around his waist.

"I am happy with tonight. And tomorrow."

"Just happy?" I teased, smiling.

"Fuckin' over the moon thrilled, I swear," he corrected, growling and pushing with his hips.

The way he held me, the movement pressed the hardest part of him against the softest part of me, and I gasped. He laced his hand in my short hair and pulled my head back so he could kiss the front of my throat. The bond flooded with wicked desire, and the sensations made my toes curl.

Those torturous little tingles rippled down my body while he muttered against my skin, "I've waited and I can't anymore. It feels like it's been forever since I've been imagining how it would be, how it would feel to sink inside you and make you take it how I want to give it."

My heart fluttered. I was down with skipping the foreplay this time. The water was only to his mid-thigh, so I was moving, trying to position myself. "Why wait any longer?"

He moaned, holding my waist while he adjusted us, positioning his cock at my entrance, and pulling me down.

When I opened my eyes, I screamed, "Finn!" He moaned my name, trying to hold me still while I scrambled to get out of his arms. "No! Finn, they're stealing it! The blade!"

Someone was digging through our clothes on the beach.

He muttered, "What?" and then blinked, finally coming to his senses. "Oh, shit! Hey!" Finn dropped me into the water, and he was already shifting, giving chase to the vampire who hissed over his shoulder, his eyes glowing red.

I fought to wade out of the water after him, shifting to Hana to follow Shaw in pursuit of the enemy.

CHAPTER 19

KAT

WE LEFT THE BEACH, running again into the dark alleys of Rio de Janeiro. Vampires were fast. Faster than wolves. I'd caught Shaw by the time he rounded into a dark alley, and Hana stopped in her tracks with a whine. More than a dozen pairs of glowing red eyes greeted us, the scent of decay permeating the air. Shaw wasted no time jumping into the fray with a growl. The vampires converged on him, but he was ruthless. A truly powerful killer that could tear head from shoulders in a single bite. Their attention was lost on me, a small fox, and I looked past the group, watching the thief crawl up a wall with the athame.

'There it is!' all three of us, Rieka, myself, and Hana said together, jumping onto a dumpster to skirt around the vampires and fall into a fierce pursuit.

Someday, if I lived long enough, Hana might grow enough tails to fly. Elderly kitsune could do that, an act of ancient magic. For now, I could use my singular tail as an oar, flapping it as I jumped up the alleyway, leaping from wall to wall to climb the narrow space. I made it to the top of the building, glancing back as Shaw continued his fight. He would win, I expected, but I couldn't wait for him. The athame would be lost.

The vampire thief leaped from this building to the next, and Hana followed, pursuing with her feather-light stride. Jumping the gaps was easy, and I was gaining when he dropped into an alleyway and disappeared from sight. A smarter person might stop and assess before they followed, but I was me, and I leaped down after him.

I landed at the feet of two vampires. The thief was handing the athame off, and he turned to hiss at me.

"Calm, calm," the other said. A woman. "It's just the little fox."

Her accent was eastern European, but I couldn't place it past that. Her dark amber eyes flashed in the moonlight that poured over the buildings into the alley. All the vampires I'd ever seen were gross. Red-eyed stinking demons. She wasn't. She was composed and strikingly beautiful, with her dark curled hair and pale skin. Eris had talked about this kind. They were called counts or countesses, old enough to lose the red glow of their eyes and control their thirst.

She snickered and held up the athame. "Looking for this?"

I bared my teeth and tried to take a step back, only to hit the brick wall behind me. A vampire was one thing, but a countess was a different fight.

She grinned and said to her subordinate, "Go. Ready my plane to return to Mistress Edana. I will handle this." He scurried away, leaving us, and she looked up the side of the building where I'd jumped from. "I don't think your big alpha wolf can follow you here, little fox. They're too oafish, aren't they?" Her grin widened, her canine teeth growing past her lips as she added, "He will find your husk, eventually. Until then—"

Hana jumped up and bit her wrist, already tired of the villain monologue. The countess hissed but didn't drop the blade as I'd hoped she would. With a flick of her arm, she sent me flying into the brick wall with a yelp. I barely had time to register the pain before she had my scruff, lifting me and hissing in my face, her fangs elongating down toward her chin like needles.

"You are going to taste so sweet!" she crooned, opening her jaw wide.

But Rieka said, '*My turn!*' and before I or the vampire realized what was happening, we shifted. From fox to wolf. I'd never done that before.

Rieka was five times Hana's size, and the vampire's eyes widened. Her mouth formed an "o," and I thought I heard the first breath of the word, "Wait." My wolf did not oblige, and with a ruthlessness I didn't know Rieka possessed, she turned in the vampire's hand and latched onto her throat.

The crunch of bone and flesh made me nauseous as a conscious bystander, and I said, *'Holy shit!'*

Just like I'd seen Shaw do to others, Rieka ripped her head off with a couple of brutish yanks.

We stood for a beat of silence, the three of us watching the body gush blood from the neck stub through Rieka's eyes, and then Hana cheered, *'That was brilliant!'*

We were all talking at once, with me shouting, *'Oh my gods! Rieka! That was wild. You're wild! How did you do that?'*

'You like that?' she boasted, her braying laughter filling our head. *'I don't know. I just did!'*

'Did we just defeat a countess? By ourselves?' I asked. *'We? Us? The inept trio of perpetual disaster?'*

'I think we did!' Hana said. *'Mostly Rieka, though. I could never tear someone's head from their shoulders!'*

Rieka checked the alley for others and found it empty. *'We would've never caught her without you, Hana. I cannot run so fast or climb buildings.'*

'Grab the athame, and let's get out of here,' I said, worried more vampires would return when they sensed her death.

Rieka picked it up and turned, all three of us yelping when we ran into something. Another wolf. Shaw. His bushy black eyebrows were the most expressive I'd ever seen on an animal, surging up his forehead as he looked past us at the dead countess. I could see the shadow of Finn there, lurking behind the wolf's expression. Rieka offered a little growl, bobbing her head back and forth and prancing on her two front feet as if to say, "Yeah, I did that."

Hana was laughing in her high-pitched chitter. *'Look at his face! He can't believe it.'*

Shaw barked, and rubbed his cheek against Rieka's, licking the blood on her muzzle. Our three hearts fluttered in unison, and Rieka offered him the athame, following him out of the alley after he took it.

Like two black shadows, we slunk through the sleeping city, the human occupants unaware that the beasts they told stories about passed under their windows. The beach was empty, and we entered our bodega. I shifted, and heard Finn shift behind me, followed by the lock of the door.

I spun with my hands on my cheeks, squealing. "You should've seen me, Finn! The three of us!"

He was checking the window for anyone who might have followed, but whipped around, throwing his hands out. "Kat! You just, like, saved the friggin' world!"

I didn't think, in all of my life, that anyone had ever looked at me the way he was. A broad smile, but more than that. A shine in his eye. Was it pride? I stared at him, my eyes filling. He asked, "Kat?"

"What?"

He'd said something, but I hadn't heard.

"What happened out there? Tell me!"

"Oh! Well, Hana chased the runner down, and then he gave the athame to the countess, and she had us by the scruff, but we shifted. From fox to wolf! We've never done that! I was just as stunned as the vampire!" He was walking toward me, and I laughed when he grabbed my waist, picking me up so I could wrap my legs around him. My cheeks were warm as I finished the story. "And, uh, Rieka just ripped her head off. Like, just..." I made a motion with my hand across my throat, giggling because we were naked, and my heart was still racing, and he was so handsome, smiling up at me.

"Well, no one else in the world can do that, so I imagine she was shocked," he said, winking. "You're pretty special, you know?"

I shrugged. "I guess."

"You are."

I put my hands on his cheeks and ruffled his beard, giving him a little scratch like I might a dog. His eyes closed, and he leaned into my left hand, a silly smile spreading across his face.

When I laughed, he did too, and said, "You can do that anytime."

My hands went from his beard up to his auburn hair, scratching his scalp, and he sighed, leaning forward to kiss my chest. When he turned his head up, looking for my lips, I gave them.

He said into the kiss, "I love you, Kat."

And everything screeched to a halt, my heart flatlining before jumping into a race. My eyes flew open, and I nearly fell out of his arms, throwing myself back to escape the loaded words. He let me down, and I glanced in the mirror to my left.

"Oh, my gods!" I was covered in dried blood from my mouth to my chest from Rieka's bite. I brushed at it, but it was caked on. "Gross. Why didn't you tell me?"

He shrugged. "It doesn't bother me."

The segue to hygiene did nothing to cut through the heavy tension that invaded every corner of the room.

"I'm gonna shower," I said, pointing to the bathroom.

He nodded and picked up a menu. "I'll order some more food?"

"Yes. Yes," I said, clapping my hands once. "I am ready for dessert. Starving." I wasn't, but I didn't know what else to say.

"Well, we'll take care of that," he said, picking up the hotel phone to call the restaurant.

I slunk away to the bathroom, unsure if it was love I feared, or if it was what always came after that frightened me. The anchor of love was pain. That I knew.

Chapter 20

Finn

THE RIO SUNRISE GAVE us a grand goodbye, coloring the sky with oranges and yellows as we boarded the jet early the next morning. Kat's body practically hummed with excitement as we walked up the stairs to the waiting open door.

She looked at me, beaming. It struck me how much I could see the fox in that grin. She said, "This is crazy. I feel like I'm the president or something."

I chuckled, despite my sour mood. I'd blown it last night with my declaration of love, and I felt like I was going to burst out of my skin with how badly I wanted her. "Wait until you see the inside."

Our father had purchased this asset, sparing no expense. He hated flying, so I guess he wanted to make it as comfortable as possible. It was a business jet with over eight hundred square feet of floor space, leather seating, couches and tables, flat-screen TVs, and a full bedroom suite and shower. Even for us, it was extravagant, and Gideon talked regularly about exchanging it for something more practical.

Kat gasped, spinning in a circle in the middle of the living room area. "Holy shit! And I thought first class was nice!"

The pilot approached me, nodding her head. "We're ready to take off, sir, if you want to sit until we're in the air."

We both sat and buckled. I watched Kat as she gazed around the cabin, reveling in her amazement. A totally different woman from the one I'd found in that cemetery. When we were at cruising altitude, the pilot gave us permission to move about the cabin, and Kat explored. She opened every cabinet, gasping at the contents of each one.

"It's a little much, isn't it?" she asked, wrinkling her nose. "The pack house mansion and the plane and all of it." She held out her arms. "Such luxury almost feels dirty to me for some reason when there are so many suffering in the world."

My brows lifted. "I assure you my brother has a lot of money, but he pays his fair share of taxes to Uncle Sam every year."

She tilted her head, looking unconvinced.

"Plus," I added, standing, "I want you to think about your time in the pack. Did you see a homeless person? Someone panhandling for money or food?" There had been plenty of them in Los Angeles. Lost souls searching for a scrap under million-dollar skyscrapers. I understood her feelings, as it had made me uncomfortable, too.

After a moment of thought, she shook her head. "I didn't see anyone struggling."

"That's because they don't. We're a pack. We're a family. All are taken care of. We are a society built of ranks—Alpha, Beta, Omega—but I can't imagine living in a world where we allowed a single wolf to live on the streets. I'm not the Alpha, but I know my brother, and I knew my father. They believe that the success of your reign is determined by the health and happiness of your omega class."

"That seems like a fairytale to me after growing up in the human world," she said.

"To us, it's common sense. It's natural. No one should suffer such indignity as not to have at least their most basic needs fulfilled while others sleep in silk sheets. The pack is connected through him. He's the link, and part of his power is drawn from that relationship. If the Alpha didn't care for the people, their loyalty to him would weaken, and along with it, his power, until another wolf of strong blood could challenge and defeat him."

She said nothing, only nodded, a small smile curling the corners of her lips.

From the cockpit, the pilot called, "Beta? Would you like the itinerary?"

"Excuse me," I said, squeezing Kat's hand as I walked by.

I went to speak to the pilot about any stops we might have and what our estimated arrival time was. When Kat walked back towards the bedroom suite, I smiled to myself.

Kat

"Oh, my gods." I couldn't stop saying it. Everything on this plane was the nicest thing I'd ever seen. The Jackson Pollock hanging above the bed caught my eye, and I nearly choked on my own spit when I got close enough to realize it wasn't a print. I kicked off my shoes and climbed onto the bed to get a closer look. The door opened and closed behind me, indicating I was no longer alone.

"You hang an original Jackson Pollock on your plane?" I demanded, leaning closer to smell it even though it was behind glass.

Finn chuckled. "It was a gift."

My brows lifted. "From who? This is worth half a million dollars, at least! I'd bet more than that."

"Really? The fae king gave it to my brother as a sign of our ongoing diplomacy and partnership. Gideon thinks it's hideous." He snorted. "We had no idea someone would pay money for something like that."

"Hideous?" I gasped. "I might slap him for that."

Finn chuckled. "Do you want it? It's yours if you want it. Hang it wherever you like. In your room at home."

The words were casual, but I felt their intention, insisting that I had a room to return to in his lavish pack house with his fancy Jackson Pollock to woo me.

"Mine?" I whispered, touching the glass like it was a newborn infant, and I was afraid to harm it. "I couldn't."

"No one will even know it's missing. You might have to paint a new one to fill the spot, though."

Another subtle insistence that I'd be there long enough to craft a replacement.

I sighed, never imagining I'd witness one outside of a museum. "A real Jackson Pollock. I can't believe it."

Finn didn't answer, and I yelped when music blared out of the speakers. The volume slightly decreased as the intro to the song started.

I spun around to find Finn facing away from me. "W-what are you doing?"

He answered by shimmying his hips, then glancing over his shoulder and wiggling his eyebrows. "Would you like a dance, my lady?"

"Oh, no," I said, covering my mouth to hide my smile. A giggle bubbled up my throat, accompanying the heat that rose into my cheeks.

My brows flew up when he spun on the ball of his foot and fell toward the counter, grabbing it and executing a pushup that ended in a deep hip thrust.

Cupping my hand around my mouth, I shouted, "Woo!" and flopped onto the bed to watch the show. "How are you *so* good?" I asked, laughing and clapping when I realized his dance moves were far above average. He had excellent body control. The eye contact was simmering when he grabbed his t-shirt at the neck and ripped it, revealing the swollen mounds of his pecs and the washboard of his abs. He followed the trail of hair down his stomach with his hands, hooking his thumbs into his belt line and thrusting his hips again. More than once. I covered my eyes, peeking through my fingers and giggling.

Hana chirped, *'Oh my,'* and Rieka, I felt, was speechless.

"Gods," I mumbled, swallowing as my face burned hotter. No one had ever danced for me before.

He grinned, and I left the bond open, allowing the pulse of my feelings, my desire, to roll across it. I had to wonder how long he'd been planning this. His routine had no awkward pauses, as if he'd choreographed it all beforehand. When the song was ending, Finn jumped onto the end of the bed, rolling and grinding his hips into the mattress while his eyes told me what he really wanted beneath him.

He crawled up the bed, up my body, until his arms straddled my shoulders and we were nearly nose to nose.

"That song is longer than I remembered, and that was harder than I thought it would be."

I touched his forehead. "You're sweating. Don't have a heart attack." His gaze softened, and his eyes drifted up and down my face. "I wouldn't dare. I'd be pissed if I died before I got to do this."

My hand drifted from his forehead to his cheek. "Do what?"

Finn pressed his lips to mine, pushing my head back into the plush pillow. The kiss lasted through my shirt being pulled over my head, and the unlatching of my bra. My heart raced, sounding in my ears as if it was playing percussion to the new song pulsing out of the speakers.

His mouth was on my breasts, taking my nipple between his lips. I gasped at the warmth, and at the beat that throbbed in my core, aching.

He kissed between my breasts and moved to the other one, swirling his tongue over the bud. His teeth grazed it, making me gasp, and I held fast to the headrest of the bed, watching him.

"Oh, gods," I whispered, still aware we were on a small plane with other people when he slid my panties off and tossed them, making his way down my body.

He kissed my inner thigh by my knee, and his facial hair tickled me, the sensations growing more intense as he moved higher. At one point, he stopped, focusing on one spot and sucking the sensitive flesh into his mouth.

Trying to be quiet, I gasped, my hand flying up to cover the sound. My thighs tingled, and there was a deep throb between my legs. I squirmed, giggling and saying, "Finn! Gods!" I couldn't help it when the sensation became too much, and I reached down and smacked him lightly on top of the head.

He chuckled, pulling his mouth away to study the hickey he'd left on my leg. His hands on my hips suddenly yanked me toward him, and he gripped me under my knees, opening them. It left little to the imagination as far as what he could see, and my cheeks warmed.

He stopped, and staring directly between my legs, said, "My gods, you are beautiful."

The heat in my cheeks filled my face. "Do you say that to all of your many, many women, Finn?"

He looked up at me. "No. Only the one that calms my soul and sets my flesh aflame at the same time."

I swallowed. Sometimes he did that; just dropped something serious and surprisingly poetic into the conversation when I didn't expect it.

A slow smile turned my lips. "Are you on fire for me, Finn?"

"Of course, I am. Twice now I've been moments from having you only to be denied at the last second. You won't escape again."

With a soft moan, I flexed my hips toward him. "Show me how bad you want me."

And he did—my gods—he did. My back arched at the first touch of his lips, and his grip on my hips tightened to keep me still.

It was a riot of sensations, whirling in my core and through my blood. I didn't expect tentativeness, but his entire mouth was on me. Devouring me. I actually sputtered, "What are you—what?" because I couldn't understand how it was *that* good, and the growl of approval that rumbled in his chest only made it better.

My head dropped back, and I squirmed in his hands, fighting and submitting at the same time to the bliss. To the torture. That tight curl in my core that spun and twisted with every slide of his tongue. What he was doing was the only thing I thought of, my entire body focused on him. Two of his fingers joined the heady torture, stretching me and moving in an upward angle.

I cried out, threading my hands into his hair. "That's gonna make me come. You're gonna—"

The encouragement doubled his already diligent efforts, and the twist in my core unraveled. I arched my back, shouting his name. Praised it. This had to be something close to Elysium, to the gods.

My body was quivering when he lifted his head. His lips were glossy in the dim light, and he asked, "Do you know how good you taste?"

He didn't wait for an answer, putting his glistening fingers on my lips. I opened, tasting my own pleasure, and his kiss followed right after. It was rough; it felt like a claiming, his mouth on mine. This man. This man woke the wolf in me that I'd worked so hard to repress. He made me wild.

I put my hands on his chest, running them down the patch of hair that trailed to his stomach and lower. He'd already unbuttoned his shorts, so I pushed past them, taking his hard length in both hands.

His lips parted slightly against mine, and he moved his hips, rolling them. I reached farther, cupping his sack, and the deep sound he made sent a flush of heat through my veins. I felt his splash of surprise in the bond.

"Is this a competition to see who's naughtier in bed?" he asked, his voice rough.

I nipped his lip. "It can be."

He kicked his shorts down his legs. "This is the first time I've ever hoped to lose."

I pushed his shoulder, and he understood, rolling to his back and yanking me on top of him. Straddling him, I was dancing to the music, grinding on him, barely avoiding penetration. His tongue shot out, sliding over his lower lip, and he grabbed my waist trying to guide me to take him. I turned around, thinking I would continue the dance; continue the teasing, but his arm wrapped around my waist, and he trapped me, sliding me slowly back and entering me as I sat down.

"Ah—oh, gods," I moaned, because he pulled me down without giving me time to adjust to the intense stretch. I whimpered when my bottom was pressed to him, and he was seated deep inside me.

"Why'd you stop?" he growled, a little tease in his tone.

I moved my hips in circles to the rhythm of the song, moaning when he grabbed my waist and lifted me, only to drop me again. I cried out, but found my footing and took over the movement, saying, "Gods, you feel so good."

His hand lifted in my periphery, and he spanked me, growling in his chest.

My body flushed with pleasure from the light sting. When he felt it in the bond, a dark chuckle rumbled through him. "You are perfect."

The dance continued until Finn lifted me, so my hands fell back on his chest, and I was in a wide reverse straddle over him. He grabbed under my thighs and started his own ruthless rhythm that had nothing to do with the music.

I looked down and I could see where our bodies connected, and how tan his hands were against the creamy skin of my thighs, and how my breasts bounced in a pretty, perfect rhythm.

My head kicked back, and I moaned his name, totally forgetting the other people. The angle of his thrusts elicited sharp slices of pleasure, and I was soon begging him to keep going.

"Ah! Oh, my gods!"

The climax was quick, whipping through me until I was shuddering on top of him, my pretty red nails digging into his chest. Finn sat up, his arm around me as he flipped us and seized all control before I returned to reality. I was on all fours, him behind me and still inside me, and the world spun, his thrusts deeper, harder, and longer.

After that climax, it was a torturous assault of raw sensations, and I shied away, pushing back on his hip with my hand and dropping to my stomach.

Finn spanked me, twice, and then his weight pressed on my back. "Where are you going?" he growled, lifting one of my legs to open me wider. "Running from me?"

"Of course not," I gasped, barely able to speak.

"Good." His hand was between us, finding my entrance again with the head of his length, and then he sank into me. I was caged by his arms, at his mercy, and I melted like cheap chocolate into the embrace.

We were frantic and wild, the same brutal rhythm, and my voice turned into a keening hum while every thrust pushed me into the soft duvet, sending satin-wrapped shards of pleasure through every nerve of my body. It was a delicious contrast when Finn delicately laced our fingers, holding my hand. He slowed and cursed. "You take it so well. Gods."

He was close. Trying to last. I grinned and rocked my hips back and forth, grinding against him. Unsure what wickedness possessed my tongue, I said, "Give it to me. I *love* it."

Another cool burst of surprise and his hand wrapped under my chin, pulling my face back to look up at him.

Our eyes collided, and he asked, "What'd you just say?"

"I said I love it. I want it. Hard."

His pupils exploded, nearly blotting out the fiery hazel. He growled and picked up his speed again, rougher this time. His hand wrapped around my throat. "Is that what you want?"

I matched his rhythm with my voice. "Yes, yes, yes!" The bed knocked, smacking against something. It was so rough, I wondered if I could handle it, only for his other hand to push under me, finding that sensitive bud with his fingers. I was ensnared by the buildup of pressure in my core, caught in the web of too much pleasure. "You're gonna make me come again!"

He said, "Holy gods, Kat," while my legs shook and I cried out, squeezing the bedding in my fisted hands.

When the climax ebbed, I smiled and stuck out my tongue, giggling almost manically at the way my body trembled. I felt as if I were floating.

Finn cursed again. "If you're asking for it, you better keep your naughty mouth open."

I did.

He pushed off of me and moved around near my face. Understanding, I took him with my hand and my mouth, listening to him groan long and loud and feeling the pulse of heat against my tongue as he came. His grip was tight in my hair as I ran my hand up and down his length until his body twitched.

Finn flopped onto the bed next to me, and with a happy sigh, mumbled, "Well, I lost."

CHAPTER 21

---◆◇◆---

FINN

I T WAS A DREAM. This was all a dream, I was sure of it as I lurched awake, sitting up. The cabin of the plane came into focus, and I chuckled, unable to believe it. It was real. The goddess really had paired me with the most deliciously naughty woman I'd ever met. No other had ever let me be so rough; push so deep. And she'd loved it.

Kat asked, "Are you okay?" her voice thick with sleep.

"Yeah. I just thought you were a dream."

She giggled. "Well, I am, aren't I?"

"Gods, yes." I rested on my elbow and kissed her, running my hand down the front of her bare body. "I'm going to go see where we are."

She yawned, saying, "Okay," and hugging the pillow like she had no plans to move.

I stepped out into the seating compartment, and Lucien glanced over the top of his magazine. His lips were curled at the edges, and he greeted me with a simple, "Beta."

The other warrior, who was freshly nineteen and didn't have his mate yet, greeted me as well, but a full grin cracked across his face.

Sure that they'd heard plenty and not caring, I nodded and smiled. "Morning, fellas... or afternoon? Where are we?"

"Pilot says in about half an hour we'll touch down and refuel in Miami."

"Thank the goddess. I can't wait to give this to my brother." I patted the athame at my waist.

"He called. Rumor in the realm is that Diamond Moon has the other artifact secured."

"Secured," I said, and laughed dryly. "I fucking doubt it. They don't have an Enid."

KAT

A car waited for us at the Seattle airport, accompanied by three black SUVs full of warrior shifters. Gideon was not taking the safety of this artifact lightly. Finn kept it on his belt and took over the driver's seat while I sat on the passenger side.

We drove for hours, the landscape becoming more wilderness as we moved inland until tall pine trees flanked the road on both sides, making it impossible to see anything else.

I smiled. They reminded me of Finn and his pine and coffee scent. When my heart skipped a beat and my skin erupted with tingles, I knew we'd crossed the barrier of the realm. The magic prevented any humans from wandering into supernatural territory and condensed the massive area so it couldn't be seen from the air. There was an entire forest here, thousands of acres that humans didn't know about. The world was much bigger than they realized.

Finally, after what seemed like forever, we arrived at the pack house in the late afternoon. Between the jet lag and the constant exhaustion of the trip, I wasn't even sure what day it was. Finn and I boarded the elevator, riding up in silence. Our tired reflections stared back at us, and he wrapped his arm around my waist, pulling me into his side so I could lay my head on his shoulder.

"We did it," he said, sighing.

Finn opened the door to Gideon's office without knocking. Gideon and Eris were both waiting, and Eris was wringing her hands, her face tight. Enid and two other women were also here. From their appearance, I assumed they were the witches Finn mentioned.

"Hi, Finn and Kat!" Enid said, the only cheerful person in the room.

"Hi, Enid," we mumbled in unison, and I waved like an idiot for some reason.

Eris hurried around the desk to hug me. "I'm so glad you're both safe."

Finn unsheathed the athame and held it out to his brother, who took it, frowning.

"It definitely holds some sort of power," he said, handing it to the blonde witch. "What do you think, River?"

She looked at it and then closed her eyes. The office was silent, waiting for her conclusion.

"Yes, this has to be it. This is ancient magic."

Gideon nodded and stood, clapping Finn on the shoulder. "Good job."

"Couldn't have done it without Kat. She killed a countess by herself."

Gideon's brows lifted, and he smiled. "Good job, both of you."

"What do we do with it?" Finn asked.

"We have to keep it out of the hands of the dragons. As we speak, a vault is being constructed underneath the pack house. It will be warded with magic and technology, the best of both. Once it's finished, the athame will stay there under constant guard. Until then, I'll keep it with me." Gideon took the blade back from River and continued, "Unfortunately, Diamond Moon recovered the bell in Egypt. If the vampires were watching you, I assume they were watching them as well. I fear it's only a matter of time before the dragons attack here, Diamond Moon, or both, and try to take the artifacts."

Finn grabbed my hand, squeezing it.

River looked at Enid. "We all need to be ready."

Enid nodded, her smile not wavering. I couldn't believe she was only sixteen and the fate of the entire pack rested on her shoulders. The entire world, really.

"There is another pack meeting in four days at Emerald Moon," Gideon said. "They want to discuss our movements going forward. Lyrion has convinced quite a few of the Alphas that I'm determined to be Alpha King. They want both artifacts brought to the location."

Finn balked. "What? They want to make it that easy for the dragons to get them both?"

Gideon shook his head, obviously annoyed. "Trust me. I have argued the point extensively, but no one wants to listen to me."

"So, we'll all be going?" Finn said, indicating everyone in the room.

Gideon nodded. "Yes, I believe that's the best move. If the dragons attack, we need Enid there, and I want River and Rhia to confirm that the bell is an authentic artifact."

Finn agreed. "Sounds good. Well, it's been a long week. If there's nothing else, I'd like to go to bed."

Gideon nodded, and Eris made me promise to visit later and tell her about the trip. Finn and I trudged like zombies to the elevator, but on the way up he asked, "Do you want your own room?"

"What?"

"You always catch me off guard with that one, so I thought I'd ask in advance."

"I definitely don't want my own room."

"Good. You are mine."

My eyebrows shot up. "That's a little possessive."

"Well, you may not be willing to admit it yet, but we belong together."

My lips curled, and I reached over and took his hand, threading our fingers. It surprised him, probably expecting me to argue, and he brought my hand up and kissed my knuckles.

I snuggled into him in bed, listening to the steady rise and fall of his chest, and to the strong beat of his heart against my ear. Before the beach, I still thought there was a chance this would just be a fling, but that idea was quickly dissolving.

A life with Finn suddenly made sense, but I had to talk to him about something. He deserved to know the truth before we made a commitment, and I was terrified that it would bring all of this to a grinding halt.

CHAPTER 22

KAT

I SLEPT A LOT over the next two days, feeling exhausted from the trip. It still felt like I hadn't even rested after the dragon's keep. My brain couldn't reconcile that I'd been chained to that wall only weeks ago when it felt like a lifetime had passed since then.

The sketchbook became my obsession, and I poured my soul into it. I sketched Finn as Indiana Jones, and him sitting on the lanai in Rio with whiskey in his hand, and in the alley with his t-shirt loincloth. Then, so I never forgot it, I sketched the room with the mural, the skeleton warriors, and the scene with the undead dragon crushed by the bell.

Everyone was busy, even Finn. When I saw him again the second night, he was exhausted, and we had lazy sex before drifting to sleep.

They were all getting ready for this meeting and working on keeping the athame safe. I felt bad, like I didn't have a place here or a way to help. An outsider. A feeling that I was all too familiar with.

It was late morning on day two when I heard a knock on the door. Eris was waiting with a tray of food, and I welcomed her inside.

"You've been hiding up here. So, I thought I'd come join you."

I shrugged and bit my thumbnail. "Not hiding, but not really sure what I'm supposed to do. I don't know anything about being in a pack."

She laughed. "You can just come hang out with me in my office! Trust me, I can find you something to do." Her face soured. "I really don't like the printer."

I smiled. "Really? I can just come in there? Your job is so important."

"Of course, Kat," she said with a soft look in her eyes. "You have a place here with us. You are family."

"Thank you. I've been feeling a little lost since I went back home and..." I choked on the last words, still struggling to say it.

Concern broke across her features. "What is it, Kat? What happened?"

"Finn didn't tell you?" I croaked, a little surprised.

She shrugged. "We only knew you were feeling extreme emotional distress, and that's why he went to find you. He never elaborated."

I took a deep breath trying to compose myself. I closed my eyes, and two tears ran down my cheeks. Eris grabbed my hands and held them tightly, waiting.

"When I got home. My parents..." I choked up again, trying to control my emotions. "My parents disowned me." I was having trouble saying the rest, realizing I hadn't actually had to inform anyone Celia had been murdered. Finn had figured it out himself. Gods, it was hard to say the words.

She gasped. "What? Why?"

"Because when the vampires took me, my sister was there and they—and they..." I was sobbing now and finally whispered, "They killed her."

She answered with a sharp gasp, her dismay genuine. "Oh, my Goddess, no. Kat... I am so sorry."

"It had to be the vampires because if the dragon had done it, I know he would've used it to torment me like you and Daro. I had no idea she was gone. My parents blame me. They never want to see me again."

She hugged me. "I pray the vampires that did it all died at the dragon's keep. I hope they suffered."

My brows lifted. It wasn't what I was expecting to hear while she rubbed my back with gentle circles, but that was Eris.

"I'm so sorry, Kat," she said again after I'd cried some more.

"So, when I found out Finn was going to Brazil, I wanted to go, you know, to get away. And I learned this mate bond thing isn't so bad," I said, some heat rising in my cheeks.

Eris giggled. "Yes. It's not so bad."

She'd resisted Gideon at first but had given in and learned to love again.

"I noticed you're not marked, though," she said.

"Eris. How important is it to a shifter to have pups?"

Her brows shot up at the unexpected question for an answer. "It's very important. Family is everything to shifters."

"I see," I whispered.

"Why?"

"Oh, it's just something I have to talk to him about. It's kind of why, you know." I waved my hand at my marking spot. "I know he wants to. Really badly," I said and chuckled awkwardly, trying to skirt the subject.

"Finn won't mark you unless you ask him to. That I promise. It's totally up to you, Kat."

"Oh. Is that like a rule or something?"

"It's tradition, or etiquette, I guess. Marking someone without their consent is one of the worst things a wolf can do. It's spiritual rape, really. To force someone into a bond..." She trailed off, her face scrunched with disgust.

"I guess I can understand that."

"It's a story we're told as pups. My mother told it to me when I was small," she said, her eyes traveling to another place.

"Will you tell it to me?"

Her eyes lit up. "Yes, of course. Every wolf should hear it. It starts with the Alpha King called Darius, paired with his wolf called Wroth. All shifters lived under his rule. He was a firm but fair ruler, although tortured because he hadn't found his Luna and he was nearing his thirtieth birthday. He had his fair share of dissenters, the most prominent being a wolf named Rike, who had dubbed himself the King of Rogues. Finally, a she-wolf named Sarah visited the Alpha King's court, and Darius found she was his mate. That evening there was a huge celebration, meant to be her Luna ceremony, but Rike dressed as an old woman, snuck into the castle, and stole her before she and Darius could mate or mark each other."

"That's terrible."

Her face darkened. "It is. It's unfathomable, and it gets worse. Rike and his human cruelly mated and marked Sarah, against her will. Once a wolf is marked by another, it cannot be undone. It's the most sacred part of the mate bond, a melding of souls."

"So, what happened?"

"Sarah, unable to face her fate, walked into the ocean and was never seen again. The Alpha King went insane. He became a cruel and violent leader, which led to revolts and civil war. It was what Rike had wanted all along, and he swept in, killing Darius. He proclaimed himself the new Alpha King, but he was also a brutal and paranoid leader. The wars continued until he was killed. The suffering of wolf shifters was immeasurable at the hands of these two rulers. Afterwards, the treaty was written that there would never again be an Alpha King. Many alphas won their right to rule by participating and dominating in a tournament, which is still honored every summer. Several packs were formed to strike a balance in each realm, and everyone agreed, no more kings."

"Wow, so that's why everyone is so freaked out. They think Gideon wants to be Alpha King, huh?"

Eris nodded and looked at her hands. "Yes, everyone is so worried about it they can't see the bigger picture. It's terrifying, actually." She sighed and waved her hand. "Anyway, the story. It's now customary for the she-wolf to start the marking out of respect for Sarah and what she went through. Finn has certainly been told the same story as a pup, and he would never disrespect it, even though male wolves especially can be pushy to their human counterpart."

"His wolf wants him to mark me?"

"Oh, yes. I'm sure he's had an earful from Shaw."

"Why doesn't Rieka know any of this?"

"Wolves don't remember everything from their past lives. Since you weren't told the story as a child, it makes sense that neither of you would know."

"I see. Well, I don't know. I don't know, Eris. It's all so crazy and so fast!"

"You'll know when the time is right. Finn can wait. He deserves it after being such a philanderer." I snorted a laugh, but she was dead serious and obviously unamused by Finn's pre-bond promiscuity. Eris plated some food for me and smiled. "Now, I want to hear about your entire trip. I heard the artifact was in an old temple."

"Oh yeah, it was awesome! It was just like Indiana Jones!"

Her eyebrows knit together. Eris didn't understand any pop-culture references.

"It's a series of movies where a daring archaeologist professor goes on epic adventures."

She nodded, and I continued, regaling our tale in all of its awesomeness and showing her my sketches for emphasis.

"See, this is Finn dressed as Indiana Jones," I said, blushing.

She grinned. "Oh. Like Finndiana Jones."

I cackled, loving it, and we chatted the afternoon away. The sun was sinking below the trees when her eyes glazed over.

"Gideon is looking for me," she said, and I caught a hint of a mischievous blush on her cheeks. "But we can hang out every single day." She shrugged. "If you want. You're my best friend."

"Really? What about Enid?"

Her brows knit. "Enid is my heart, but she is weary of my protectiveness. She craves people in her life who are not me. Hm." Her mouth pulled into a small frown. "I don't... make friends easily. But it's easy with you."

"You really just want me to hang out in your office?"

"Yes! Please. Do you know anything about printers? Mine is my mortal enemy."

"I could probably help," I said, slapped with the realization that I had a place here. All I had to do was be bold enough to take it.

It was early the next morning, and the light was gray in the window. When I heard the first bird chirping its morning song, I decided I couldn't wait any longer. Finn had his arm over my waist, breathing gently, and I turned to him.

I put my hand on his cheek and ran my thumb over his cheekbone, my throat tightening with emotion.

"Finn?" He didn't stir, so I cleared my throat, and said, "Finn?" a little louder.

"Kat?" he asked around a yawn, but his brow furrowed when he felt my feelings in the bond. "What's wrong?"

"I just have to tell you something. I don't think it's okay for us to continue this, you know, until I do."

"Gods, okay," he said, a burst of anxiety in the bond. He sat up on his elbow, rubbing his eye with his finger. "I'm ready."

"I don't think I can have children."

His finger froze. "What?"

"I don't think I am capable of conceiving a child. Because I'm a hybrid."

"What does that—why?"

"Like a mule, you know? Or a liger. Their chromosomes are weird, so they're sterile, and I think I am, too."

"But why do you think that about yourself?"

"I just... have a feeling? I sense it about myself. Female intuition? I mean, I don't know. I just want to warn you. If we were to do this... be together. I might not be able to give you a pup."

My eyes filled with tears, but I cleared my throat, fighting them.

He was devastated. It was like a cold hole opened in the bond, but he buried it as quickly as it appeared.

"Well, we don't know for sure, so we shouldn't make assumptions. Even if it's so, Kat, we can figure it out. We can still be parents. My family—we've got money—we can do everything we can."

"What if it doesn't work, and I just can't?"

He searched for an answer. "Then, then..."

"I don't want you to answer now," I said, running my hand down his arm.

"But I want to answer."

"This is something you should really think about, Finn. It's your future. I think you should take some time to really digest it before you decide."

FINN

Gideon drove to Emerald Moon, although I should've taken the wheel with how stressed he was. The ladies, Kat, Eris, and Enid, sat in the back seat. River and Rhia told us they would get there by themselves.

We rode in dead silence. Gideon was on edge. I could tell because he was talking to the steering wheel, his lips moving like he was having a conversation in his head. It was a habit that only emerged when he was really keyed up. His alpha aura was projecting like an angry black cloud, pulsing around the cab. Being accused of trying to overthrow the government to become Alpha King could do that to a guy, I guess. If he could make it through this meeting without killing Lyrion, I would be proud.

He wasn't the only one on edge. Bringing both of the artifacts to the same place was the most idiotic thing I'd ever heard. And although I was glad to be going to Emerald Moon because Rudy was a loyal ally, his pack was much smaller and less equipped to handle a fight with dragons.

Kat was strong, and she was more agile than any wolf I'd ever seen, but she didn't have any official training as far as fighting goes. I was anxious about bringing her into a situation where there could be an attack, but she had absolutely refused to stay at the pack house.

'And she's still unmarked,' my wolf reminded me, *'in a room full of other alphas and betas!'*

'And that.'

'Mark her! Mark her when we get there. Better yet, tell your brother to pull over. Five minutes—'

'You want to take Kat out into the woods and mark her while everyone waits in the car?'

'Why do you say it like that? I think it's very practical.'

'Gods, Shaw. This brings me back to the original argument of, she didn't ask!'

'That's because you clammed up this morning!'

'It was like five a.m., and she just sprung that on me!'

'You should've just said the truth!'

'Oh, yeah, what?'

'That you love her. That you're in love with her and you want her forever.'

'What if she can't have pups?'

'Oh, you're going to reject her?'

'What? Of course not!'

'Of course not, you dense oaf!' he repeated, and whined in my head, beyond annoyed. *'So, what's to think about? We'll deal with it later, and if we're not meant to be a father in this life, we will accept this fate dealt to us by the gods. We can still serve our pack. It has nothing to do with taking Kat as your mate because she is our future. She is our happiness. Besides, if we're going to war, there will be orphans everywhere. No one will notice if we snatch a couple. Voilà, pups.'*

'Oh, my gods. No stealing children, Shaw.'

My heart pinched at the thought of never having a child of my own, but he was right. I would never reject Kat for it. She was the love of my life, and I had no doubts.

I glanced in the rearview mirror. Kat was biting her thumbnail and staring out the window. Eris was wringing her hands in her lap, probably drowning in the tidal wave of my brother's feelings.

The only person who seemed calm was Enid. She petted Hades on her shoulder, and when we made eye contact in the mirror, she offered a cheery, closed-lipped smile.

Between her aura, Gideon's aura, and the magic pulsing from the athame, I felt like I needed to roll the window down for some fresh air.

My brother smacked his hand on the steering wheel and didn't seem to notice it made everyone in the car jump. This was going to be a long drive.

We finally arrived, and I stepped out, sucking in the fresh air. Kat did the same, and I wrapped my arm around her waist, pulling her towards me.

"Wow, being in the car for that long with Enid was... an experience," she whispered.

I nodded and glanced at Enid. Her cat was laid across her shoulders, watching as the valet approached. We walked around the front of the car, and I was not shocked to see that River and Rhia were waiting for us at the door of the pack house.

I leaned over and muttered in Kat's ear, "See, that's creepy."

She giggled, rolling her eyes.

We all walked inside together and were led to the conference room. When we stepped through the doors, the conversations all stopped. Distrustful eyes turned to my brother, scrutinizing him.

I thought back to the last Pack Conclave just a little over a month ago, the one Eris had been kidnapped from, and I was stunned by how quickly things could turn. Several of these alphas had been our father's friends. They had known us our entire lives, and now they thought Gideon was trying to pull off some kind of coup d'état.

I linked him. *'This is not good.'*

'I know. I don't know how they all turned so quickly,' he said, his hand sliding to the athame sheathed at his waist. *'We have to protect the artifact at all costs, Finn. We can't let them take it today. I won't relinquish it, even under threat of retaliation.'*

I scanned the room. *'Well, who is still with us? Definitely with us?'*

'Rudy, Brutus, and Odin all voted with me the other day. That's it.'

Dread settled in my gut. This was going to be a disaster.

CHAPTER 23

KAT

I COULD FEEL THE tension rolling around the room in stifling waves. There were more people than I expected. Alphas, Lunas, and Betas sat around a giant table. Several warriors from different packs crowded along the walls. Obviously, some were expecting this not to go well.

A man called attention at the front of the long table, indicating everyone should sit. Eris had done her best to describe important people to me, and I assumed this was Rudy Black, Alpha of the Emerald Moon pack.

A smug-looking blond man, who I pegged as Lyrion Cain, Alpha of Diamond Moon and Gideon's greatest dissenter, spoke first.

"Did you bring your hoard of witches to intimidate us, Alpha?" he asked Gideon while eyeing River, Rhia, and Enid.

Several of the other Alphas eyed Enid in particular. I could see fear dancing in the back of their eyes, even though they tried to hide it.

Gideon glared at him. "I brought them to save your life when the dragons attack us and try to take both artifacts."

Lyrion's eyes flashed with anger. "I don't need your protection."

"I guess time will tell. Besides, this goes beyond just our kind. All supernaturals should know the threat looming over our realms. As I've already told—"

"Enough, you two," an older man interjected. "We're here to discuss the fate of the artifacts."

"There's nothing to discuss," Gideon said. "We agreed less than a fortnight ago that whoever found the artifact would protect it. The athame stays with Gold Moon."

Several people murmured, glaring at Gideon.

"That was before we realized the items carried more power than expected," the old man countered.

"A witch I consulted with informed me that this bell holds ancient, powerful magic," Lyrion said, presenting a small, plain-looking copper bell from his pocket and placing it on the table.

Gideon glanced sideways at River, and she nodded, confirming that it was the real deal. The third artifact.

"We assume you've discovered the same thing about the athame," Lyrion finished. "May we all see it to confirm you have it in your possession?"

Gideon hesitated a moment and then pulled it from the sheath, laying it gently on the table in front of him.

"Alphas," River interjected, "these artifacts do indeed contain power, but I don't believe it can be wielded aside from the ceremony to unlock the apocalyptic beast."

Several people glared at her; some even scoffed as if they were offended she even dared speak.

"We don't know that for sure," Lyrion said. "And why would we trust you? You work for Gold Moon."

"My wife and I work for no one." She placed her hand on Enid's shoulder. "It is our path to help the Pythonissam Viridi accomplish what she was sent here to do."

Lyrion shook his head. "I don't believe you."

Several other Alphas jeered in agreement, and River stared at him, her expression as flat as stone.

Gideon sighed, rubbing his temples. "What are you playing at, Lyrion?"

"I vote that Gold Moon keeps the Green Witch, Diamond Moon protects the bell, and Ruby Moon protects the athame."

An older, portly Alpha startled, sitting up in his chair. His eyes widened on the athame. "I didn't make preparations to protect this item!"

"The athame and the bell should be with Enid," Gideon stated. "She can protect them."

One Alpha scoffed. "She's just a girl. What is she, sixteen? You think she can do a better job than a grown man?"

'Ugh, what a sexist creep,' I said.

Hana yipped in agreement, but Rieka had been acting strangely since we'd arrived.

'Rieka, are you okay?'

'I don't know.' She whined. *'I feel that something isn't right here.'*

'Yeah, well, no kidding. These old farts all suck.'

"Obviously you weren't at the dragon's keep, Alpha Amos," Gideon said, pulling my attention back to the debate. "That battle was lost until she arrived."

"Well, I second what Lyrion suggested," the Alpha replied. "It makes more sense to have the girl and the artifacts split up. That makes it harder for the dragons to get all three together."

There were several ayes around the table, and Gideon glared around at his peers.

"I'm telling you now. I am not leaving this meeting without this athame."

Several of them bristled and then started arguing, tempers flaring. They quarreled for over three hours but accomplished nothing. Things grew more tense until people started getting aggressive and showing signs of shifting, eyes flashing yellow around the table.

Rudy finally called a halt to the meeting, suggesting everyone take lunch to calm down. Gideon stood first, storming from the room with Eris at his side, her shoulders square and her head held high. Enid disappeared with River and Rhia.

"Well... do you want to eat?" Finn asked, and I nodded.

Finn grabbed my hand and led me, obviously familiar with this pack house. I could feel his unease through the bond, and his face was etched into a deep frown.

Lunch was in a large dining room, served buffet style. It was quiet, Alphas whispering amongst each other in small groups. I noticed they were watching Finn to make sure he couldn't hear.

It was so somber, I was surprised when he asked, "Can I answer now?"

No one was close to us, but my cheeks still flushed. "Now?"

"Kat... I really want to have pups. I do."

My heart sank.

"But, I don't unless it's with you. And if we're not supposed to be parents, then we'll just be the coolest aunt and uncle that ever lived."

"You're sure? You're not going to regret—"

"I'm in love with you."

He'd said it so casually I thought I'd misheard.

"What?"

"Don't shut down on me again with those words, please. I am in love with you. Desperately. Hopelessly. And I don't care what obstacles the future brings. It doesn't change my heart or my mind."

I smiled and looked at my hands, picking at my cuticles. He took my fingers with his, running his thumbs over my knuckles.

I cleared my throat. "Do you think you can just move into my heart like you own the place and tear all the walls down?"

"I'm just trying to build my life, and I'm wondering if you're free. Forever."

"Finn. Love. It's been like two weeks! I mean, that's a lot..."

"I know. You wanted me to take time to answer, and I want you to do the same. You don't have to tell me anything right now."

I looked up at him, our eyes colliding. It was like we weren't in a crowded dining room. He kissed me, his hand holding my cheek, and I leaned into him, resting my hand on his thigh.

A plate dropped on the floor. The clanging brought us back to reality, and we snickered into the space between our lips.

I asked, "Do you want dessert? I'm going to get some."

He nodded, smiling as he released my hand.

'You love him,' Hana said as I walked across the room.

'But do you, Hana? That's the real question. Can a kitsune be happy in a wolf pack?'

'Well, I don't hate him,' she admitted, and I smirked.

'We both know Rieka loves him,' I teased, knowing my wolf had been smitten since the beginning.

She didn't answer, and my brow furrowed, worried about her.

'What is wrong with you today, wolf?' Hana asked.

'I have a feeling. A bad one. I can't discern its origin, though.'

Hana yipped. *'Then we must stay alert.'*

I was standing at the dessert table when Rieka became restless in my head. With a strong tap on my shoulder, I turned, staring into the golden eyes of an older man I didn't know. Rieka growled and then whined in my head.

He smiled, but it was tight, like it was made of plastic. "Who are you?"

"Uh, Kat."

Rieka whimpered. *'Careful! Let's get back to our mate! This man is the source of my feelings. He's... he is our sire.'*

Dread clawed up my chest, seizing my heart in an iron grip. I glanced down at his wrists and found diamond and gold cufflinks. My mouth dropped open. They were inscribed with the letters RC.

CHAPTER 24

FINN

I WAS SITTING AT the table thinking about how absolutely fucked we were when a sharp pang of fear shot through the bond, immediately bringing me to my feet. I scanned for Kat, finding her by the dessert table where she said she'd be.

'Why is Royce Cain talking to Kat?'

Shaw snarled. *'I don't know or care. But he should stop. Not so ridiculous now, my proposition to mark her during the commute, is it?'*

Royce was the last person I wanted around Kat. The former Alpha of Diamond Moon, and Lyrion's father, he was a notorious womanizer that openly disrespected the mate bond. He'd rejected his true mate, a lower-ranking omega wolf, and taken Lyrion's mother, Mary, as his chosen alpha mate with the intention of producing pureblood pups.

Mary was the daughter of the former alpha of Obsidian Moon. Her brother, Brutus, was the alpha now and had an obvious distaste for his brother-in-law, explaining why he still allied with Gideon even when almost everyone else had turned on him.

Mary and Royce were far from a happy union, and I'd only seen her a handful of times, hearing rumors she spent most of her time tucked away in her room in a depression. She was probably horrified that her mate slept with every woman on their household staff and any other that would have him.

Shaw was ready to start a fight. It would be a challenge. Royce was a strong and well-trained wolf. He often bragged about defeating our father in the tournament championship when they were teenagers, always forgetting to mention he'd lost to Dad the next year.

Lyrion favored his mother's looks, inheriting her blonde hair, blue eyes, and pallid skin. Royce had black hair that he kept cut short, military style, and was tan, like he spent too much time in the sun. Age was just showing in small wrinkles around his golden eyes, and he had perfect teeth that were so white they looked fake.

I hurried over to them, trying to control Shaw. Kat had a look of unspeakable horror on her face, and I couldn't imagine what he was possibly saying to her. I pushed up beside him and grabbed her, pulling her to my side. His face had been fixed in a sneer and quickly relaxed, offering me a smug smile.

"Beta Finn. I was just getting to know your sweet little mate."

"I see that. What are you even doing here, Royce?"

He shrugged. "My son's Beta is welcoming his first pup today with his mate. I came in case things get out of control."

Kat trembled against me. She said nothing and just stared at him, her eyes as wide as I'd ever seen them.

"Well, if you'll excuse me," Royce said, inclining his head. He looked at Kat and winked. "Catch you later, sweetheart."

She stiffened next to me, and Shaw snarled, infuriated, making me growl low in my chest. Royce chuckled, smirking, and then walked away.

'He threatened her right in front of us!' Shaw spat, wanting to shift.

I turned to Kat. Her eyes were wide and glassy, like she was trying not to cry.

"What was that?" I asked, searching her face. "What did he say?"

"Can we go somewhere else?"

I nodded and led her down a hallway toward a balcony. Emerald Moon was beautiful, named because the trees were so thick they looked like a sea of green. The pack house sat right next to a small mountain lake, and the cold air was biting, making Kat shiver when we stepped outside. I wrapped her in my arms, hugging her and regretting letting her go anywhere alone with how tense pack relations were right now.

"What happened?"

Kat looked up at me, tears flowing down her cheeks. "My-my wolf says that man is my.... He's the diamond cufflink creep in the parking garage. He's the one who attacked my mom!"

Never, ever, in a million years did I expect her to say those words.

"What? Is she sure?"

Her eyes glazed over, and then she nodded. "One hundred percent."

Holy shit. I thought maybe he was threatening her, or me, or Gideon, or something. I scrubbed my hand down my face and then hugged her against me.

"I'm so sorry, Kat. That must've been horrible for you," I said, rubbing her back.

She sobbed, and anger blossomed in my chest. I wanted to tear Royce to pieces. He was more than just a womanizer; he was a rapist piece of shit.

I linked Gideon. *'Where are you?'*

It took him a moment to answer. *'Our room.'*

'Seriously? Gods, you two.'

'Hey, it's stress relief,' he countered, and I could hear the humor in his voice. *'And are you—you, Finn Greenwood—scolding me about my sexual habits? Do you know how much I had to deal with...'*

'What room?' I interjected. *'You better have clothes on when I get there because we've got gigantic problems.'*

The humor dissolved. *'Third on the right when you leave the dining room.'*

'We'll be there in thirty seconds.'

I looked down at Kat. "We need to tell Gideon and Eris. Is that okay?"

She nodded and leaned into me. I could feel her immense sadness through the bond and sighed. As if she hadn't been through enough already.

I led her back down the hallway and knocked on the door. Gideon opened it, still buttoning his shirt. He looked at my face and then at Kat tucked under my arm.

"What happened?"

KAT

Finn and I sat on the bed, and Eris came over to sit on my other side, putting her hand on my back. I was trying to collect my thoughts, but they were scattered, and it felt like I had bugs crawling all over my skin.

Finn was blunt, not sugarcoating my origins. "Kat was conceived as a result of an assault that happened to her mom in LA. They never found who it was."

Gideon tilted his head. "That's horrible. I am so sorry, Kat."

Finn sighed. "Well, we just discovered Royce Caine is the one who attacked Kat's mom. And he's her... father."

"Sperm donor," I corrected, never willing to associate that man with being my father.

Eris squeezed my hand and looked at her husband, her mouth hanging open.

Gideon ran his hand through his hair. "Gods. You're sure about this?"

He'd asked Finn, but I answered, "My wolf recognizes him. She's sure."

"What did he say to you?"

"Nothing. He asked who I was, and then Rieka said who he was. I was so stunned I couldn't even say anything, and then Finn showed up. But I felt like he wanted to threaten me."

"I'm sure he knows the truth as well. A father recognizes his pups," Gideon said.

Finn's face was red. "He threatened her when I got there! He said he'd 'catch her later' right in front of me!"

"I'm sorry you had to find out in such a horrible way," Eris said, holding my arm.

"So am I," Gideon agreed. "And Royce, of all people. I'd like to say I'm surprised he'd do such a thing, but I'm not."

Finn shook his head. "Not at all. Kat's mom is probably one of many."

"This stays between us for now," Gideon said, looking at everyone. "I highly doubt Royce is going to tell anyone, and I'm not sure what to do with this information. I really wish we had more proof." He rubbed his chin, his brow drawn in thought, and then looked up at me like he might've offended me. "Not that I don't believe your wolf. It's just, Royce is a powerful man. It's going to take finesse to bring him down."

I nodded, and Gideon glanced at his watch. "I need to get back to the meeting, and you need to come with me, Finn. If they keep pushing me, I'm going to secede from the pack union."

Finn's eyes bulged. "You're not serious?"

"They aren't taking this artifact from me."

Finn's brow furrowed, and he looked at me. He didn't want to leave me.

I put on a brave face and a close-lipped smile. "It's okay. You need to go."

I didn't want him to, but I knew there were a lot of things in motion right now and Finn needed to be there as Beta. From how tense things were earlier, I wouldn't be surprised if the meeting turned violent.

"I'll stay," Eris said, hugging me with an arm around my shoulder. "No one will harm Kat as long as I'm here."

Finn kissed my forehead. "I'll be back as soon as I can."

CHAPTER 25

FINN

I WALKED NEXT TO my brother, as nervous as I'd ever been. When I glanced at his face, I found it set in a determined glare. The current Pack Union had been in place for almost three centuries. If he seceded, it would be an unprecedented move, no doubt followed by chaos. Civil war, when a holy dragon war already threatened to break out on the horizon.

Before we entered the conference room, I linked him. *'You're sure about this?'*

'Not really. But my gut is telling me if I let this artifact go, it'll be the end of us all. I will not walk out of this building without it.'

I nodded, trusting his instincts, and pushed the doors open. I expected the conversations to all die like they had before, but it was dead silent in the room.

Confused, I looked around the table. Enid sat alone at our spot, stroking Hades in her lap. She was smiling, a soft turn of her lips, and it was one of the most bizarre things I'd ever witnessed. This petite teenage girl calmly petting her cat at a table full of hostile alphas.

We sat by her, and she said, "You're late," but her smile stayed.

"Apologies," Gideon said aloud, but his eyes glazed over and knew he was talking to her through the mind link.

"Well," Amos huffed, "now that everyone has finally arrived, let's settle this matter."

I looked at the old man, who'd quickly become Lyrion's greatest supporter and biggest advocate, and refrained from rolling my eyes.

For the next several hours, Gideon tried his best. I had to give him that credit. He delivered his argument calmly, making good points. He kept insisting on a re-vote even though he'd lost three times already. It was almost one in the morning now, and most of the Lunas had retired along with Enid.

Lyrion growled. "Fine. One more vote. Alphas, cast your votes regarding the Green Witch staying at Gold Moon, the bell artifact at Diamond Moon, and the athame artifact at Ruby Moon."

The twelve alphas cast their votes. Rudy, Brutus, and Odin maintained their loyalty to Gold Moon. One other Alpha had changed his opinion, now siding with Gideon, and he himself, of course, voted nay as well. The other seven stubbornly cast their ayes. I watched the look of smug victory cross Lyrion's face.

"The ayes have it. The final vote stands seven to five," Amos hissed. "Relinquish the athame to Ruby Moon, where it will stay."

My brother stood and gripped the table so tightly it groaned under the pressure. I thought surely it would snap, but it held.

"Gold Moon puts forth the motion to secede from the Pack Union."

Several eyes bulged at the proclamation, gasps sounding.

Amos stood. "On what grounds?"

"That Gold Moon is being forced to overturn assets it fairly gained."

"Outrageous! Think about what you're doing, boy!"

"I am no boy," Gideon spat. "And I know exactly what I'm doing. If you want this athame, you can take it by force." He leveled his gaze at Lyrion, who was grinning, and started loosening his tie. "You want it that bad, Alpha Caine? I challenge you for it. You and I. Let's go. Outside right now."

Royce sat up in his chair, glaring at his son. "Accept."

There were murmurs around the table. An Alpha's challenge. A fight to the death or forfeit, whichever came first. It had been a long time since one had been proclaimed. Everyone looked at Lyrion.

His smile evaporated, and his skin blanched, his face going white. "I decline."

I relished the look of disgust on Royce's face as he glowered at his son. I couldn't help myself. I giggled under my breath and received several glares from around the table.

"Anyone else?" Gideon asked.

No one said anything, and Amos sat back down in his chair.

"Then I'm done here," Gideon finished, looking at me. "Get the car."

I nodded, following him out of the conference room.

Rudy chased us down. "You'll start a war, Gid!"

Gideon stopped, yelling so they could all hear, "We're already in a war! That's what nobody seems to understand!"

To his credit, Rudy didn't flinch, nodding he understood. "Well, at least stay the night. It's nearing two in the morning."

Gideon glared at the conference room. I realized he didn't trust the other alphas not to do something drastic.

"I'll post guards at your door," Rudy added, noticing his hesitation as well.

"Fine."

Gideon looked at me. "You and Kat are staying in the room with Eris, Enid and I. I'm not taking any chances after everything that happened today."

I nodded and followed him back to the room.

Later that night, I laid on my back, staring at the ceiling. Kat was against me, and she leaned up to my ear. The soft words she whispered in my ear sent a rush through my veins. "If you're sure, then I am, too. I do want it, Finn. This. You and me. I love you."

I stiffened, my eyes going wide as Shaw whirled fully awake in my head. *'What'd she just say? Did I hear that right?'*

Glancing at the other bed, where Gideon and Eris were, and the couch where Enid slept, I whispered, "What?"

Her lips were still against my ear. "I want you to mark me." I could tell she felt a little awkward about it because she giggled. "I guess I'm supposed to ask."

"And you ask right now?" I hissed, looking over at her in the dark.

"Is that bad?"

"Is that? Oh, gods." I sighed and ran my hand through my hair.

Shaw erupted in my head, a happy howl, and then, *'There it is! She asked! Do it!'*

I took a deep breath. *'Easy, big fella. There's a literal child in the room.'*

Shaw didn't care, and a flush of pure testosterone rushed me, courtesy of him. Never in my life had he pushed me so hard, trying to take partial control and do it himself. It was so bad I gritted out loud through clenched teeth, "Calm down."

I leaned over to Kat, and my voice was rough because of my wolf. "Nothing is bad, it's just I really need to fuck you. Like, right now. It's very sexual, the marking."

"Oh! Well, no one told me that."

"Oh, my gods," I whispered, and wrapped my hands around her waist, pulling her into me.

We kissed, and I was grinding on her, hard just thinking about marking her. For a second I considered just doing it, but I knew this wouldn't be a quiet event. There was no way everyone in the room wouldn't know what was happening. Eris and Gideon? I didn't care. I really didn't. But Enid was too young.

Another wave of testosterone crashed through me, and I cursed my wolf, then whispered, "I'll be right back."

"Where are you going?"

"I just need a second."

"Okay. I'm... sorry, Finn."

"Don't be. My wolf is being difficult."

I stood and found the t-shirt I'd been wearing, pulling it back on.

'Where are you going?' Gideon's voice echoed in my head.

'To get a drink. Kat just asked me to mark her! Gods.'

He snickered aloud from his bed. *'Be careful out there. If you're not back in ten minutes, I'm coming to look for you.'*

'Okay.'

I stepped out into the hall and nodded at the two warriors guarding our door before heading towards the dining area. There was a bar, but obviously no one was there at this time of night. I knew Rudy wouldn't mind, so I went around and made myself a drink.

Shaw was harping on me. *'Go get her. Find a better place. Do it.'* We walked past what had to be a storage or custodial room, and he said, *'There!'*

'You want to mark our mate in the janitor's closet?'

'If it were up to me, it would be done already. Human halves and their need for privacy. It's a natural and beautiful event, the marking!'

I returned to the balcony on the lake and leaned against the rail, trying to calm my wolf. A soft snow fell in the still air, and I breathed, letting the cold shock my system while I debated with him.

'It's dangerous. We're surrounded by potential enemies.'

As if to confirm my worries, the smell of tobacco smoke invaded my nose. I stiffened, hearing someone walk up beside me, and looked to find Royce sucking on a cigar.

"Nice night, Beta Finn."

I didn't answer, eyeing him. I wanted to punch him and toss him over the balcony. He offered me the cigar, and I shook my head, my lip curling at the thought of sharing anything with this man.

"What do you want, Royce?"

His voice was smooth and low, almost friendly, but the undertone carried his real, threatening intentions. "To tell you that whatever that little mate of yours is saying, it isn't true."

"I don't know what you're talking about. But you saying that makes me think you have something to be worried about."

He smirked. "I'm not worried about anything. But whatever that little half-blood might think she knows is the truth would be a lie. Her mama and I shared a nice evening, and that was that."

I bristled. Degrading Kat by calling her a half-blood, not to mention what he implied about her mother.

Royce clicked his tongue. "I feel for you, Beta Finn. It's cruel when the Goddess pairs you with a weak woman. I know that personally. My true mate was an omega, but at least she was a wolf. To get a half-breed... terrible." Royce shook his head but kept talking. "Although I will admit those little foxes are pretty, aren't they? And quick. Once you get your hands on them, though, they're so feeble. Fragile things."

He smirked, winking at me, and I stared at him, rage roiling in my gut. "How dare you?"

"Hey, calm down, son," he said, guffawing as if he didn't understand why I was upset. "I just noticed you hadn't marked her yet. There's still time to make the right choice. Not that the Greenwoods give a shit about keeping a pure bloodline. I told Henry not to take that omega trash as his Luna all those years ago, but he wouldn't listen. He said he loved her." He scoffed and added, "Pathetic when an alpha can't do the right thing for his people."

I squared up to him, getting in his face and grabbing the front of his shirt. Talking shit about my mate, and now about my mom!

"I should kill you right now," I snarled, my fangs elongating.

He barked a laugh in my face. "You can try, boy, but I can tell you favor that weak mother of yours. I may be older, but I'm tougher than I look." He took a long drag on the cigar and blew the smoke in my face. "And your arrogant brother has already gotten himself and your pack into a pretty precarious diplomatic situation. Might not look good for his Beta to go off half-cocked and attack an old man who's just out for a smoke."

Shaw was clawing at the front of my mind, snarling and desperate to get out. I kept him in check, knowing what Royce said rang true. The peace between shifters was fraying, and I'd be a fool to let some asshole talk me into making a mistake that furthered his son's efforts to alienate Gold Moon.

"Your brother, though," he said, tapping the cigar to break the ash, "obviously favors Henry. And he was gifted with that alpha girl as his mate. A true healer, too. What I wouldn't give to have her mated to my son instead. If that barren bitch he's with now doesn't produce a pup soon, I'll kill her myself."

"You're a sick fuck, Royce."

He laughed and shrugged. "Maybe I am. But what I came out here to tell you is that it's best to let it go."

Royce leaned into my face, the tobacco on his breath accosting my nostrils. He pushed the cigar into the snow on the rail, between my thumb and first finger. It was close enough that I could feel the heat, but I didn't flinch.

He sneered, "Because no one is going to believe that half-breed bitch over me."

It took everything I had to stop myself from hitting him. I snarled in his face, and he grinned, turning on his heel and walking inside.

I took a deep breath. When my wolf was under control, I looked down at the cigar on the rail, picking it up so I didn't touch the area where his mouth had been.

I held it up in front of my face. "We'll see about that, you stupid prick."

CHAPTER 26

KAT

I was lying there, feeling bad about what had just happened. Finn was mad. Really mad. I could feel it in the bond.

'I didn't know it was supposed to be, you know, super private, I guess,' I told my fox and wolf.

'It's okay,' Rieka said. *'He knows that.'*

'But he's so angry—'

I sat up because the anger turned to rage, and he was disgusted. It seemed a bit much for being disappointed he couldn't mark me here.

"What is Kat? Is it Finn?" Gideon asked, sitting up, too.

"I don't know," I said, rubbing my chest where his rage was so hot it burned. "He's really pissed about something."

Gideon stood, pulling on his shoes. The anger ebbed, still hot, but tinged with a small feeling of satisfaction.

Gideon dropped his shoes and sat back down on the bed, running his hands over his face. "He says he'll be here in a moment."

Less than a minute later, Finn rushed in.

I stood, going to him. "What happened?"

"Oh, just a friendly chat with Royce out on the balcony."

My eyes widened. "What did he say? You were so mad!"

"You don't need to worry about that," he said, rubbing my arm.

So, it was bad then. I was sure he didn't have nice things to say about me at all.

"But," Finn added, turning to his brother, "I got this."

He presented a half-smoked cigar like it was a gold medal. Gideon stared at it, and Eris put the pieces together.

"Brilliant, Finn," she whispered, grinning. "Royce's DNA."

The guest rooms were just like hotel rooms, complete with a little coffee maker and everything. Finn took one of the little paper cups out of its plastic bag and went to place the cigar in the bag.

"No, wait," Eris said, moving towards him. "Plastic is not the best way to store DNA."

Finn arched an eyebrow at her, and she shrugged.

"I don't like television very much, but I enjoy the true crime genre."

Gideon nodded with a sigh. "Yes, she really, really does."

Finn laughed. "Well then, don't piss her off. It's like a guide on how to kill someone and get away with it."

Eris grinned and then grabbed the paper cup, holding it out. "Here, use this. Paper is better. It breathes, so moisture doesn't collect and break down the DNA."

Finn dropped the cigar in, and Eris put the lid on. We all looked at each other, smiling.

"This is exactly what we needed," Gideon said, clapping Finn on the back.

"What is going on?" a voice asked behind us.

We all jumped at the question and looked at Enid. I'd forgotten she was there, asleep on the couch.

She was watching us with her head tilted, and the girl never stopped smiling, I swear. Her lips were curled at the edges, and she petted the cat. Hades looked less than amused, stretching in her lap and turning his back to us.

Eris gave Enid a quick rundown of the whole situation. Enid listened and then agreed that she wouldn't tell anyone about any of it.

"Well, let's all try to get some sleep," Gideon said, going to lie back down.

We all nodded and settled back in. A dangerous hope blossomed in my chest. I knew I didn't owe my mom anything, but I still felt awful for her and for what she'd been through. She didn't have to have me or raise me, but she had. I liked to tell myself that she did her best considering what she was facing, and I wanted to get her some justice, even if she never knew it. Royce deserved to pay for his crime.

And now we had a chance to make that happen, thanks to super spy Finn. I pushed my happiness through the bond to him, and his arms tightened around me.

"I thought all of that anger was for me," I said, keeping my voice as quiet as possible. "I'm happy to find that's not the case."

"I don't think I could ever be angry with you, love."

My heart fluttered. There it was again, that sweet little name. *Love.*

"Although I'm going to get no sleep tonight thanks to you," he added, and turned so he was spooning me.

He pressed against me so I could feel how much he wanted me. His desire spilled through the bond, and he ran his hands up under my shirt, grabbing my breasts. A moan nearly escaped my lips, and I bit my lip hard to trap it. He kissed my neck, where I knew his mark would go, and a race of tingles flowed down my body, settling between my legs. I couldn't help it, and rolled my hips back into him, grinding.

"You have no idea what you're doing to me," he whispered in my ear. "If Enid was not in this room, Kat, I swear."

I ran my hand over his cheek, pushing my desire, and my humor, through the bond. It was horrible how much I enjoyed teasing him.

With his lips still on my ear, he said, "Or maybe you do. You're gonna pay for being such a tease. Cruel little fox."

I turned so my lips were whispering against his cheek. "Looking forward to it."

His desire flooded the bond again, and he kissed me, his tongue in my mouth and his hands still roaming over my body. He stopped and sighed. "Gods, help me. This is going to be the longest day of my life."

CHAPTER 27

KAT

T HE CLOUDY SKY WAS colored gray with early morning light when we all walked out of the building. Our car was waiting there for us, but so were several of the Alphas. I was relieved to see that Royce was not in the crowd.

"This is your last chance, Gideon," Lyrion said, his arms crossed over his chest. "Just give us the athame and you get to keep the Green Witch."

Gideon opened his mouth to reply but was cut off.

"I am not an object and no one 'keeps' me," Enid said, and I glanced over at her, my mouth half open.

Several of the Alphas shifted on their feet, eyeing her.

"I choose Gold Moon because they are my family and my pack. You couldn't make me go elsewhere if you tried, Alpha Cain," she said, leveling a subtle challenge at all of them. "The athame will return with us, and I will keep it safe, because I'm the only person who can. I don't say that to be arrogant or boastful. I say it because it's the truth."

Hades growled, and I swear to the gods, it sounded like, "Yeah."

The group in front of me looked like she'd smacked them across their faces. I covered my mouth with my hand, hiding my smile. Hana and Rieka both cheered in my head, in awe of this powerful, tiny girl. I wished I hadn't been knocked out when she and Eris killed Xeron. It must've really been something to see.

Lyrion opened his mouth but was so stunned no words came out.

The old man, who I now knew was called Amos, spoke instead. "You would be smart to learn to respect your elders, child."

"Respect earned is respect given," she said sweetly, her expression soft. "I owe you nothing just because you're old."

Finn blew out a raspberry next to me, trying hard not to laugh, and failing. It was like in school, when you were in trouble, but your friend started giggling and you couldn't help but join. I kept my hand clamped over my mouth, snickering. Alpha Rudy was struggling, too, and rubbed his mouth with his hand to wipe his smile away.

Amos' face blossomed red with anger, but he addressed Gideon. "Alpha, if you are choosing to disobey the vote, we have the right to find Gold Moon treasonous."

Gideon was inspired by Enid and put on his own sassy-pants. "I'm sorry, but you can't find me treasonous because I'm seceding from the Union."

"That, in itself, is treason!"

Gideon motioned for us to get in the car. "I'll expect your declarations of war on my desk by tomorrow."

Gideon and Eris sat up front, and I sat in the back, with Finn and Enid on either side. We drove down the long driveway in silence, and when we turned onto the main road, Finn barked out a laugh.

We all jumped, looking at him.

"Enid! You and that cat are the most fearless duo I've ever seen, and you are bundled in the tiniest packages. I owe you nothing just because you're old! Craziest shit I've ever seen in my life, I swear," he said, laughing and laying his head back.

The rest of us laughed, too, and Enid smiled, stroking Hades across his back. He purred, seeming to accept the compliment.

"Where did River and Rhia go?" Finn asked, knitting his eyebrows together. "They weren't at the second part of the meeting yesterday."

Enid shrugged. "River said that she didn't think they could do anything else to help, and they have a lead on another piece of Dragonsbane."

"Cool," Finn said. "I hope they get it."

Everyone was quiet after that, and I laid my head on Finn's shoulder. Even with the shocking discovery of my biological father, I knew I wasn't facing it alone. These were my people. My friends.

They're alright, ' Hana agreed. *'For a bunch of wolves.'*

FINN

I could feel how happy Kat was through the bond, and it put me in a light mood despite how much of a disaster the meeting had been. Gold Moon was the biggest pack, but Diamond Moon wasn't that far behind. If the alliances split along the same lines as the last vote had, wolf shifters could be looking at a vicious civil war.

I trusted my brother, and I believed in him as Alpha. He was focused on the bigger picture. The dragons scared him. I could sense his fear of them, and I knew that would be a hard pill for any alpha wolf to swallow.

He understood their power more than anyone else because Xeron had nearly killed him only a month ago. If the Moon Goddess and the Goddess of Witches, Hecate, hadn't gifted him with a mate that could miraculously heal people, he would be dead.

He was talking to himself again as I studied his reflection. The wheels of his brain turned rapidly behind his eyes, and I thought of something my father used to say. They're playing checkers, and I'm playing chess.

I smirked. He would come out of this on top, someway, somehow. That was just Gideon.

Eris held Gideon's hand and rubbed circles on his thumb with hers. His and her eyes kept glazing, indicating they were deep in a private conversation with each other.

I was glad that I wasn't Alpha. The amount of pressure my brother faced every day? No, thanks.

Kat slept against my shoulder, her mouth hanging open while she snored softly. I chuckled, amazed at how quickly she could fall asleep. But her neck was exposed again, and the soft skin beckoned me to mark her. I grinned inwardly, knowing that I would get to before this day was over.

I laid my head against the window, napping on and off.

A bump in the road rocked the vehicle, waking me sometime later. Kat was up next to me, watching the trees go by out of the window. Sensing we were close to our pack lands, I grinned.

Desire bloomed in my chest again, and I pushed it to her. Her cheeks flushed, and she smiled, biting her lip. Enid was still sleeping, so I put my hand on Kat's bare leg. She was wearing a skirt, and I pushed my hand up as far as I dared. I could feel the heat between her legs as her desire raged through the bond.

I took a deep breath and looked out the window, wondering why I tortured myself like this. A familiar mountain appeared, peeking over the trees in the distance, and I was able to discern our location.

Twenty minutes. I could make it.

What seemed like an hour later, we pulled up outside. I hopped out, dragging Kat with me, and started towards the door.

Gideon called after us, "I asked everyone to the conference room for a quick briefing, and then you can have the rest of the day off."

I ground to a halt, turning to look at him, my eyes pleading. "Can't you do it without me?"

He gave me the big brother look that I had been the recipient of many times in my life.

"We might have just started a civil war. You should be there."

"You're using the word *we* pretty loosely," I muttered, and sighed, trudging inside.

I could feel Kat's disappointment, but also some humor as she giggled at my despair.

We all sat in the conference room. Lucien, the acting gamma, was there, as well as our top three warrior officers. Someone had cajoled Leo into leaving his room, and he sat by Daro, the unicorn boy that was rescued from the dragon's keep. Mom was here, too, her brow drawn in concern.

Enid went and sat on the other side of Leo, and I swore I glimpsed a smug look of victory on his face while Daro's eyes clouded with jealousy. Both expressions were so quick to appear and then fade that I wondered if I was imagining things.

Kat exclaimed, "Daro! What are you doing here?"

He stood, and they hugged. My already crazed wolf was not impressed, but I did my best to suppress his jealousy.

"Didn't you hear? I'm the diplomatic representative of all unicorn kind," he said with a dramatic flair while he put his hands on his hips and puffed out his chest.

Kat and Enid giggled.

"That's awesome. I'm glad you're here," Kat said.

"And I'm glad you're here, foxy. Now I'll have someone else to hang out with who knows nothing about wolf shifters."

'Foxy? He wants our mate! Kill him,' Shaw growled, his jealousy flaring hot in my chest.

'Oh, my gods, no he doesn't. Kill him? Really?'

He grumbled, and I pushed the aggression down, trying to calm him, but I could tell Kat felt it through the bond. Her humor sparked again, and she came to sit down by me, patting my shoulder.

Gideon started talking, but I couldn't pay attention. Kat was pushing her desire towards me, wave after wave of it coursing through the bond. Our chairs were so close our legs were touching, and I was so perceptive of her I could feel the heat of her bare skin through the denim of my jeans.

When I felt her hand slide up my leg, I was already struggling for control. I stiffened at the touch, and looked over at her, begging for mercy. She didn't stop. Her expression remained calm, pretending to pay attention, while her hand traveled all the way up my leg until she was rubbing my erection that strained painfully in its denim prison.

My hands were flat on the table, and I was focusing on the feel of the cool wood under my fingertips. I was holding my breath, just trying to keep my face normal, when I realized everyone was looking at me. Kat had stopped what she was doing, and I glanced at my brother, who was looking at me expectantly.

Shit, he must have asked me something.

I cleared my throat, and with no idea what he'd actually asked, gambled by answering, "Yes."

"Yes?" His eyebrows lifted, and I could see humor hiding in his gaze. He probably didn't know exactly what was happening, but he had a basic idea.

'Weren't you scolding me just yesterday?' he asked, and I sighed.

'I told you to do this meeting without me.'

I saw his eyes glaze for a second and heard Eris cough, hiding a giggle. I didn't even dare look at my mother.

Aloud, Gideon said, "Okay, so Finn will work on fortifying the fences. I don't want fences. I want walls."

Kat's hand fell back onto my leg, and I said, "Uh, yeah. Walls. I can handle that."

Gideon took mercy on me and wrapped things up quickly after that. When he finally called an end to the meeting, I grabbed Kat's hand and pulled her out of the room without saying another word to anyone.

My bedroom was one floor up, but I didn't have the patience for that. I walked four doors down to my office and clicked in the code, trying to keep my breathing even.

She had teased me. All night and all day. Mercilessly. Right now, she was still pushing her feelings of unfettered desire toward me. Provoking my wolf and pushing my control.

It was time to settle the score.

Chapter 28

Finn pushed my back to the office door as soon as it was closed behind us, his hands jerking at the clasp of my skirt.

Our faces were close together, and I whispered, "You seem to be in a hurry."

"That's because you tease me until I can't stand it anymore."

"Are you complaining?"

He stepped closer, grabbing my wrists and bringing them over my head. My smaller frame was pressed to the door by his bulky weight, his legs pinning my lower body. There was such hunger in his eyes that my breathing quickened, and a flutter of excitement tightened my thighs and stomach.

"I'm never complaining as long as you're willing to accept the consequences."

"And what are those?"

His eyes shifted more golden, like his wolf wanted to answer. "That I'm going to claim you. And protect you. Provide for you. Pleasure you..." His jaw tightened. "Possess you. You'll be mine."

"Threatening me with a good time again?"

"Are you sure? You've been coy with me on the marking."

"You want me to ask again?"

His hands drifted down my lifted arms, making my body erupt with tingles. "No."

"No?" I asked, my voice shakier than I expected.

Finn gripped my waist, caging it and pulling me into an arch against the door. I reciprocated, pressing my breasts forward.

"No," he said again, with finality, and his eyes drifted back up to mine. "You're gonna beg for it."

My brows lifted, and I scrambled to think of something to banter back to that, but his lips closed over mine, cutting off the words. He squeezed my breasts through my shirt, firm enough to make me whimper into the kiss.

Finn fisted the material and then ripped it in a swift pull. His hands branded me with their touch. He caressed me with desperation; a wildness. When he yanked my skirt up around my waist and cupped me through my panties, I felt a rush, a flutter in my stomach that settled as a heavy dampness between my legs.

A whispery moan parted my lips, and my hands were searching for a place to rest, roaming over the ropes of his muscular body.

He kneeled, leaving my hands empty. His desperation slowed, and he kissed my thighs. With each press of his lips, Finn asked, "How many times do you think I can make you come?" Kiss. "One?" Kiss. "Two?" Kiss. "Three?" Kiss. He paused and asked, "How about four?" and took the tendon at the apex of my thigh into his mouth, sucking while I melted against the door, moaning.

My panties were gone, pulled down to my knees, and he teased me with his thumb, running it up and down the slit of my core. I arched into him, seeking more. He chuckled. "You like the sound of four, don't you?"

"Of course I do," I said, giggling and pressing my hips to him. "Not sure I believe it, though."

He made a small sound of amusement, and his thumb pressed, finding my swollen bud of nerves and circling it without actually touching it.

I gasped. I moaned. My toes flexed, and he circled, steadily applying more pressure. It was torture. I wanted to climb the mountain to bliss faster, and I mindlessly rolled my hips, searching for deeper contact.

"What, you need more?" he asked.

"Yes. Yes."

He was suddenly and annoyingly calculating. "What would you do to get my finger inside you?"

I yanked my bra down, and cupped my breasts, pushing them together and saying, "Give it to me."

As I expected, his desire burned in the bond with a new flush of heat. His finger pierced the soft flesh of my core, and I tossed my head back, smiling and moaning.

He asked, "Another?"

"Yes. Yes."

"You want three? You need to be filled?"

"Mm-hm," I said, gasping.

"By who?"

"By you."

Finn groaned in his chest, and I felt the sharp stretch of two fingers joining the first. The effect was immediate and devastating. He pressed them deep, curling, and his other hand took the place of his thumb, moving in firm circles. I did not climb the mountain to bliss—I teleported to the top.

"Oh-I-fuck-oh-gods," I sputtered incoherently, grabbing the doorknob and squeezing it. My thoughts scattered, the climax barreling through me with an intense ferocity.

When it was ebbing, he kept stroking my too-sensitive bud with his thumb, making me laugh and twitch and moan.

"There's one," he said, and I could hear the smug grin on his face. "You want another one standing here or do you want to move to the couch?"

Determined to keep up with the teasing, I said, "I want to taste what you've done to me."

To my surprise, Finn stood, and I put on my best pouty face, looking up at him.

He kissed me and pushed the ripped shirt off my shoulders, unfastening my bra and letting it drop to the floor.

I went to slide my skirt off, but he said, "That stays."

Finn worked his way down my body, licking and kissing until I was breathless, my hands in his hair. He kneaded and sucked on my breasts, taking his time and focusing on them until I was trembling. The ache in my core grew as he kissed my stomach, nipping the skin.

I pushed his head down, lost to him. He released the control he was holding over his emotions, and his lust overflowed in the bond, tinged with frustration. Teasing him was fun; it was a thrill. It was a lonely person's kink to be so intensely wanted by another.

His tongue dragged up the slit of my core, and I ached. I needed the next climax like I needed my next breath.

"Gods. Yes, yes," I chanted over and over, saying his name while I tried to understand how he could do such things with his tongue. Flicking, lapping, rubbing. Gods. I was consumed.

I should've gone to the couch because my knees weren't going to survive this time. They were trembling, and, using his tongue and fingers in rhythm, he drove me to another climax. It was so powerful, I informed everyone on the business floor of its grandeur with my enthusiastic cries. I was wild, holding his hair so tight it had to hurt him.

This time, he was breathing hard when he surfaced for air. He ripped off his shirt and used it to wipe his face before he tossed it. My hands were drawn to his body like magnets, touching. I unzipped and freed his cock. He was hard, as hard as I'd ever felt a man, and he moaned in relief when I ran my hands up and down.

He worked his pants off and picked me up. "That was two."

My body felt like my bones were made of jelly, and I wasn't sure how to handle climax number three or a seemingly impossible number four.

"Finn..." I whispered, but he set me on the arm of the couch, and with his hand splayed on my chest, shoved my back into the leather.

I drew my legs back, bending them and grabbing my own ankles so I was as open as I could be. I was still wearing my black Converse high tops, and they were the sexiest things I'd ever seen elevated like they were, my red nail polish striking a stark contrast against them.

Finn groaned and grabbed the skirt around my waist, holding my knees open with his elbows. He pushed into me with a wicked thrust that stole my breath.

With a long, hard stroke, he said, "You are mine," and with another he groaned and said, "You are perfect."

It was a claiming. His possession of me, where my body belonged to him.

FINN

I watched her expression. Her soft eyes, her perfect mouth and her flushed cheeks. She was wild, moaning, and I knew my brother was probably in his office next door cranking up his music and trying to get his work done.

Good. Let the world know. Let everyone know it. She was mine. I was never letting her go. With all of my thoughts on claiming her, I drove deep and hard between her thighs, reaching the end of her sheath. Her eyes flew open with a look of helpless shock, and her legs clenched around my arms.

I shook my head to clear my thoughts. "If I'm too rough, you tell me."

She moaned, grinning, and grabbed my wrists, digging her nails into my skin. "I love it."

I tightened my grip on the skirt around her waist and thrust harder. "You sure?"

She hummed. "Yes. I want you to make me take it."

I closed my eyes. "Kat. Gods."

She laughed, knowing what she did to me, and my shaft throbbed inside her, wanting to come just hearing those words. I fought it. There was more to be done. I said four, and I fucking meant it.

I put her ankles up by my neck and lifted her hips, taking full control of the movement because I knew I could hit *the* spot easily in this position. Kat's back bowed in an arch, and she was twice as loud, her hands flailing and then grabbing the couch.

I ran my hands over her flawless, inky skin, entranced by the rhythmic bounce of her breasts; topped by those perfect coral pink nipples that begged for my mouth, even when I'd already had them. I stopped at her stomach, my thumb dipping lower and caressing that bud of nerves. Her eyes opened, her brow knitting, and her mouth opening in a wide, soundless "O." That wonderful look of sensual surprise.

Her body clenched in my grasp. "Oh, Finn! Oh, gods! I'm coming!"

I squeezed her hips in my hands, feeling the satisfaction of victory as her core clenched around me. The fourth would be the easiest, despite her doubts.

I didn't stop. No breaks. I grabbed under her knees and held her open wide. She was incredibly flexible—probably because of her dancing—and I was living for it. My hips slapped against her, and I shuddered with pleasure. It was as deep as a woman had ever allowed me.

"Please, Finn, please, please give me your mark," she whined, grabbing for me and pulling me to her.

Finally, the prize. The moment I'd dreamed of, not only for these past weeks since finding her, but for my entire life.

Shaw rushed me with his aggression, a partial shift that sharpened my teeth. This was complete possession. I pierced her soft flesh. She tasted so sweet, every inch of her, and she yelped then moaned wildly, her core clenching me again. Number four. I was flooded with awareness of her. Her heat and her soul; her essence joining mine.

Our scents danced together in the surrounding air, fusing to become one.

I opened my mouth to ask her to mark me because my shaft was already swelling, pulsing with the need to fill her, but she grabbed my head, and I felt her fangs before I could say anything.

Pure, unbridled ecstasy rolled through me. I lost track of reality. It was magic. The good kind. Moaning, I didn't have a thought of pulling out of her, my climax erupting to fill her. When I was nearly finished, she bit me again, on the other side of my neck. Smaller teeth.

I shouted, stunned as the sensations rocked my world again, giving me the longest and most torturous, most intense orgasm of my life. My fingers ripped the leather of the couch at a seam where I held it so fiercely.

Then it was quiet. Our breathing wild as our souls danced together, intertwined forever.

I dropped to my knees and laid my head on her stomach, still trying to find breath.

'You about killed me,' I linked her, laughing and cherishing that we were now fully connected.

She giggled. *'Hana really wanted a turn.'*

'Told you I'd win her over.'

She said, *'Wow. I love you, Finn Greenwood,'* and my heart soared on those words. So high, I was sure it would never find the ground again.

'And I love you, Kat. Every day. Every second. Forever.'

CHAPTER 29

KAT

A HANDFUL OF DAYS had passed since the pack meeting where Gideon had declared his secession from the Union. It was a strange time for me. Here we were, with impending doom and apocalyptic threats hanging over us, and I floated around the pack house on a cloud of bliss.

I spent a lot of time with Eris, helping her as much as I could. She was the strongest, most determined woman I'd ever known, but her weakness was modern technology. Trying to teach her how to use her laptop, the printer, her new smartphone, and everything in between was like trying to teach a fish to climb a tree. At least we had a lot of fun and a lot of laughs in the process; me teasing that it was worse than trying to teach elderly people how to use a remote control.

It was dinnertime, and Finn held my hand, leading me towards the dining room. He made a lot of effort to make as much time as he could for me, despite how busy I knew he was. They now had to prepare for a civil war while still making plans for someday soon fighting dragons.

Finn tightened his fingers on mine, and a light excitement thrummed through the bond.

'What's going on? Why are you so excited?' I asked through our link, now completed with the marking.

'It's lasagna night.'

I furrowed my brow. *'You're a bad liar.'*

He didn't answer me, only chuckled. I was increasingly suspicious as his excitement sparked higher the closer we got to the dining room.

When we walked in, it was empty except for the Alpha's table. All of those closest to me stood around it. Eris, Gideon, Finn's mom Diane, Enid, Daro, and even Leo were all there.

"Surprise!" they all yelled when I walked in.

A hand-painted banner hung on the wall that said, "Welcome to the Pack, Kat!"

"Aww," I cooed, fanning my eyes as they tried to fill with tears. It was all so perfectly cheesy and wonderful. My face was hot. Finn was beaming at me, and I shook my head. "You didn't have to do this!"

He squeezed my hand, and I looked at everyone else.

Eris came up and hugged me. "I'm so happy to have you as my friend, Kat."

"Thank you," I said, my voice thick.

She whispered, "I hope you like it here because I'm never letting you leave me alone with that printer again."

I laughed, sniffling. It was the sweetest threat I'd ever received.

Gideon was next to her and asked, "Are you ready to become an official part of the pack?"

"Really? Yeah! I mean, yes. I didn't even know this was a thing."

He placed his hand on my shoulder and said, "I, Gideon Greenwood, accept you, Katarina Kimura, as a member of the Gold Moon pack."

As he said it, I felt the magic of the pack bond enter my head. Suddenly, I was connected to everyone in the pack, all of us sharing one link. It was intense, and I sucked in a breath, my mind adjusting to this unfamiliar presence in my head. It was already crowded as it was.

Rieka was so happy. She howled in my head as something she didn't know she was missing made her feel complete. The outcast wolf finally had her pack.

I realized I could feel, almost see in my mind's eye, hundreds of life forces. I knew which one was Gideon's. He had a dark, powerful aura, and I could feel Finn's, of course. It was similar to his brother's. Eris' ambience was strange, a combination of dark and light, her Alpha and Maiden auras both present. One was dominating. It was a pastel green color, and its immense power took my breath away. It was so large and bright that it was painful to focus on it too much. Enid's, no doubt.

"Careful," Finn said. "Digging into the bond too much is hard if you're not the Alpha. It'll give you a headache."

I focused on Eris and said through the link, *'Eris? Can you hear me?'*

'Yes!' she replied instantly, and I opened my eyes, grinning.

"Wow. That's incredible." Tears filled my eyes as a flurry of emotions rolled through me, and I choked out, "Thanks, guys. This is so great."

Finn squeezed my hand. *'Are you okay?'*

'This is the first party I've ever had thrown for me,' I admitted, wondering if I should say thank you again.

He put his arm around my shoulders and squeezed me. *'Well, I promise it won't be the last, Kat.'*

FINN

The next few weeks flew by without incident. Every day we expected a dragon to show up and rain down fire upon the pack, but nothing happened. It was almost worse that way, the constant waiting and living on edge. Gideon grew more paranoid with each passing week. More insistent on fortifying our pack lands, which was nearly impossible in the middle of winter.

The other Alphas hadn't declared war, and everything seemed to be at an impasse. No one wanted to make another move. Gideon had not officially withdrawn from the Union yet. He didn't want to, but he would do it if he had to. As long as no one actually tried to take the artifact, he was going to put it off.

Yule was upon us. The Winter Solstice celebration was happening tonight, and I had a big surprise in store for Kat before we started the party. I was trying not to think about it too much because I didn't want to tip her off. I found her in Eris' office, where she always was when she wasn't with me.

"Can I borrow my mate?" I asked, smiling.

They were both hunched over Eris' laptop, deep in focus.

"Yes, of course," Eris said, plopping down in her chair and rubbing her temples. "I can't stare at this blasted screen any longer, anyway. I hate spreadsheets!"

Kat giggled. "You'll figure it out. We can work on it again later."

I led Kat to the elevator, trying to keep my cool.

"What do you have planned now?" she asked, eyeing me suspiciously.

"Nothing." I tried to look innocent.

She wasn't convinced, humming, "Mm-hm," as the doors slid open on the fourth floor.

I led her down the hall towards our room but went on past it and typed in the code on the next door.

"Okay, close your eyes."

She smiled but did as I asked as I led her into the room.

"Okay. You can open them."

She did and blinked, her eyes wide and her hand flying up to cover her chest. "Finn! What is this?"

"Your art studio!"

"You said they were remodeling this room for Gideon and Eris!"

"I had to explain the noise somehow. What do you think?"

She walked around the room, running her fingers over the various supplies.

"It's... I couldn't have even dreamed it. How did you do this?"

I grinned, liking that answer. "Well, honestly, Leo designed the entire room. He's into this stuff, too."

We had completely replaced the out facing wall with floor-to-ceiling windows, allowing as much natural light as possible. Leo had insisted the walls be left white, unless Kat wanted them a different color, so that the color palette of the wall wouldn't influence her art. I'd never admit it to him, but I owed him one. He'd nailed it.

There was a giant oak desk on one side of the room. Behind it on the wall, I'd framed and hung all the loose pictures and sketches from Kat's duffle, including the one of Celia in the garden.

She walked over to them. I could feel her emotions fluctuating between joy, sadness, guilt, and longing. And then humor when she saw what else I had there. I had found an original 1981-issued poster for *Indiana Jones: Raiders of the Lost Ark* signed by Harrison Ford.

"And of course your Jackson Pollock," I said, motioning to the splattered painting, and still unable to understand what she liked about it. She laughed, running her fingers over the frame.

Kat walked to the center of the room, where there was an oak-finish tilt-top drafting desk for sketching. It swiveled so she could have the light at her front or back.

"And watch this," I said.

I clicked the switch on the wall, and metal window covers collapsed over the windows. When they closed, it was completely dark. I flicked the one next to it, and the ceiling lit up with special bulbs made specifically for art studios. She looked at me, her expression somewhere between a pout and a smile. There was more, and I watched her take it all in. More pencils, paints, canvas, and paper than I ever knew existed. All different sizes and colors.

"I know sketching with colored pencils is your thing, but I got paint, too. I don't know. Anything you want for the rest of your life. It's yours. I want to give you everything, Kat."

"You already have," she whispered, sighing and wiping under her eyes with her fingers, trying to spare her makeup.

I wrapped my arms around her waist, hugging her back to my chest. "I love you."

"I love you," she said, her hand coming up to caress my cheek.

"So, you wanna break this desk in?" I asked, and she served me a heated look over her shoulder that stirred my soul. I groaned low in my chest, struck by her, and found her lips with mine.

CHAPTER 30

FINN

LATER THAT EVENING, WE were at the Winter Solstice party in the ballroom. I sat by Gideon, who seemed distant.

'What's going on?' I asked. I'd known the man my entire life, and I knew when something was wrong.

He leaned back in his chair, resting his chin in his hand. *'Eris is pregnant.'*

My brows shot up, and I found her in the crowd. She was dancing with Kat, who was trying to show her some modern dance moves. They were both laughing so hard they were hanging onto each other for support. Obviously, it was too early for Eris to be showing at all.

'Holy shit! Congratulations, Brother.'

His mouth turned up in a slight smile. *'Thank you.'*

I frowned. *'This is a good thing, right?'*

'Of course it is. It's always a good thing,' he answered quickly. *'It's also the most terrifying thing of my entire life. A dragon could attack us at any moment. Maybe more than one. And we're on the brink of civil war. My mate is going to be vulnerable, but I know she won't stay out of the fight. I thought I couldn't worry more, and then the pups happened...'*

His voice trailed off, and he sighed, leaning forward to grab his drink and then draining the rest. A realization struck me.

'Pups? Like more than one?'

'*Yes, two pups.*' I could hear his pride this time, as well as some disbelief.

Wolf shifters almost never had multiples. It was so rare I couldn't think of anyone in our pack who had a twin brother or sister.

'*That's fucking crazy,*' I said, stunned. '*And that's why you've been so paranoid these last few days?*'

'*You're the only other person who knows. We're telling everyone else after the new year, but I just wanted you to know. Eris is stubborn. Like I said, if there's a fight, she won't stay out of it. I want you to be aware and do your best to help me keep her safe if something happens.*'

'*You know I will.*'

KAT

It was the first day of the new year, and we were all at breakfast. Diane sat next to me, chatting about her mate, Henry, and telling me about Finn as a little boy. She was describing to me how, for the entire year between two and three, she couldn't keep clothes on him. She'd dress him and turn around to do something else, and the next thing she knew, he would be naked again.

'*I guess old habits die hard,*' I linked him while I was laughing.

He snickered, shaking his head.

Diane was so sweet, and I was so lucky to have her in my life. There were times I felt almost, I don't know, jealous or something. I couldn't help but wonder what my life would have been like if I'd had a mother that loved me.

Eris and Gideon stood, pulling me from my thoughts.

"We have an announcement," Gideon said, smiling.

Everyone stopped talking, giving him their attention.

I knew what they were going to say already. Eris had told me days ago and sworn me to secrecy. I had been dying not being able to tell Finn.

"Eris is pregnant."

Gideon gazed at her with so much love in his eyes that I involuntarily said, "Aww," because I was so struck by the intensity. My thoughts tried to trail to my fertility again, and whether I could ever give that to Finn. I didn't let them, reeling them back in. This was Eris and Gideon's moment, and I would be happy for them.

Diane was over the moon, standing and hurrying to them. She was crying and fawning over Eris when Gideon finished his announcement.

"With twins."

There was a stunned beat of silence, and then everyone started jabbering. Daro looked very confused by the commotion. I had been, too. I didn't know wolf shifter twins were so rare. Enid leaned over and explained it to him, an expression of understanding crossing his face.

Growing up in the human world, it all seemed so fast to me, but Eris explained that wolf shifters, especially true mates, didn't wait long to have pups. I hoped Finn wasn't in a big rush.

'You probably should've thought about that before you had unprotected sex with him like a thousand times,' Rieka chimed in, snickering.

I blushed, knowing I didn't really have a retort for that.

I pushed all thoughts of pregnancy away, noticing Finn wasn't surprised by the announcement either.

'You knew?' I demanded.

'Yes. I'm sorry I couldn't tell you! I was sworn to secrecy. Please don't be pissed at me.'

I laughed through the link. *'I knew, too.'*

He sighed, shaking his head in exasperation. *'Seriously? Goddess, it's been killing me not to tell you!'*

'Me too!'

'Should we just tell each other next time and then pretend we didn't?'

'Sounds good.'

After a few seconds of quiet, he said, *'Gideon just linked me asking if we would meet him in his office after this.'*

We finished breakfast, and Gideon, Eris, Finn, and I rode the elevator up together. Gideon walked around his desk, picking up some papers.

"There is only one laboratory in the world that is geared for supernaturals. It's in Sweden, but I had them rush the DNA test," he said, looking at me.

I nodded, putting my hand over my mouth. Here it was. The indisputable proof of my mother's pain.

"They emailed the results yesterday afternoon, but I didn't check my email until this morning."

Finn squeezed my hand. "What's it say?"

"Your wolf was right. Which isn't really a surprise. I wouldn't doubt her instincts."

My heart dropped, then kicked into a race. "So now what? We should tell someone, right? He should be arrested."

Gideon looked pensive, unsure. "Would your mom be willing to come here? To testify?"

I shook my head vigorously. "Nope. No way. I'm one hundred percent sure she would not."

He sighed and sat in his chair, running his hand through his hair.

"Then I don't know," he said, frustrated. "Obviously, there's a law against rape, but there has to be a complainant, and the accused has the right to face their accuser in court. There are also jurisdictional issues since it took place out of the realm. Plus, I believe the statute of limitations may have already run out."

"So, there's nothing we can do?" I asked, my heart sinking. "He just... gets away with it?"

He looked at me, and I could tell he felt awful. "If we tried, I know Royce would just say it was consensual. Without your mom to dispute that, there would be no case against him."

I nodded my understanding and looked at my hands, trying to keep tears from falling. Finn put his hand around my waist and pulled me close.

Eris was not as accepting. "This is outrageous! He is a danger to other women. We can't just do nothing."

Gideon tapped his pen on his desk. "Let's just keep this between us for now. Give me some time. I'll look at the laws. I won't let this go so easily."

Eris smiled at me. "He won't get away with it. I promise. We'll find a way."

CHAPTER 31

FINN

W INTER PASSED WITHOUT INCIDENT. As soon as the ground thawed, Gideon was hurrying me to get the walls built. He had also ordered the construction of two large bunkers, enough space for the more vulnerable pack members to keep safe during a dragon attack. I was in charge of all the finer details, and I sat in my office discussing numbers with the head of construction when Gideon linked me.

'I need you in my office.'

I wrapped up my conversation and walked down the hall to Gideon's office, knocking twice and entering.

River and Rhia stood with him. They'd been absent since the pack meeting where Gideon had threatened secession. I noticed with a start that Rhia's right arm was gone from just above her elbow. No one said anything about it, and I wasn't about to ask.

I nodded greetings to them and looked at my brother. On the desk in front of him, there was a sword piece. It had to be another chunk of Dragonsbane, the only sword in existence that could kill a dragon.

Gideon looked at me. "What weapon do you favor? What do you want made for you?"

I glanced at the wall where his own reforged weapon was displayed, a retractable spear crafted from the first piece of Dragonsbane the witches had discovered. Eris used it to kill Xeron last fall.

I considered all my options. Although wolf shifters didn't fight in human form often, we had training with various weapons.

"I'm not bad with a bow. And if they're going to be flying around, it's probably the best bet, don't you think?"

River spoke first. "I think that would be an excellent choice."

Gideon looked at the sword piece.

"We can probably have some arrows made," he said, more to himself than anyone else. "Each one tipped with a piece of metal from the sword." He glanced up at me. "You'd better have good aim. They're fast."

"It's been months. You're sure they're coming?"

River tilted her head, lacing her fingers at her waist. "Beta Finn, these dragons have been alive for centuries. Weeks, months, and even years mean very little to them. They'll wait as long as they feel necessary. We cannot let our guard down."

I nodded, feeling like I'd been reprimanded by a teacher. The sentiment that the dragons weren't coming had been echoing around the other packs, too. Other Alphas were making fun of Gideon for being too much of an alarmist. I'd had some conversations with Rudy on the phone. He was worried about how paranoid Gideon was becoming, but we both understood his intense need to protect the pups.

Eris was about halfway through her pregnancy now, and every day Gideon grew more protective. I didn't know if he even slept anymore. I glanced at the corner of his office, where the trapdoor to the vault had been installed. An entire chamber had been added, descending through the house and into the ground underneath.

The athame was below us right now, accessible through several locks made of the highest technology available. We're talking eye scans, fingerprint scans, and, most incredibly, a lock that pricked your finger and took your blood. Gideon and I were the only ones who could currently access the chamber. A magical ward kept us from touching it, though. One of the witches would have to be present for the blade to be taken.

Gideon stood, staring out of his window at the endless forest. "I know what they're saying, you know, that I'm crazy. But I just know that they'll see soon. I feel bad for the other packs because they are not prepared for what's coming."

I nodded again and updated him on the progress with the walls and the bunkers. He listened intently and was happy it was moving along so well.

When I sensed the conversation was closing, I checked the clock on the wall and decided I'd be done for the day. I searched through the bond for Kat, and I could feel she was peaceful. A strong sense of bliss and happiness. That meant she was in her studio.

KAT

I was sitting at my elevated desk in the middle of the room, sketching a picture of Eris and Enid together that I thought was cute. Leo was at my desk, hunched over and working on something in his sketchbook. I'd invited him to use the room whenever he wanted. He'd designed it after all, and there was so much here I could never use it all by myself. I noticed Leo rarely used color, though. He sketched everything with pencil and charcoal. Not that I'd ever actually seen his drawings. I shared some of my work with him, but he never reciprocated.

We were here a lot together, but we didn't really talk. Leo was certainly one of those people who were more comfortable without conversation. It wasn't awkward, though. The quiet was peaceful. Sometimes it was just us in the room's silence, the scratching of our pencils the only sound, and sometimes he played music on his phone. He liked a variation of rock and metal, which was fine by me.

I heard the door pad beeping. Finn was here. When I stood, I knew I had been sitting there longer than I realized, and I stretched my legs and neck.

Leo looked up from his work when Finn walked in. He slammed his sketchbook shut and stood. We, coincidentally, had the same one.

"Wow, I didn't know we'd been in here so long," Leo said, stretching. I smiled. "Yeah, me neither."

Leo walked around the desk, heading for the door and typing on his phone. Finn cherished every moment that he could antagonize his little brother and kept stepping in front of Leo while he tried to get around him.

He was laughing, and Leo rolled his eyes. "Gods. You are so dumb!"

Finn finally let him pass, and he was nearly out the door when he came hurrying back in and grabbed his sketchbook.

A light blush colored his cheeks. "Wouldn't want to forget this. Later, Kat."

I nodded. "See you at dinner."

He hurried back out the door, pushing his older brother aside this time with more force than Finn was expecting. I felt Finn's shock and humor, laced with a bit of pride, through the bond. Leo was a big kid, a gentle giant, but I suspected he could beat someone's ass if he wanted to.

Finn sauntered over to me, pulling me into him.

"Well, my love, we could go to dinner, or we could go to the room," he said huskily, running his hands down my back.

I leaned up and kissed him, our desire sparking together, but I broke the kiss before it got too heated.

"First, I have to show you this."

I hurried over to my sketchbook. I had drawn Finn again in front of the dragon temple, this time with pink sweats, and I thought it was hilarious.

I opened the sketchbook, and it took me a moment to realize it wasn't mine. I saw only the first two pages, but both sketches were of Enid. She and Hades in the back gardens, flowers around them. The other was her smiling and holding a guitar. I stared at it, stunned by the detail. It looked like a black-and-white photograph rather than a pencil sketch, with every hair on her head delicately defined. Realizing I was snooping, I slammed it shut, blushing.

"What is it?" Finn asked, confused by my embarrassment.

"This one is Leo's."

He gasped and hurried over, grabbing for it. I held it protectively to my chest.

"No way! You're not looking at it. It's private."

"You looked at it!"

I danced out of his grasp. "I didn't mean to!"

'Leo, you took my sketchbook by mistake. There're sexually charged sketches of your brother in there, so you probably don't want it,' I joked through the link.

'Oh, gods, gross. I'll be right back.'

He made it back in record time, and he was breathing hard, like he'd been running. I handed him the sketchbook and took mine.

He glared at Finn. "You better not have looked at it!"

"What if I did?" Finn drawled, tormenting him.

Leo's face darkened to the color of a raspberry. "If you say anything about—"

"I wouldn't let him look!" I said, saving him from the embarrassment.

Relief crossed his face, and his lips pulled up into his little half-smile. But he looked at me and flushed again, probably realizing I had seen some of it.

"Thanks, Kat."

"Leo... how long does one of those sketches take you?" I asked, unable to help myself.

"Um, I don't know," he said, shrugging. "A hundred hours for one, maybe?"

My brows lifted. "I've never seen anything so detailed. Your talent is incredible."

Leo shrugged, but his already red face deepened three shades. He mumbled, "Thanks," and then turned on his heel, leaving again.

Finn looked at me. "He's that good?"

"He's that good," I said, staring at the door.

"Well, what in the name of Hades was in there to have him so flustered, then?"

"Don't worry about it."

"Oh, you're gonna tell me," he said, grabbing me and tickling me.

I laughed, trying to squirm out of his grasp.

"Never!" I yelled, being dramatic. "Artists have to stick together!"

We fell to the floor, wrestling. The mood shifted from innocent play to not, and Finn pinned me to the floor, so I wrapped my legs around his waist. I ground my hips up against him, and he growled in his chest. He grabbed my hands and held them over my head with my wrists.

"Fine," he said, kissing me, "keep your secrets. But I expect something good in return."

I laughed. "I bet I can figure something out."

CHAPTER 32

FINN

IT WAS NEARING MID-SUMMER when the declaration of war arrived on Gideon's desk. Diamond Moon and the other packs were finally going to make their move.

Eris was only one week from her due date, and everyone, especially my brother, was on edge, knowing it could happen any day.

Rudy and Brutus had traveled here with their mates to meet with Gideon about our course of action. We all sat in Gideon's office, talking about battle strategies. I looked out to see the sun was sinking behind the trees. We'd been at it all day.

Diamond Moon was our border pack. The walls on that side would need to be stronger and better manned. Rudy and Brutus' packs bordered each other, so they could help each other if need be.

The phone rang, and Gideon answered. I was talking to Brutus but stopped when I realized the nature of the conversation.

"Now? They're there now?" Gideon asked, standing. He listened, nodding at whatever was being said. "Do your best, Bruno. We're on our way!"

Bruno was the Beta wolf of Diamond Moon. Gideon hung up the phone and walked around his desk, grabbing his spear. "The dragons are at Diamond Moon. We need to mobilize now. I linked Lucien. He's getting the warriors together."

"Dragons?" Rudy asked, standing. "How many?"

Gideon hesitated at the door, hand on the knob. "Five. The pack has already sustained mass casualties. Lyrion is dead."

"Fucking five?" I sputtered. Killing one had been nearly impossible. There was a stunned silence, and then Gideon was moving again, running down the hall.

I headed to my office, grabbing my new bow and arrows. We hurried down the stairs, not bothering with the elevator.

"We can run there in twenty minutes," Gideon said.

"Yep. I'm ready."

KAT

We were sitting in Eris' office chatting with the two visiting Lunas, Beth and Emily, when Eris stiffened, looking concerned.

I panicked for the hundredth time this week. "What is it? The babies?"

"No. But something's wrong. Something's happening."

Her eyes glazed over, and I knew she was talking to Gideon. A horn blared outside the pack house, and Eris stood.

'Finn? What's happening?' I asked.

It took him a second to answer, and he sounded distracted. *'Dragons at Diamond Moon. They've called for our aid.'*

I gasped. *'And you're going?'*

Foreboding dread set in my gut. I knew this day might be coming, but the thought of Finn fighting dragons made me want to vomit.

'Of course. We need to save the artifact if we can. Gideon needs you to keep Eris here. Take her to the bunker.'

'How am I supposed to do that? Have you met this woman?' I demanded, equally frightened of her as I was of dragons.

She pushed past me towards the door, waddling as quickly as she could.

"Eris? Where are you going?"

"He thinks he's leaving me here," she spat, as if she couldn't believe her husband didn't want her fighting dragons days before she was due to give birth.

I jogged after her, throwing my arms out. "Well, yeah. No offense, but look at you!"

"I know I can't fight, but there are lives I could save. My sister will be there. She could need me, and he is out of his mind if he thinks I won't be there for her!"

I followed her to the elevator with Beth and Emily. Eris was determined, with her face set in a stubborn frown.

"Eris," I started, but she glared at me, and I shut my mouth, putting my hands up in surrender.

She's not going for it,' I told Finn.

'Great.'

We left the elevator and walked to the front of the house, where everyone was gathered. A loud siren blared, warning all non-fighting civilians to get to their designated bunkers.

We broke apart, looking for our mates. I found Finn in the crowd and ran to him. He was doing busy work, instructing people, but saw me and hugged me, holding me close.

"How bad is it?" I whispered.

He looked concerned, as if he didn't want to tell the truth. "There are five dragons there."

My heart leaped in my chest. Finn had never seen the true power of a dragon. I had experienced it firsthand.

Rieka and Hana both whined in my head, their fear mixing with mine.

I clenched his arms in my hands. "The artifact is already lost. Don't go." My eyes filled with tears. "Please, please, Finn. Don't go."

He closed his eyes and took a deep breath. "I have to go. Innocent people are dying."

I was panicking, tears rolling down my cheeks. "Let me come then. I can help!"

He frowned and shook his head no, putting his hand on my cheek and catching a tear with his thumb and wiping it.

"I'll come back, Kat. I love you too much to leave you."

"No, you won't! Finn. Five dragons!"

I pressed my face into his chest, breathing in his scent and trying to compose myself.

Gideon's voice boomed above the mad scurry of people, causing everyone to pause. "You are NOT going, Eris! My gods!"

He had a hold of her shoulders. Eris's body was shaking, and her hands were clenched in fists. She opened her mouth to say something, but he cut her off.

"One more word and I'll use the Alpha command to compel you to stay here. I will protect my children!"

She blanched and glared at him, a dry, homicidal laugh parting her lips. I thought she was going to punch him in the face, I really did. Their eyes glazed over, both of their faces set in stubborn frowns. They must have been linking furiously with each other.

She hissed, "Fine! You're wasting time. You need to go."

He rubbed her arms and then placed his hands on her stomach. My eyes filled with tears as I watched. They could all die. The darker side of me said they would all die. Five dragons. It was insurmountable.

Eris' face softened, as she had the same thoughts, I was sure. She leaned up and kissed Gideon, whispering something. They held for a moment, everyone watching, and then the kiss broke.

Gideon looked at Finn, who nodded he was ready, and then shouted, "Let's move!"

He shifted, and someone hung the spear over his neck with a leather strap. I heard the sounds of hundreds of other shifts happening simultaneously, and turned to find that Finn was still human, looking at me. He pushed his love to me, and I choked on a sob, pushing mine back. He handed me the bow and arrows, showing me how to strap them to his wolf.

He kissed me swiftly once more, and then I heard the cracking of bone as he shifted. I stood on my tiptoes, strapping the weapon to his back. Everyone else had already disappeared into the treeline.

'I love you, Kat.'

Tears rolled down my cheeks. *'I love you, too.'*

And then he was gone, bounding out of sight beyond the trees.

I turned and realized it was just Eris and I left. Emily and Beth must've gone as well.

I wiped my cheeks. "It'll be okay, Eris. Let's get to the bunker."

Eris turned on her heel, her stride an aggressive waddle back toward the garage.

"Eris?" I yelled, running to catch up. "The bunker is this way, by the stables."

I knew she knew that already.

"I'm not going to the bunker," she said as she typed in the garage code.

The door lifted, and she walked in, climbing into the seat of one of the SUVs.

I caught the door so she couldn't shut it. "Eris! What are you doing?"

"You can go to the bunker if you want, Kat," she said, staring at me with an intensity that frightened me. "I have to help. I'm the person the goddess chose to give the ability to heal mortal wounds, and I'm going. These dragons chose this exact time so I would be indisposed, but they underestimate me. So, either hold your tongue and get in, or get out of my way!"

I laughed, surprising her. It was obvious she wasn't going to listen, and I figured it was better not to let her go alone.

"I've always known you're a crazy bitch, Eris! Now get out. I'm driving. You're the worst driver ever, and that's coming from a Californian. We need to actually make it to the battle if we're going to help!"

It was true, and I didn't say it to be mean. She was a crazy bitch. I knew it the day I watched her spit in Xeron's face and then take the lashings without making a sound. She was kind and caring, but she also had a beast lurking inside her, and it scared me. Eris Dragonslayer. You didn't get a name like that hiding in the bunker.

Eris nodded and slid out, waddling around to the passenger side. I jumped in and started the engine, taking a deep breath.

"Block your bond," she instructed, clicking her seatbelt. "They'll be distracted if they know what we're up to."

CHAPTER 33

FINN

I CAUGHT UP WITH Gideon as we ran through the forest connecting Gold Moon and Diamond Moon. We had one hundred and fifty warriors with us, and I hoped it would be enough.

They waited until there was no way for Eris to be part of the battle. They didn't want to fight her and Enid,' Gideon linked me, growling.

'How do they know?' I asked.

'I don't know, it's not like her pregnancy was a secret. Everyone in the realm knows about it. Some fae could've forfeited the information for all we know. It is frustrating that our enemy knows everything about us, and we know virtually nothing about them.'

I agreed. The smell of smoke hit us like a wall as we drew close. It was dark now, so we could see the glow of fire up over the next ridge. The scent of blood mixed with everything, accompanied by the telltale smell of decay. There were definitely vampires here.

The screams came next. My ears picked up the horror waiting over the ridge, and I felt my adrenaline spike. The sounds of agony and fear increased, and we crested the hill and got our first glimpse of the battlefield.

It was dark, but the entire city was on fire, and the glow lit up the valley, casting long shadows in every direction. We had been told there were five dragons, but right now I could only see four. A golden-colored one and a dark blue one flew in circles around a clearing just east of the town. The dark blue one was huge, probably three times bigger than the golden one. Enid was there with River and Rhia. They battled the two dragons furiously but seemed to be at a stalemate.

The golden one swooped down on Enid, blowing a torrent of fire on top of her. She put her hands up and seemed to form some kind of shield. The fire rolled around her but didn't touch her. She was controlling the air element. The dragon screeched, and several of our warriors flinched at the noise.

'Steady,' Gideon linked everyone simultaneously. *'That's a sixteen-year-old girl out there fighting. Steel your nerves, warriors.'*

The other two dragons were shifted, but on the ground. One was ruby-red, the smallest of the group, and the other was a jade green color. They walked through the city streets, plumes of fire erupting every few seconds as they scorched everything in their path. I watched the green one pick up a Diamond Moon warrior in its jaws and throw him, catching him again with a sickening crunch of bones and then swallowing him while he was still screaming.

The vampires flooded the streets, cackling as they ripped the throats out of anybody they could find. It was the most evil I'd ever seen. The slain bodies of women and children piled in the streets, the scent of their blood filling the air.

'All these pups, my goddess, help us,' Shaw lamented, his sorrow thick in our blood.

The Diamond Moon warriors were practically gone, but they had done some damage. I saw countless ash piles among the dead.

Gideon linked me again. *'You need to go help Enid. I can't do anything against the airborne dragons. I will take everyone else, and we'll try to save the civilians that are left. Maybe I can kill one of the dragons on the ground, too.'*

I took off toward the clearing. *'Good luck, Brother.'*

KAT

I tapped the steering wheel nervously, driving as fast as I dared. At one point, I turned on the radio, but then I immediately switched it off. That was dumb. I was a ball of nerves, barely able to think.

I glanced over at Eris and watched her tense, stroking her belly. I had noticed it several times already, and I braked, my mouth falling open.

"Fuck sake's, Eris! Are you in labor? Was that a contraction?"

"It's just Braxton Hicks from all this excitement. I'll be fine. Just keep going."

I shook my head but pressed the gas down again. "If I somehow don't die today, Gideon will surely kill me, anyway."

"I won't allow that. We're almost there," she said, and rolled the window down. The sharp smell of smoke and decay filled the cab, and I gagged at the overwhelming scent. An orange glow peeked through the trees just over the horizon. "Have you ever experienced déjà vu?" she asked. I looked at her and saw a stray tear trickle down her cheek. She wiped furiously at it and then set her face in a mask of determination.

We made it over the last hill, and I gasped at what unfolded below us in the valley. "Oh, my gods!"

"Stop here," Eris instructed, remaining calm and collected as we climbed out. "I can't shift Kat. I'm too far along, and it will hurt the pups. You need to help protect me from the vampires. I know you don't have any official training, but your wolf will know what to do. Let's just try to make our way towards Enid. I can heal some along the way, hopefully."

I looked at her, my mouth falling open. She was insane. "You can't shift? You could've dropped that bombshell a little sooner! Eris, I don't know what I'm doing!"

'Don't worry!' Rieka snarled, and I almost giggled, having never heard her be so aggressive. *'I won't let any of those bloodsuckers hurt our Luna!'*

Eris reached over and squeezed my hand. "Just do your best, Kat. I believe in you."

I nodded and undressed, shifting to my wolf. Rieka shook out her fur, flexing her claws, and I swore she was excited about this.

I kneeled so Eris could climb onto my back. She did, grunting with effort, and I bounded down towards the edge of the city, warily eyeing the two dragons near the center, destroying everything in their path.

We encountered our first vampires as soon as we crossed the boundary of burning buildings. They were feasting on a felled shewolf. A young girl, maybe three years old, sat to the side sobbing and calling for her mother.

Eris was right. Rieka jumped them, ripping the head off of one with ease and throwing it. She circled the other, and he hissed, the shewolf's blood dripping down his chin.

He made a move, lunging at me and slashing my shoulder with his claws. Ouch. Neither of us expected Eris to kick him hard in the face with her booted foot when he did. It disoriented him, and that was all Rieka needed, grabbing him by the throat and ripping his head off as well.

Eris approached the child. The girl was terrified, and Hana whined, *'Oh, this poor baby.'*

I felt sick. She had just watched her mother torn apart and eaten.

"Hey, sissy, what's your name?" Eris cooed, reaching her hand out to her.

The girl was hiccupping through her sobs but answered, "Sierra." She couldn't quite say the "r" sound yet, so it sounded like Siewwa.

"Hi, Sierra, I'm Eris. I'm a Luna. Do you know what a Luna is?"

She nodded. "Our Luna is the mommy of the pack. My Luna is Natasha."

Eris smiled. "Good, that's very good, Sierra. I know Natasha. Are you hurt?"

She shook her head no.

"Okay, then I need you to be really brave for me and run. Run up that hill and find my car. It's black. Climb into the back seat and wait there for me, okay?" Eris pointed in the direction we just came from.

Sierra nodded and started walking, trying to look at what was left of her mother. Eris stopped her by stepping into her field of vision and pushed her gently on the back.

"Go, Sierra. Run as fast as you can, okay? Run, run, run."

Sierra's lip quivered, but she started running. I watched her until I was sure she'd cleared the wreckage.

Eris turned to me, her eyes haunted. She'd watched her own mother die. "See. What would've happened if we weren't here? We must keep going."

I kneeled again, and she climbed on.

We continued in that fashion. Killing vampires and trying to save people, but there weren't a lot left alive to save. It was a massacre. So much death. I had to turn off my emotions before I drowned in the horror.

Eris did her best. She was healing as much as she could. A broken leg or broken ribs, just enough so people had a chance to run. But those fatally wounded she couldn't help without Enid, or else she'd pass out.

When we were in a calmer area, I stopped her and looked at her face. She was exhausted. I watched her stiffen in pain again, a small groan escaping her lips, and I shifted back.

When she cried out, doubling over, I panicked. "Oh, shit! Oh, gods! You are in labor, you liar! You need to take a break, Eris. I'm worried about the babies."

We were deeper in the city now, and I was on high alert, ready to shift back at any second. I pulled her down a side street. We tripped over a man's body, and he groaned.

"Bruno," Eris whispered. "Oh, my Goddess."

She got down next to him and put her hands on him.

"Luna?" he gasped, obviously surprised. "What are you doing here?"

She ignored the question, closing her eyes. I could tell he wouldn't make it. The lower half of his body was practically gone. So much blood.

"I'm sorry, Bruno," Eris said. "I can't heal you."

He nodded in understanding. "Tell your mate I'm sorry. We should have listened. They took the artifact! The bell is lost. One dragon took it and left. I'm so sorry!"

He was overcome by a wet coughing fit. Blood peppered Eris' face, but she didn't move.

She shushed him and held his hand. His breathing grew more erratic and then finally shuddered to a stop. I remembered that his mate had just had their first pup last fall.

Eris stood, and I wiped the tears from my face. This was all too much. So much death and pain. The ground shook beneath our feet, and we turned, holding our breath. The jade dragon rounded the corner, roaring when it saw us.

I pushed Eris. "Run!"

A torrent of fire escaped its maw, funneling down the alley. We ducked, the flames licking my naked back. Eris hurried down the alley as fast as she could.

I stopped, shifting to Hana. "Keep going!"

Another blast of fire pushed her further away, and she shouted, "Kat!"

I avoided the flames easily this time as my nimble fox gracefully maneuvered the alleyway. We ran towards the dragon, darting beneath its legs. It turned, roaring and following me. I sighed. At least Eris was safe for now.

'Gideon? Eris needs help. She's on the east side of the city; we got separated. I'm so sorry she wouldn't stay home. I'm leading the green dragon away from her, but she can't shift. She also might be in labor...' I prayed he could hear me.

'Are you fucking—' His furious growl echoed in my head. And then he said, *'I'll find her, Kat. Don't you dare die, either.'*

I heard a howl that I knew was his, and I was relieved that he was closer than I expected. I just hoped he would find her in time.

CHAPTER 34

KAT

I SCAMPERED THROUGH THE streets, choking on the smoke as I got deeper into the city. The dragon was easy to lose once I ducked under a few gates. I was disoriented, though, unsure what direction to go. With no sun and no way to see the stars, I had no bearings.

'Eris?' I tried the link. *'Please tell me you made it.'*

'Yes, I'm here! Gideon found me. We're trying to kill the red dragon!'

'Okay. I don't know where I am, but I'll try to find you.'

I heard a roar somewhere off to my right and thought I might as well move towards it. As Hana, I wove through the alleys, avoiding the vampires and sticking to the shadows. The roar sounded again, closer this time, and I followed the sound. I ducked under one more gate and found myself out in the grassy clearing where we'd seen Enid.

I stepped back out of sight, watching and breathing a sigh of relief. Finn was here, taking aim and firing an arrow at the smaller dragon. The beast rolled in the air, blocking it easily, and then descended upon him. My heart nearly stopped, but when the torrent of fire blasted at him, some kind of force-field stopped it.

I looked to see Enid, arms out in front of her as she controlled the air around Finn. I didn't even know the air element had manifested for her. She was someone I didn't recognize. Her eyes were glowing bright yellowish-green, and all the purple veins in her face were visible under her pale skin. Covered in dirt and soot, her singed skirt blew around her, waving like a flag in the heat of battle.

'The Green Witch has entered the chat,' I said to Rieka and Hana, watching Finn nock his bow. I knew they'd only been able to make ten arrows. I watched, hoping one would hit true.

FINN

I let another arrow fly, my aim right on, only to have the golden dragon deflect it again at the last second. It splintered, falling to the ground in two pieces. I growled in frustration, knowing I'd already used eight of my ten arrows. The dragons were too fast, too aware of my shots. They were also annoying and deadly. The big blue one had a nasty-looking, razor-sharp piece of silver attached to his tail that he whipped when he swooped down upon us.

'What is this?' I asked Shaw when a coal-black dragon, much smaller than the others, swooped in from the night.

It blasted a stream of fire into the face of the golden dragon, who screeched in response. The black dragon was small, but agile, as it danced through the sky. The blue and golden dragons roared, focusing their attention on this new target.

'Who is that?' Enid linked me, confusion in her voice.

'It's attacking the others?'

'It looks like it.'

'I've lost eight arrows already. They're too fast.'

With the dragons distracted, Enid ran towards me.

"Take aim," she instructed, "and fire when I tell you."

I complied, aiming at the distinct orange glow of the heart of the golden dragon. I tracked it, waiting for the signal. Enid kneeled in front of me, and we waited, observing as the battle ensued in front of us.

The black dragon was outsized and outnumbered. It was struggling, but dove in towards the golden dragon once more, blasting another stream of fire into its face.

'Now, Finn!'

I let the arrow fly, holding my breath. Enid stood as soon as it cleared her head, and I watched as she manipulated the air around the arrow, spinning it faster and increasing the speed to a rate that would've been impossible to achieve otherwise.

Everything happened in slow motion. The golden dragon snapped angrily at the black dragon and then saw the arrow, the metal tip glinting as it turned. The dragon flailed, trying to lift its leg to block it like it had the others.

The arrow was a fraction of a second too fast, and it buried itself into the dragon's chest. My ears rang from the unholy screech that rang out, and then the golden dragon started falling from the sky. As it fell, it shifted back to its human form. It was a woman, and she dropped unobstructed, hitting the dirt with a disgusting thud.

I could hear the others behind me in the city screeching as well, like they were in pain. The blue dragon roared and went after the small black dragon with a new intensity. He whipped his tail, and the silver razor tip hit true, slicing the black dragon across the right thigh and wing.

The black dragon bellowed and fell into an uncontrolled dive, trying to flap but failing as the air just passed through the ripped wing. The beast crashed into the forest, trees snapping violently at the impact.

I heard more wings flapping behind me and looked to see the other two dragons rise into the air from the city streets, the air off their wings fanning the flames of the surrounding buildings. I thought they would join the fray, but to my surprise, they flew off in the other direction. They called behind them, seeming to beckon to the blue dragon. He bellowed furiously at them. Even I could tell he was pissed at their cowardice.

His eyes fell on Enid again, and I nocked my last arrow, taking aim. She kneeled in front of me, and he started his descent, bearing down on us like an avalanche.

'Now!' she ordered.

Taking a deep breath, I released the arrow, watching as it soared towards its destination. Enid stood, pushing it like she had the one before.

Without the black dragon's help, the beast deflected it with its front leg, and it snapped in half, falling back down to the earth. I was officially out of ammo. He flew just over us, whipping his silver tail wildly. We both tried to evade, but it struck Enid on the upper arm, cutting her to the bone as she shrieked in pain.

I crouched over her, ripping a piece of her shirt so I could tie it around the wound to stop the bleeding. She held her hand up to stop me and stood. The petite features of her face were shadowed with anger, and she laid her hand across the flayed skin. Small flames erupted, cauterizing the wound. The smell of burned flesh filled my nose as I stared at her, not knowing whether to be impressed or horrified. That was definitely the most metal fucking thing I'd ever seen.

She glanced at my quiver, seeing I was out of arrows, and said, "Go help the others, Finn. There's nothing you can do here," then hurried back towards where River and Rhia stood.

"Okay, rude," I muttered, but stilled when a familiar scent drifted into my nose and fear curdled my blood.

Shaw was beside himself. *'Is our mate here?'*

I whipped my head around, searching for Kat. She was standing at the edge of the clearing, and she had obviously been in her wolf or fox form because she was stark naked. I watched her bend down, picking up half of one of my broken arrows. The fletching was gone, and it was about eight inches of shaft and the arrowhead.

The metal tip glinted in the firelight as she turned it in her hand. Kat glanced up at the dragon, who was now assailing the witches with unending fire. I could see the wheels turning in her head, as if she was making a plan. I didn't know what she was thinking of doing, and I didn't care. She shouldn't even be here. She wasn't even a trained warrior.

'Don't you dare,' I linked her.

She jumped at my voice in her head, and she looked at me, her chestnut eyes dancing brightly with the flames.

CHAPTER 35

KAT

I LOOKED AT FINN. His expression was warning me, and he shook his head, telling me not to do whatever I was about to do. My lips curled at the edges in a half smile, and I turned away from him, running towards Enid.

'*Kat!*' he snapped in my head. '*Why are you here? Go home!*'

'*I love you,*' I answered, and then blocked the bond.

The dragon was solely focused on Enid now, and she, River, and Rhia stood together. River was crafting giant mud projectiles that looked like icicles, and then Rhia was launching them, pushing them through the air at incredible speed towards their target. The most effective shots were when they tore through the soft webbing of the dragon's wings, but he healed so quickly it wasn't doing any permanent damage.

Enid was defending, holding the air shield to stop the fire and creating giant earthen walls to stop the massive silver-barbed tail from cutting them.

'*Enid, the next time he's close to the ground, I need a boost,*' I linked her.

She scanned and found me, looking confused.

'*Kat...*'

'*It's okay. I've got this. Just get me some air.*'

'*You'll have it,*' she said, and I appreciated her confidence in me.

I put the arrow in my mouth and held it there, shifting to Hana and opening up my stride so I was running at full speed. I was set on a course to intersect the dragon from the side as he dove at the witches head on.

He neared the ground, blasting fire at Enid. She held her air shield and then placed her other hand on the ground. Stone steps rose out of the ground in front of me, and I leaped up them, not losing speed. The dragon's body was passing in front of me as I jumped from my platform, spinning my tail for a boost and aiming for a spike on his lower back.

I realized, disappointed, that I hadn't jumped far enough and he was going to be just out of reach. I prepared myself for the impact of the ground when I felt the air stir beneath my feet, giving me the extra little push I needed to grab him.

I shifted back to my human just in time. My hand caught a bony spike, much lower on his tail than I wanted to be, and I held on tight, extending my claws and digging them in. I felt like my shoulder nearly left the socket as the momentum of the dragon's incredible speed pulled me roughly upward.

"Oh, shit! It actually worked!" I slurred around the arrow in my mouth.

I brought my other hand around and grabbed on with it, too, trying desperately to stabilize myself.

Hana hissed, *'This is so embarrassing, flapping in the wind naked like a skin flag! Get it together, Kat!'*

'I am trying!' I snapped, grunting as I brought my legs up to wrap around his tail.

The wind whipped around me, stealing my breath, and my stomach dropped out as we started climbing in altitude.

FINN

I watched with my mouth hanging open as Kat's plan came to fruition, and then actually fucking worked. She clung to the end of the beast's tail. I couldn't breathe. I wasn't even sure my heart was beating. The dragon ascended rapidly into the sky, roaring when he realized he had a tiny passenger.

He whipped his tail, trying to shake her. She barely clung on, wrapping her legs around the tail and holding fast.

"Ah! Ah! Oh, shit!" I shouted to no one, putting both of my hands in my hair and watching.

The witches started their assault again, River and Rhia working together and Enid on her own. The earth projectiles launched at incredible speeds, peppering the dragon's body and wings.

"Don't hit her!" I yelled, running towards them.

They stopped, and all looked at me with flat expressions, like, "no shit."

"Please," I whispered, desperate for Kat to survive this somehow.

River and Enid's expressions softened as they went back to work. Rhia still looked at me like I was an idiot, pushing the next projectile forward.

The onslaught helped, distracting the dragon enough that he turned his focus back to them. I watched Kat pull herself up the tail, using the huge spikes to climb.

KAT

Okay, so this was much more difficult than I expected it to be. The pure G-force of riding this beast was insane. I worked slowly, pulling myself from one spike to the next. They were growing in size as I made my way up, and the one I clung to now, just above the base of his tail, was the size of my entire upper body. The wind generated by his giant wings whipped the air around me, threatening to knock me off balance.

He was irritated by the airborne earth clods, and he flew erratically to avoid them, plus the dirt was windborne everywhere around me, getting into my eyes. I closed them, trying to clear the debris out.

When I opened them again, the dragon was glaring at me over his right shoulder. Fear iced my blood as I stared into the giant, slitted, yellow eye. The pupil dilated, and he growled, his entire body rumbling beneath me.

'Oh boy,' I said.

Rieka barked, *'The tail!'*

I looked back with just a moment to spare, ducking and sliding down his side while the silver tip buried itself into the spike I'd just been clinging to. That weapon certainly had more range than I was expecting.

I was on his right side now, using his scales as hand and foot holds. They were smooth against his body but were sharp like obsidian glass on the edges. I cried out. They were cutting into my hands and the bottoms of my feet. Fresh blood slid down my wrists, the slickness making it more difficult to hold on.

I turned to see what he was doing and screamed. He was biting at me, and the massive teeth clacked shut just three or four feet away from me. His hot breath fanned my body as his enormous maw opened. I could see the fire rolling to life in the back of his throat, and I knew I was about to get roasted.

"Oh, shit!" I shouted around the arrow still held in my teeth, squeezing my eyes shut.

The flame never came. The small black dragon appeared again, crashing into the neck of the blue dragon and sending us into a tumble, saving my life.

I screamed like I was riding the world's worst roller coaster, clinging to the sharp scales as we tilted off-balance.

The blue dragon roared, and my eardrums nearly burst at the colossal sound. He leveled out again, seeking the black dragon and forgetting about me. It seemed personal between them. I took advantage, scrambling up his side and back to the spikes. The bigger they grew, the quicker I moved. I reached the largest one, the size of my whole body, just between his shoulders. The massive muscles he used for flying moved underneath my feet as I crouched by the spike and clung to it.

He was fighting the black dragon, rolling and turning in the air, so everything was thrashing around me in chaos. I wrapped my arms and legs around the spike and held on for dear life, realizing I needed to get around to his chest and stab him in the heart.

'Well, now what, Kat?' I asked myself, hoping maybe Hana or Rieka would have an idea. They didn't.

Without warning, the dragon turned straight down, diving at a rapid speed towards the earth. My stomach dropped out again, and I screamed until my voice broke. He did a barrel roll, turning several times in the air. I shut my eyes and clung to the spike, unable to think of anything but holding on. Where I sat now, he couldn't reach me with his tail, his mouth, or his fire, so he was determined to fling me off.

When he leveled back out, growling in frustration at the pest still attached to his back, I looked over at his wing. It flapped at a constant rhythm, straightening and then bending far underneath his body. My mind hatched an idea, but even I had to admit it was truly insane, boasting a low chance of success.

'Oh well. Fuck it,' I thought, adjusting the arrow in my mouth and positioning myself to jump.

CHAPTER 36

KAT

T HE BLACK DRAGON FLEW up alongside us, eyeing me. I needed him,
or her, I wasn't sure, to start their next attack.

We stared at each other. This one's eye was blue instead of yellow.
The dragon I was riding, the jade dragon that had chased me earlier,
and Xeron all had yellow-orangish eyes.

The black dragon snorted, and smoke curled out of its nostrils. I
steadied myself and then, timing the flap of the wing, nodded when I
was ready.

The black dragon dove into the face of the blue dragon, blowing
flames and scratching at its eyes. The blue dragon tilted to the side as
its wing came up, and I launched myself at it, catching it about midway
down the length. The wings were fleshy and easy to grab, so I sunk my
nails in and clawed toward the tip.

The blue dragon roared and tried to bite at me but was met with a
stream of fire from the smaller dragon. My heart hammered, a wild
animal caught in the cage of my ribs. The world faded away, my
thoughts going out like snuffed candles until I had one goal, one focus.

The heart. The kill.

It was one of those rare times when something I planned actually
worked. I reached the end of the wing as he flapped, and I rode it
down towards the underbelly of the beast. My hair whipped around
me, and my queasy stomach flip-flopped again, full of nothing but pure
adrenaline.

When the wing reached the apex of its downward journey and curled, I jumped, grabbing for the scales of the dragon's belly and chest. If I didn't catch hold, it was a long way down. They were sharp, slicing into my hands and feet again, as expected. Fresh blood slicked my hands, but the pain wasn't there.

My arms and legs shook, holding my entire body weight as gravity sought to ruin my day. With a deep grunt, I sank my teeth into the wooden shaft of the arrow and pulled myself towards the orange glow of the heart. The entire act had only taken ten seconds, but it felt like two hours, time moving as if we were trapped in resin.

I needed to hurry. It was only a matter of time before the blue dragon—

The massive tail whipped up, striking the glass scale just inches from where my right hand clung. Trying to watch for the next strike was pointless; the world was a blur of night sky and dark trees. I scrambled and was no more than a yard away from the heart when the blue dragon's entire body started rocking.

My heart dropped. The black dragon's back leg was caught in its jaws, and the blue dragon was thrashing its head, like a dog would with a chew toy. The black dragon screeched, clawing at the blue dragon's face while spurting blood fell in mist toward the ground.

This was it. I knew it. The realization settled in my bones. Either I did this, or the war was already over.

Growling around the arrow, I pushed myself, clambering towards the heart. The tail whipped again, and I screamed at the silver slicing into my left calf. The bones in my lower leg snapped, and my foot fell away from the dragon's body, flapping uselessly in the wind.

Fuck you. Fuck you, I thought. This dragon wouldn't stop me, and he certainly wasn't about to take the family I'd just found.

Everything I had was in this last push, this last move up. Ignoring the painful complaints of my body, I lunged up one more time.

My eyes were level with my target now. The orange heart thundered just behind a thin layer of flesh and skin.

Not caring if I fell, I let go with one hand and yanked the arrow from my mouth, screaming as I plunged it home.

FINN

I was going to pass out. My heart thundered so hard I thought it would seize. Kat was more agile than any wolf could ever hope to be.

After some crazy moves using the blue dragon's own wing, she ended up clinging to his chest. She was so close to the heart that I wondered if she was actually going to pull this off somehow.

"Ah!" I shouted to no one when his tail whipped, nearly striking her.

I stood next to the witches now, who had stopped their onslaught when dirt started getting in Kat's eyes. We all watched in silence. Enid had her hand on my shoulder, and I didn't know if she realized her nails were digging in.

The black dragon, who was definitely fighting for our side, attacked again. Big blue was ready this time and snagged its back leg. It shook the smaller dragon, nearly ripping the leg off, and whipped its tail at Kat again. This time it found her, striking her lower leg. Blood poured from the wound, and her foot hung at a sickening angle, flapping in the wind.

"Fuck, fuck!" I yelled, snapping the bow in my hands in half and dropping it. My hands fisted my hair. "Come on, Kat!"

Kat didn't stop, lunging once more and leveling herself with the beast's heart. She did it, sinking the arrow into its chest. I felt no satisfaction because she lost her footing and held on with only the arrow and the scale in her bloody hand, her legs dangling wildly.

The blue dragon screeched, releasing the black dragon from its jaws.

Enid shrieked, "Oh, no!"

The tail.

She couldn't hear me, but I yelled, "Kat! The tail!"

The barbed tip whipped around, striking Kat one last time. Right on target and impaling her with vengeance in the gut. Through the gut, so the sharp silver barb gleamed in the moonlight where it stuck out of her back.

The witches gasped while Shaw howled in my head.

"NO!" I bellowed, shifting to him and loping across the valley towards them.

They were at least five hundred feet in the air. The blue dragon shifted to its human form, its tail disappearing and pulling out of Kat's belly as it did. They fell limply next to each other, their bodies twisting with the passing currents of air.

I wouldn't make it in time. To do what? I didn't know. I couldn't catch her and save her. The fall would certainly kill her if she wasn't already dead.

'Enid?' I begged, hoping she could slow her down.

'I'm trying!' she said, her voice thick with tears in the link.

She didn't have to. The mysterious black dragon swooped down, catching Kat on the base of its neck. The human body of the blue dragon finished its fall, thumping like a bag of dropped rocks less than twenty feet away from me.

The black dragon glided down, and I shifted, pulling Kat from its shoulders.

"Oh, my gods. No, no, no, no," I said when I saw her.

The black dragon eyed Kat, letting out a sad chortle. Then it flapped its wings, taking off and flying away over the treetops.

"Kat, Kat," I repeated, patting her cheek.

Her eyes fluttered open, but it was bad, worse than I could've imagined. A gaping hole that gushed blood at an alarming rate. A puddle quickly formed under her body, her skin losing all of its color.

Her eyes were on me, and tears rolled down her cheeks. She opened her mouth like she might say something, but thick blood poured out, cascading down her face and into her ears.

"Don't talk, love. Don't talk," I said, pressing my hands over the wound in a failed attempt to staunch the bleeding. "It's okay, Kat. You're gonna be fine."

She opened the bond, and her pain, fear, and sadness hit me all at once.

'I'm sorry,' she said.

'No. No, no, no,' I answered, sniffling to keep my eyes from filling. *'You are not dying on me. We both know you're too stubborn to die.'*

River was at my side. She pulled a bottle of orange powder out of her robes and dumped it into her hand. She then stuck her hand deep into the open wound. Kat's body clenched, and a horrible smelling orange foam erupted. It slowed the bleeding.

"She is healing fast. Faster than I've ever seen," River said, breathless. "But it's not enough. She's going to die."

I shook my head, glaring at the witch. "No, she's not!"

She looked around the valley. "We need The Maiden or she's not going to make it."

CHAPTER 37

FINN

'*ERIS!*' I SCREAMED INTO the link.

  '*I saw, Finn. I'm coming... I'm trying.*'

Her voice was strained, and I stood scanning the edges of the clearing. The battle had ended with the death of the blue dragon. I couldn't hear fighting anymore, just moans, cries, and sorrow intermingling with the crackle of the burning city.

Eris pushed through a group of warriors, trying to get into the clearing and going as fast as she could. I ran towards her. I would carry her to get her here faster if I had to, but my brother's black wolf howled behind her. The crowd scurried to get out of the way, and Ivailo stopped, picking Eris up and running to us.

I kneeled down by Kat and smoothed her hair. Her eyes were closed now, and her breath barely rattled in her chest. Her skin was chalky, and the pretty red of her lips faded to a dusty pink.

'*Hang on,*' I begged her through the bond.

She didn't answer.

'*She's dying!*' Shaw howled in my head. He wanted to shift, but it was just panic. There was nothing he could do.

I looked up as Gideon placed Eris on the ground. Her face was pinched in a tight grimace, but she laid her hands on Kat and gritted, "Not today, Kat!"

Enid was by her, giving Eris extra power, and they sang their mother's lullaby together. I gasped, having never seen the power work on a physical wound before. Kat's flesh quickly weaved together like someone hit fast forward on healing. No less than a miracle.

Eris smiled up at me, a grimace smile, and grabbed my hand, squeezing my fingers.

She gasped out the words, "I think she'll make it, Finn," and doubled over again, clutching her belly.

She cried out and whimpered, and I thought she'd tear my fingers right off my hand. I glanced at my brother, who stood there with a slack jaw, his eyes wide with panic.

River gasped. "Luna! You are in heavy labor!"

Eris leaned back up, and I saw that her leggings, which had been a light gray, were now stained dark and soaking wet.

"Is the hospital intact?" I asked, referring to the one in Diamond Moon.

"It's burning as we speak," Gideon said and ran his hand through his hair.

Eris was moaning again, and unfortunately my fingers were still in her hand. My knuckles popped, but I squeezed back, trying to comfort her. I wasn't well versed in women having babies, but I knew when contractions were this close together it was go time.

When it passed, Gideon asked her, "Can you hang on? If I shift, can you ride? I can get us back to our hospital in twenty minutes."

She nodded and went to stand, but River stopped her. The witch cast a spell over her own hand, and when she was finished, her hand was spotlessly clean. She kneeled by Eris and put her hand down the front of her pants.

Eris whimpered again, and River shook her head, casting the same spell over her hand again when she removed it.

"I'd better come, too. I don't think you're going to make it."

Gideon nodded. If you didn't know him well, he appeared to be keeping his cool. But I could tell he was like a duck. Calm on the surface but kicking like a madman underneath to stay afloat.

River addressed Enid and Rhia. "I will go with the Luna. You two help pull survivors from the rubble."

"Good luck, Eris," Enid said, her eyes wide, and then she and Rhia jogged towards the city as Gideon shifted.

River helped Eris climb onto Ivailo's back and then removed her robe, handing it to me for Kat. Underneath, she wore a black long-sleeved shirt, black leggings, and bare feet. River hopped up behind Eris, and Ivailo took off, growling at anyone even relatively close to his impeding path.

I watched them go, and then wrapped Kat in River's robe, handling her like she was fine china. The robe smelled of herbs and earth, and I sat there cross-legged on the ground holding her to my chest.

I was numb—my body, my mind. Nothing felt real.

Oh, Kat.

She was still unconscious, and the blood on her face was dried and cracking. I felt for her life force and found it. It beat strongly through the bond. She was still pale, white as a sheet, but I knew she was going to be okay.

I didn't think I would be, though. How could I ever recover from what I'd just seen? The image of her honey eyes staring into mine with the fear of death in them, and thick blood sliding down her face. I clamped my eyes shut, willing the image away, and Shaw whined in my head.

I held her closer, staring at the trees. The city burned behind me, and I thought I should go. I should help. But I couldn't move. I couldn't leave her again. I sat for a long time, trying to gain control of my emotions.

My mind wandered to the small black dragon. I owed him or her my life. They saved my mate more than once, and I wondered if I would ever know who they were or what their motives were here today.

I glanced over at the fallen dragon. He was an enormous man, nearly seven feet tall, with coal-black hair and a huge scar over the left side of his face.

The broken arrow still stuck out of his chest, a stark symbol of Kat's victory.

"Fuck you. I hope you burn in the flaming river," I spat at him. He'd nearly taken everything from me.

"Finn?" I heard a soft voice behind me and jumped in surprise.

Enid stood over me, her face drawn in sorrow. "You should come and see this. It's probably best if you tell Gideon."

I stood, cradling Kat to my chest, and followed her. A deep sense of dread set in my gut. I knew I was not going to like what she had to show me.

CHAPTER 38

FINN

I WALKED INTO THE medical wing of the pack house. Gideon had it added when our mom was sick, so she could be home. He and Eris were here with the babies.

I still carried Kat, finally relinquishing her to a nurse in one of the private rooms. She instructed me that Gideon and Eris were two doors down.

I shuffled down the hall and stood at the wooden door, staring at it. No part of me wanted to do this. I didn't want to ruin this moment for them.

Instead of knocking, I established the link with my brother. *'It's me. I'm at your door.'*

Gideon opened it a moment later. He held a tiny baby bundled tightly in the crook of his arm. I glimpsed Eris behind him in the bed. She was resting, her eyes closed, and the other baby was on her chest with her hospital gown pulled up over them.

Gideon beamed, whispering, "Finn."

My throat tightened. I had a sudden recollection of a Yule morning when we were boys, and he was waking me, whispering my name with the same jubilant excitement. He presented the baby to me, pride written across his face.

"My son," he announced. "Henry Gaylon Greenwood. After our dads."

I looked at the little, wrinkled face of the baby boy in front of me and smiled.

"Wow, he's a handsome guy, like his uncle," I said, trying to match his energy.

This should be a happy day.

He chuckled and stepped aside so I could see Eris better and said, "And Ceres Diane Greenwood, our baby girl."

I nodded. "They're beautiful, Brother. I'm so glad you guys made it on time."

He shook his head, snickering. "Gods. We didn't."

My eyebrows shot up. "What?"

"River delivered them about halfway between our pack and Diamond Moon," he explained. "I sat behind Eris and supported her back, and she just... had them right there. True wolf shifters, born in the woods like in the old days."

"How did that go?" I asked, looking at the baby again.

"I'm pretty sure I still have bruises on my thighs from where she was squeezing my legs," he said, chuckling and stroking the baby's cheek with his forefinger. His smile was soft and he added, "But it was... its own type of magic." He looked up, and I could see the emotion gathering behind his eyes. "It was powerful, Finn."

"I bet," I whispered, unable to keep my sorrow buried for another second.

Gauging my expression, his face dropped. "What is it? Is it Kat? Eris was sure she'd be okay."

"No, no, Kat's fine. She's just down the hall."

My brow furrowed, and I swallowed, having a harder time than I expected.

"What, Finn? What happened?"

"It's-it's," I stuttered, trying to force the words around the lump in my throat, "it's Rudy, Gid. He's gone."

He stepped back away from me, like he was trying to escape what I was saying.

"That can't be true." His eyes glassed, and he asked, "Finn?"

"I'm sorry. I saw him. He's gone," I croaked, trying to compose myself.

He blinked several times and looked back down at his son, adjusting him in his arms. Coming to terms with the news. Then Alpha Gideon kicked in, and he went into "fix-it" mode.

"I've got to call Beth," he said, clearing his throat. "My gods. She's got to be devastated."

He took his phone out of his pocket, and I put my hand on it, stopping him.

"Beth won't answer."

He looked at me, his eyes shining as he shook his head. "Don't tell me that."

"They were together, saving people. One building was on fire. It was old, burning like kindling from what I understand. There was a baby crying upstairs and his mother screaming for help. Beth and Rudy went in. Beth put him in his little seat and threw the seat out the window. Someone caught the baby, and he's fine, but Rudy, Beth, and the mother couldn't escape. They got caught in the stairwell when the building collapsed."

I closed my eyes, the haunting image surging to the front of my mind. Rudy held Beth protectively to his chest, their fingers on one hand interlaced. They knew they weren't getting out of there.

Gideon shook his head again, a tear escaping down his cheek. He wiped it with a quick swipe of his hand and stared at his son, who slept peacefully, unaware of the horror of this world.

"They deserve the golden gates," he whispered, but glared up at me. "I told them all. I told them this would happen, and they didn't listen to me. Their hands are stained with so much blood that didn't have to be shed."

I knew he was talking about the other Alphas who voted for Diamond Moon to hold the artifact and nodded in agreement.

"Gideon? What's wrong?"

His face softened at Eris' voice behind him, the grief returning.

He put his hand on my shoulder. "Thanks for telling me, Finn."

I just wanted to be with Kat, and I nodded, turning down the hall-way.

Gideon stopped at the door and linked me. *'I want an alphas meeting arranged. Three days from today, at the wreckage of Diamond Moon. They can all see the cost of their arrogance.'*

'Consider it done.'

I stood in the doorway and watched Kat breathe. She slept, her color finally returning. She was connected to an IV of clear fluid. They had washed her face, combed her hair, and changed her into a hospital gown.

I crawled up next to her, barely squeezing in. I wasn't clean, filth still caked on my body—mostly Kat's blood—so I laid on top of the bedspread and rested my head next to hers on the pillow. Her scent filled my nose, calming me, and I breathed, trying to come to terms with this day.

I had been in battles before. I had seen people die. Today was different. It was a massacre. Pups and innocent civilians slaughtered like cattle in the streets. Rudy and Beth, meeting death in a moment of pure heroism. Kat had nearly left this world right in front of me.

I nestled in closer, trying to push the images away.

Crying definitely wasn't something an alpha wolf was supposed to do. And I didn't do it often. But now, in the privacy of this room, holding my sleeping mate, I let the tears fall.

CHAPTER 39

KAT

I WOKE UP WITH a killer headache. I was in some kind of fancy hospital room. Finn was next to me. I could hear his even breathing as he slept, and my heart clenched. I was alive. I'd actually made it.

I tried to get out of the bed as carefully as I could to go to the bathroom, but Finn stirred.

"Are you okay?" he asked, jolting up to come help me.

"Yeah. I just need the bathroom."

I closed the door and looked at myself in the mirror. It was better than I had expected. I had some color in my cheeks at least. I lifted my gown and looked at the angry red scar at the top of my stomach. It was huge, almost the size of a dessert plate, and sat just under my sternum.

"Stupid silver."

If the tail hadn't been tipped with silver, it would already be completely healed. My scars didn't stay nearly as long as other shifters' did.

'Are you guys okay?' I asked.

'Yes,' Hana and Rieka answered in unison.

Hana added, *'But let's not ever do that again.'*

'Agreed.'

Feeling disgusting, I squeezed in a quick shower, leaving my arm with the IV out of the water. When I got back out to the room, Finn was sitting on the edge of the bed with his head in his hands.

My heart pinched when he looked up at me. He was exhausted, and he rubbed his red, swollen eyes. There was a new look there, too. A haunted sadness that I'd never seen before. Between the two of us, I felt he looked worse.

"How are you?" I asked.

"Been better."

"What day is it?"

He pulled out his phone, reading the time. "It's nine in the evening. So, the battle was last night."

I walked over to him, hugging him while he sat on the bed. Finn sighed, lifting up my gown to see the wound.

He grimaced. "I'm sorry, Kat."

"It's okay. It barely hurts. Do you think they'll let me outta here?"

He nodded and stood, going to find the nurse. They returned, and she offered me some white pants and a sweatshirt, removing the IV from my arm. She gave me something for the headache and some instructions on how to watch for infection. I listened, but I could feel that I was already healed. The only thing bothering me was the tightness of the scar.

Finn wanted to carry me, and I let him, even though I could make it fine. I laid my head against his chest and listened to his heartbeat, already feeling drowsy again.

I woke up sometime later in our room and felt the bed next to me. The sheet was cold.

"Finn?"

He was close by, on the balcony, wearing pajamas and drinking whiskey. I got up and went to him, but the look he gave me caught me off guard.

"What's wrong, Finn?"

He hesitated to answer, and I felt a low ebb of anger through the bond.

"Why did you come? Why were you there?"

"What?"

"You should not have been there, Kat," he snapped, swirling the ice in his cup and drinking what was left.

"Eris wouldn't stay."

He clenched his teeth. "You almost died. I watched you bleed out on the ground!"

"Well, I couldn't just let her go alone!" I defended, back on my heels.

"Going with Eris and deciding to jump on a dragon are two totally different things, Kat!"

There was no answer to that. I didn't even know why I did what I did. It was stupid and reckless, and I should be dead.

"I just wanted to help," I whispered, not knowing what else to say.

He closed his eyes and took a deep breath, forcing it out. "Never again, Kat. You can never do that to me again. If you died... I couldn't handle it. I wouldn't survive it."

"But I didn't, okay?"

"You're not even trained to fight! You can't be there. It's a liability to everyone. Especially me."

My cheeks flared at being called a "liability." Deep down, I knew he was right. I'd survived on pure luck and superior athletic ability last night, even before I jumped on the dragon.

There was a long silence until I blurted, "Then I want to be trained. I want to learn to fight."

"No. No way."

I crossed my arms. "I should learn! We're at war."

He stood, looming over me. "You can just stay here, and you'll be safe."

"Well, I won't! Not while you and everyone else I love are in danger. Besides, they could show up here anytime!"

"Kat."

"No. I want to learn to fight, and if you won't help me, I'll just ask Eris."

We glared at each other while our mutual stubbornness waged war through our bond. When the tension left his face, riding a sharp sigh, I knew I was going to get my way.

"If anyone is going to train you, it's going to be me. But, gods, you have to be careful," he whispered, putting his forehead down to mine. "Please. I can't lose you again."

I wrapped my arms around his neck. "I'm sorry. I promise no more dragon riding."

He shook his head, pulling me closer and muttering, "I would never want to encourage you, but it was probably one of the most badass things I've ever seen anyone do. Period."

"Yeah. No big deal. Just a typical Tuesday for me, really."

He chuckled and grabbed my chin, pulling my face up to his for a whiskey kiss.

As things got more heated, he wrenched his lips away. "Are you sure you're okay?"

"Better than okay."

He smiled, picking me up and carrying me to our bed.

FINN

Two days had passed since the battle at Diamond Moon. Gideon had gone early this morning to attend Rudy and Beth's shared funeral, and he had just gotten back.

Eris and I hated that we weren't attending, but Gideon didn't want her to go with the babies, and he didn't want to leave them here without either him or me here keeping an eye on things.

We all sat in his office now: Gideon, Eris, Kat, Enid, the witches, and myself.

Tomorrow was the alphas' meeting at Diamond Moon, and Gideon had just laid out a plan that, if successful, would be one of the best political maneuvers in recent history.

We were still talking things over when something heavy thumped on the balcony. Things grew quiet, and we all stared at each other, our eyes asking if everyone else had heard it too. Gideon stood, going to look, and stopped mid-step when there was a soft knock on the door.

Gideon looked at me, and I shrugged. He grabbed the knob and yanked the door open.

A shirtless man stood on the other side. He was tall, probably three inches taller than my brother. Coal-black hair fell in messy waves around his face, contrasting dramatically with his sapphire blue eyes. He wore only black jeans. No shoes, even.

Even as a dude looking at another dude, all I could think was that no one had any business being that fucking attractive.

'What in the Armani model is going on here?' Kat asked in the link.

'What's that supposed to mean? You think he looks like a model?'

'Well, yeah. This guy should be on a runway somewhere. Look at him!' She seemed to remember who she was talking to, and her cheeks flushed pink. *'But so do you, babe!'*

'Sure,' I said, drawing out the word and glaring at Mr. Armani.

When I smelled his scent, I stiffened and saw everyone else do the same. Wolf shifters had a wild scent. Pine forests and mountain breezes were ingrained in our DNA. We'd noticed that dragons all put off the subtle scent of burned wood.

"Why are you here, dragon?" Gideon asked, glancing at his spear mounted on the wall.

The man put his hands up, grinning. "I'm not here to hurt or kidnap anyone."

Kat snapped her fingers and pointed at him. "You're the small black dragon."

He frowned. "Well, small is subjective, but yes. I am the beautiful obsidian dragon that saved all your lives, and you're the suicidal girl that rides on dragons." He arched an eyebrow at her and added, "Nude."

Kat blushed, giggling into her hand, and I already despised this guy with my entire soul. Shaw was grumbling all sorts of threats he knew we couldn't follow through on. Not that we wouldn't try.

"Glad to see you're alive. I thought you were dead for sure. She must've been there."

He pointed to Eris as he said it, and Gideon pulled her closer to him.

"Well, thanks for your help," Kat said when she'd recovered from her tittering embarrassment. "Killing him, I mean, the blue dragon."

He shrugged, pulling a cigarette out of his pocket. "Of course. He was a terrible father, anyway. Like, the worst."

He lit the cigarette with a small puff of flame from his lips, and we all stared at him.

"Wait. The blue dragon was your father?" Gideon asked.

"Yep. Ol' Pappy Typhon. May he burn for eternity, and that still wouldn't be long enough."

Kat said, "Wow. I thought I had a dysfunctional relationship with my parents."

"I bet I've got you beat. Things were rough growing up. Me being despised for being half human, and him brutally murdering my mother in front of me. All of that fun stuff."

We all glanced at each other, but he went on.

"And I'm not small," he said, apparently still stuck on that. "I'm young. Those other fossils are several centuries old, but I'm only two hundred and thirty-three."

The oldest wolf shifters only lived to one hundred and fifty, so he was certainly old in our eyes.

"Well, what do you want?" Gideon asked.

"Gideon, right? I'm Cassian. You guys can call me Cass, though, since we're friends. Except them. We are not friends," he said, nodding at River and Rhia. "And what I want is to not live in the world my father envisioned. See, the other dragons hate me, the whole half-breed thing, and they make it their business to make my life awful whenever they can." He glared at the witches. "And your kind locked me down in that fucking hole with them when I was a fourteen-year-old boy. Thanks for that, you old hags."

"Sorry we're not sorry, dragon filth," Rhia hissed, surprising everyone.

Cass chuckled, but shadows darkened his features. He moved on, not addressing them again. "I'm here to offer a truce. I want to help stop the others after they get the third artifact."

"They won't get it," Gideon said, tapping his pen on his desk. "It's safe here."

Cass laughed, hard, looking around as if we'd all join him. When we didn't, he asked, "Oh, were you serious?"

"Yes," Gideon hissed through clenched teeth.

"Wolves," he said, snickering again. "They'll get it, trust me, and when they do, I want to do what I can to help you prevent the birth of the beast and the end of days."

"Why should we trust you?" Gideon asked, raising an eyebrow.

Cassian looked him up and down, puffing on the cigarette. "Look, I know you're in charge here or whatever, Alpha, but I'm not really talking to you. I'm talking to her." He smiled and winked at Enid. "I'm here for the Green Witch."

CHAPTER 40

KAT

W E WALKED TOGETHER THROUGH the ruins of Diamond Moon. Smoky air clogged the sky. It smelled like a damp campfire after a merciful summer rain put out the remaining flames.

Three days in the heat of summer had caused the bodies not yet recovered from the wreckage to spoil and bloat. The rotting scent choked me, and I breathed through my mouth, trying not to vomit.

We were headed to the pack house, or what was left of it, anyway. Gideon ordered the conference room to be put somewhat back together so the meeting could occur. The roof was burned, so it was open to the sky, and in the middle of the charred room sat a brand-new conference table with chairs.

I had found out, and been slightly disappointed to learn, that my sperm donor had survived the massacre. His wife Mary, Lyrion's mother, and Lyrion's widow Natasha had also survived. They would represent the interests of Diamond Moon today.

We all sat under the blistering July sun, and I took a deep breath. Things were about to get interesting.

FINN

We waited while the other Alphas and their Lunas filed into the room. Many of the ladies held scented rags over their mouths and noses, and some had tears on their faces. The Alphas were pale, their expressions drawn. Royce was here, seated between Mary and Natasha. They were both dressed in black with veils over their faces, one mourning her only child, and the other, her husband.

I wondered how Royce had survived the onslaught when almost none of Diamond Moon's fighting wolves had. Lyrion had been one of the first to die, doing what he should've been doing as an Alpha and protecting his pack.

Gideon stood. His expression was shadowed and reflected his feelings over the unnecessary loss of life here. The loss of his lifelong best friend. He stared around the room, and several of the other Alphas couldn't even make eye contact with him, casting their eyes down.

He addressed the room. "Alphas. I've called you all here today to discuss the future of the Union. What remains of it, anyway. As you all know, I desperately objected to the bell artifact being left at Diamond Moon. I wanted to keep everyone safe. I wanted to bear the burden of protecting the artifacts. But you," he slapped the table with both hands, "wouldn't listen!"

Everyone jumped at the sound but remained silent.

"Now, we're down two Alphas. They killed Lyrion. And...Rudy and his mate Beth died saving a baby. Over half of the population of Diamond Moon was slaughtered and fed upon by vampires in a matter of hours. Do you now understand the power of our enemy?"

No one answered. Most of the Lunas were white as sheets, and the Alphas sat with tense shoulders. Behind her veil, Mary stared forward as if in a trance. Natasha picked at her hands, not looking up.

Gideon adjusted his tie. "So, we're here to determine the fate of Diamond Moon, now without an Alpha. And solidify the solution offered by Rudy in his last will and testament regarding his successor."

He signaled to the Beta of Emerald Moon, Linden, to take over the conversation.

Linden stood, cleared his throat and removed a stack of papers from the folder in front of him.

"Alpha Rudolph of Emerald Moon," he started, "did not produce an heir of his own in the time he was alive. Therefore, he appoints the rule of Emerald Moon to his younger sister, Glinda. Since she is only seventeen, he ordered that she is to be extensively counseled by myself and Alpha Gideon of Gold Moon until she comes of age."

Glinda was here, next to Linden, and she held her head up. The resemblance to her brother was uncanny. Short, stout, and strong, with long curly black hair and chocolate eyes. She had a dusting of freckles across her nose and cheeks, which made her appear even younger than she was.

"I accept this duty," she said, standing. "And the provisions that come with it."

Royce scoffed and looked around, but no one objected, several ayes sounding around the table.

Glinda and Linden sat, and Gideon stood again. "With that settled, we move to the fate of Diamond Moon."

Royce stood. "Request the floor? I already have a solution for that."

Gideon inclined his head, giving him time to speak, and then sat.

"As you all know," Royce started, "my son and his mate failed to produce an heir for our pack."

Natasha tensed but didn't look up from her hands.

"So, I am proposing I be allowed to take a second mate, as has been done before in historical situations, to produce another heir," he finished.

The air was heavy with shock, everyone staring at him. Mary didn't flinch.

'Bless his heart, he's going to make this easier than I expected,' Gideon said through the link.

"And who would this second mate be?" Brutus asked, his brow knit when he looked at his sister, Mary.

Royce rested his hand on Natasha's shoulder. "It only makes sense that the Luna stays the Luna."

"Gods," an older Luna scoffed, putting her hand to her chest.

"Just to clarify, you are suggesting you take your son's widow as a mate to produce an heir?" Gideon asked.

A ripple of murmurs rolled around the table.

"It's been done before," Royce defended.

"It's archaic, you cad!" Brutus snapped, and his wife put her hand on his arm.

"It's the only way for my family to continue the Alpha lineage!"

"And how does Natasha feel about this?" another Luna asked.

Natasha stood but didn't look up. "I am willing to do what's best for my pack."

'Oh, gods, that poor woman,' Kat said in the bond, reaching for my hand.

Gideon scoffed. "Well, let me be the first to vote nay."

Brutus immediately added, "Nay!"

Before anyone else could decide, Gideon continued, "It doesn't matter, anyway. Because I know, as you know, Royce, that there is another heir. She's sitting right here with us."

Kat's palm was sweaty in my hand, and I squeezed her fingers.

Royce glared at my brother. "I don't know what you're talking about, boy."

Gideon taunted him. "No? Are you sure about that?"

Royce didn't answer, so Gideon dropped the bombshell. "I present to the council that my brother's mate, Katarina Kimura, is the illegitimate daughter of Royce Caine."

Mutters of surprise erupted around the table, everyone looking at Kat and then Royce.

"That abomination," he snarled, pointing a long finger at Kat, "is not my pup! And you can't prove it."

Kat was pale, but she glared at him, and to my surprise, said, "Fuck you, asshole."

Royce gasped as if he'd been slapped, and Gideon chuckled, opening his briefcase. His grin was wry, the predator about to pounce on his prey.

He pulled out a single paper and snapped it. "Actually, Royce, I can prove it. Smoking is a disgusting habit, you know?"

Royce knew exactly what he meant. He glared at me, and I grinned, clicking my tongue.

Gotcha.

CHAPTER 41

KAT

I FIDGETED WITH FINN'S hand, watching Royce's face tighten and redden while Gideon read the paternity report.

"The alleged father, whose known DNA was collected from Sample A—one cigar butt—cannot be excluded as the biological father of the tested child, Sample B—one buccal swab, Katarina Kimura. Based on the analysis of STR loci listed above, the probability of paternity is 99.999999999 percent."

He enunciated every nine, watching Royce's face twist into unbridled rage. Gideon handed the paper to Eris, who passed it to Brutus.

"This is unfounded!" Royce said, slapping the table. "You can't prove that was my cigar."

Brutus read the report and then looked at him over the paper. "It's a simple solution. Just volunteer another sample and we'll have it tested again."

Royce looked like a ripe tomato ready to burst. "Absolutely not! I will not continue to be humiliated by this farce!"

"Then that's all the evidence I need. An innocent man would do anything to clear his name," Brutus said, glancing at the other alphas, most of whom nodded their heads in agreement.

"She didn't even grow up in a pack! She has no idea how to be an Alpha. She's from a weak breed, half kitsune."

Gideon's eyes flashed yellow, and he stared Royce down. "That kitsune is a member of my pack, and she felled a dragon here only three days ago. You should be thanking her because I didn't see you during the battle, Royce."

"I was out there!" he spat, and Natasha and Mary both looked at him, outing the lie.

Gideon said, "Right. Kat may not have grown up in a pack, but my brother did, and he is an excellent Beta. He would make an excellent and knowledgeable..." He paused and looked at Finn, a small smile curling his lips, "Luna."

Finn sighed, chuckling under his breath. Several of the Alphas were nodding in agreement.

"This is all a ploy so the Greenwoods can take control of more pack members and more pack land!" Royce said, standing and using the same old fear tactic in an attempt to win over the other Alphas. "He is still set on being Alpha King!"

"So, are you arguing against the law of succession?" Brutus asked. "Ms. Kimura has the biological right, as your pup and Alpha Lyrion's younger sibling, to be Alpha of Diamond Moon if she so wishes."

Several ayes sounded around the table, but a few Alphas stayed quiet, observing.

"This is bullshit," Royce growled, sitting and throwing his hands up in exasperation. "Two women as alphas? What a joke. Where is this world going? Are men not men anymore? My gods."

A jab at not only me but Glinda, too.

Hana huffed, *'He is an absolute pig.'*

'I would like to bite his throat out,' Rieka agreed.

Gideon said, "Welcome to the twenty-first century, Royce," and the air thickened as every Luna turned hard eyes on him.

"Well," the one called Amos said to me, sighing and rubbing his temples, "what say you, young lady? Do you accept this duty?"

Gideon looked at me and nodded, indicating it was time for me to speak.

I stood, taking a shaky breath and steeling myself. "I, Katarina Kimura, accept this duty to be an honorable Alpha of the Diamond Moon pack."

Royce barked a laugh, and I swallowed. His eyes were yellow, a flash of his wolf, and I wasn't even finished yet.

"So be it. Congratulations, Alpha Kimura and... Luna Finn," Amos said, sounding less than excited.

I cleared my throat, showing I had more to say. We practiced my lines extensively yesterday.

"My first act as Alpha of Diamond Moon is to propose a merger with Alpha Gideon Greenwood of Gold Moon. I resign my rights as Alpha to him and submit for Diamond Moon to no longer exist as is, instead becoming part of Gold Moon."

Gideon had offered the Alpha spot to Finn and me, and we had decided to decline. We didn't want that pressure in our lives. Finn admitted that he regularly thought about how lucky he was not to have to be an Alpha, and we were selfishly happy to let Gideon take over.

Royce shot back up. "Excuse me?"

Gideon smirked at him. "I, Alpha Gideon, declare that Gold Moon accepts your proposal."

Royce pointed a finger at me, his claws extending as he started to shift. "You little bitch! I swear you'll pay for this!"

Finn stood, pushing me behind him and starting his own shift.

Gideon was still smirking, and he was loosening the knot on his tie. "Do it, Royce. Make my day. My brother and I would love to tear you to pieces."

Royce's chest heaved as he glared between Gideon and Finn. The two women who flanked him scooted away, and I wondered what secret horrors those two had endured in their lives as the Lunas of this pack.

Amos sighed, sitting back and looking at his fellow alphas. They all appeared to be reeling with the understanding Gideon had just doubled his packlands and increased his population by three hundred. Only Brutus looked amused, content to watch his brother-in-law's destruction.

Royce didn't attack, but he snarled, "I will not allow this! I will fight this until my dying breath!"

"You should be imprisoned for rape," Eris snapped.

He blanched, and all eyes fell on her, confused murmurs traveling around the table.

Alpha Owen asked, "What do you mean by that, Luna?"

"I mean, we should arrest him for the rape of Celeste Kimura."

"Bullshit!" Royce shouted, laughing. "I did nothing to that little fox that she didn't want!"

Mary broke away from her forward stare and glared up at him.

"Katarina, you must be at least twenty years old?" Amos asked. "The statute of limitations has long expired for that crime. Besides, we would need the complainant herself to come forward, or this is just hearsay."

Eris crossed her arms. "There's got to be something we can do. He's a danger to women everywhere."

"There is nothing that can be done, Luna. I'm sorry," Amos answered, and to his credit, he sounded sincere. "It's the law."

Several ayes sounded, showing that the other Alphas agreed nothing could be done.

It was Royce's turn to smirk, although I could tell he was still royally pissed off. He sat, adjusting his tie, and everyone around the table glared at him with disgust.

My stomach was tied in knots. Despite our tumultuous relationship, I was sick about what he'd said about my mom. I knew better than anyone that she did not want it. We couldn't get her any justice after all.

"Then so be it," Amos said, looking like he'd aged ten years during this meeting. "The merger between Diamond Moon and Gold Moon is approved, pending ratification. Now let's all take an intermission to collect ourselves and then return to draw up the documentation."

Everyone agreed and stood, murmurs starting around the table. Royce stalked off towards the woods, shifting and disappearing.

Eris grabbed my hand. "Come back to the tent with me. I need to check on the babies and feed them."

The twins were with Diane, who'd come to care for them. We were all staying in these huge tents in the clearing where the dragons had been killed since the city was demolished.

'Don't leave her side and don't go anywhere alone, Kat. If Royce finds you, he will kill you,' Finn said in the link.

'I'll be smart, I promise.'

Eris and I left the wrecked conference room and walked towards the back door of the house, the quickest way to get to the clearing.

Natasha was waiting, and she greeted us with a sad smile. "Luna, Ms. Kimura. Can I have a word with you in here?"

She gestured to the door behind her, and Eris eyed her but finally nodded, linking me, *'Be on your guard.'*

"It's Kat," I said to Natasha, offering a smile. This poor woman deserved some grace.

She nodded, returning my smile, and then we followed her through the door. The stark smell of lemon filled the air, and I realized we were in a tiny custodial closet. It was untouched by the destruction that ruined the rest of the pack house.

Mary was waiting. At one time, she must have been an exquisite woman with long wavy blonde hair and blue eyes. She was tall and sickly thin. Her face was gaunt, with massive black circles framing her eyes.

"I know this is a little unorthodox," she said, putting her hands out to indicate the closet. "But I must speak with you, Katarina."

She was wringing her bony hands, so I smiled and said, "You can call me Kat."

Mary nodded. "I wanted you to know that even if nothing can be done and nothing can be proven that I believe you. And I believe your mother."

"Why?" Eris asked.

"My... mate," she said, the side of her mouth dipping, "is an awful man. I know from experience that he takes what he wants without asking."

Her eyes were haunted, a faraway look in them as her hand traveled absentmindedly to the faded mate mark on her neck.

I didn't catch on, but Eris hissed in her next breath. She was so upset she had tears forming in her eyes, and Eris was not a crier.

"Mary, are you insinuating that he marked you without your permission?"

Mary rubbed Eris' arm, comforting her. "He did a lot of things without my permission. But please don't cry for me, Luna. It's in the past now, and I accepted my fate long ago." She became emotional, whispering, "But I am sorry, Kat. There were so many times I thought about killing him myself, but I was too afraid. I'm so sorry about your mother for what she went through. If I had only been stronger..."

Her voice trailed away, and I wiped at a tear in my eye, shaking my head. "It's okay, Mary. I could never blame you."

Eris softened, grabbing her arm. "Mary. Tell someone. Help us put him away. Stop him."

Mary blanched, taking a step back. "I-I can't do that. I'm sorry."

"You can, Mary. We'll support you every step of the way."

"There's nothing I can or am willing to do, Luna," Mary snapped, her eyes glassy. "I'm just a sad old woman."

Eris took the hint and didn't ask again, but she crossed her arms over her chest, frowning.

Mary stuttered, "I-I only wanted you to know that, Kat, dear. Please forgive me."

With that, she pushed past us, fresh tears rushing down her face.

Natasha went to follow, but blurted around a sob, "Thank you for saving me from having to be his mate," and she hugged me.

I returned the embrace, but it was brief, and she hurried out of the door after Mary.

Eris and I looked at each other, our mouths hanging half open.

CHAPTER 42

KAT

ERIS AND I RETURNED to their heavily guarded tent, where a relieved Diane handed Eris the fussy babies. She fed them in the nice chair Gideon had brought out here just for that reason, and I laid down on the bed, wanting to rest my eyes until the next meeting.

I woke up sometime later, realizing I had fallen asleep. Eris was gone, but Diane looked up from the book she was reading, smiling and pressing her finger to her lips.

"How long was I asleep?" I whispered.

"Only about forty-five minutes."

I nodded and sat up, rubbing my eyes.

The flap opened and Eris entered, checking the sleeping babies, and then indicating for me to follow her.

"We've got to go back. Since you're the Alpha proposing the merger, you have to be there to sign the papers."

"Where were you?"

She shrugged. "I wanted to talk to Mary one more time, hoping she would change her mind about testifying against Royce."

"Any luck?" I asked, knowing she couldn't be convinced. That woman was terrified. My mom had held that same fear, refusing to report it to the police.

Eris shook her head. "No. And I didn't want to push her anymore. Despite how awful he seemed to us, Lyrion was her pup and her only reason for living, and now he's gone. I think the only reason she's still here is to make sure Natasha is okay."

I nodded, horrified for Mary. That poor woman.

FINN

Gideon and I walked together to the tent. We could've linked Eris and Kat, but he was hoping to see the babies before the next meeting. My brother would have to wait, however, because our mates met us halfway.

When Eris saw us, she stomped up to Gideon. "Royce needs to be punished. He abused Mary throughout their entire relationship. He marked her without her permission!"

Gideon blanched, and I choked on my next breath. That was the lowest of the low.

I looked between my brother and Eris. "That fucking creep!"

Gideon ran his hand through his hair. "Is Mary willing to say anything? To come forward?"

"No, she is terrified. I bet all of his victims, and I guarantee there are many, are all too scared of him to come forward. He's a powerful alpha wolf. I'm sure he threatened them; threatened their families."

"Then I don't know what to do, Eris. It's the law."

"Well, it's horrific that we live in a society where rapists seem to have more rights than victims," she hissed, pushing by him and heading back to the conference room.

He followed her, his hands out as he tried to reason with her, apologizing for things out of his control.

I turned to Kat. She giggled.

My cheek lifted, and I took her hand. "What are you laughing about?"

"Oh, just Eris. She's a force to be reckoned with."

I nodded. "Are you okay? You up for going back and finishing this?"

"Yeah. At least we took his pack from him and stopped him from forcing Natasha to be his mate," she said, looking like she could vomit at the thought.

"Yeah, that was a wild proposition, even for Royce." I put my arms around her and held her, kissing her forehead. "I am so proud to have such a strong, brave woman as my mate."

She said, "Oh, shut up, Finn," like she didn't believe me, but she blushed and tucked her hair behind her ear.

I chuckled, taking her hand. "Let's get this over with."

Detailing a merger of this size lasted the rest of the day, but by the time the sun started setting, it was finished. Diamond Moon was officially part of Gold Moon now.

Royce did not return to see his pack handed over to my brother by my mate, but it did little to lessen the burn of anxiety in my gut. If he held a vendetta against Kat, there was a real possibility he might try to hurt her someday.

We all returned to our tents, Kat and I to ours and Gideon to his. Eris was already there, having returned earlier to be with the babies.

I heard one of them now, their soft newborn cry echoing through the tents. Kat heard it too and smiled as we crawled into our bed.

"They are kind of cute," she whispered.

I pictured her with a pregnant belly. Her holding our newborn baby. Her pushing a toddler on a swing.

I took her hand. "Yeah, they are."

"I really hope I can give you that, Finn."

"Well, I guess we'll just have to find out for sure sometime."

Her anxiety spiked. I tried not to worry about it too much, but I was beginning to suspect Kat was right about her fertility issues. We'd had plenty of unprotected sex by now.

I turned on my side so I could face her. "Your ability to have or not have children doesn't change the way I feel about you. I love you more than I could ever explain, and I always will."

"I love you, too," she said, touching my cheek.

I ran my hands up her body, and she giggled.

I grinned. "You know, it's never too early to get started on making those pups."

"We're in the middle of all these tents! They'll hear us."

"So?" I answered, kissing her marking spot and pushing my hand up her shirt.

She gasped, holding my forearm. "Okay, but you have to be quiet."

I chuckled. "I don't know why you're worried about me."

She slapped my shoulder, and I caught her laughter with my kiss.

The next morning, my brother's voice jolted me awake.

'Finn, we need you outside your tent, now.'

'Why what happened?' I asked, sitting up with a start.

'Just get out here.'

Kat and I hurried and dressed, shielding our eyes as we stepped out into the already searing summer sun.

All the Alphas were gathered around, staring at me. Gideon rested his fist under his chin, studying me from head to toe.

"What's up, fellas?" I asked, putting my hand on Kat's waist.

Amos answered, "Oh, we think you know, Beta Finn."

"Uh, nope, I don't." I looked at my brother. "Will someone just tell me what the fuck is going on?"

"So, you want us to believe that you have no idea who went into the former Alpha Royce's tent and ripped his throat out last night? The man who openly threatened your mate yesterday," Amos asked, crossing his arms.

My eyes widened, and I looked at my brother.

"Holy shit! He's dead?" Kat asked.

Gideon nodded, and I tried really hard, I swear, but I couldn't contain the laughter that clawed up my throat.

'Did you do this?' Gideon linked me.

'No. Whoever did gets a high-five, though.'

'Finn,' he warned, and I realized he didn't believe me. *'If you did, I don't blame you. After he threatened Kat and everything else. I just need you to tell me the truth.'*

'I swear to the Goddess I didn't, Gideon! Trust me, I would've loved to kill that fucker, but I didn't do it.'

Gideon nodded and addressed the crowd. "Look, everyone. There's an easy way to figure this out. I'll just compel him to tell me the truth."

Amos glanced around at the other Alphas, and they all indicated that would be acceptable.

"Finn Greenwood," Gideon said, using his Alpha tone. "Did you have anything to do with the death of Royce Caine?"

I felt the command working in my brain, pulling the information to my lips. "Nope." I couldn't help but add on my own accord, "Unfortunately, I did not."

Everyone looked surprised and then Amos said, "Now, her." He gestured to Kat, and her hand flew up to her chest.

"Me? I couldn't have killed him!"

I smirked, nodding. "Yeah, I know for a fact she was too busy to be out murdering people last night."

Kat elbowed me in the ribs. "Gods, Finn!"

My brother closed his eyes, trying to keep his composure, but Amos was unamused.

"Just do it so we can all go home," Amos said, rubbing his temples.

Gideon said to her, "Did you kill Royce Caine?"

"No," she answered.

"Do you know who did it?"

"No."

Gideon looked at Amos. "See? They didn't do anything."

Amos' Beta approached, addressing the crowd. "Alphas, I feel it's relevant to share that both of the former Diamond Moon Lunas have disappeared. Their essentials are gone, like they packed a bag each and left in the night."

"Mary?" Amos asked, scoffing. "She did this?"

I glanced at Brutus. Pride shone in his eyes. His sister had gotten her own justice, after all.

"Oh, who cares who did it, Amos?" Julie, his Luna, snapped. "Royce was a monster. May he rest in the black pit. Let's go home, dear. I'm weary of this reeking mess."

He watched her walk away, and the crowd dispersed, echoing the same sentiments.

When we were alone, Amos looked at Gideon. "I'm sorry, Alpha. For not taking you more seriously about the situation with the dragons. I will never forgive myself for what happened here. We will follow your lead going forward."

Gideon nodded. "Thank you, Alpha Amos."

KAT

The drive back to Gold Moon was cheerful considering someone had been murdered last night. I never thought I'd be thankful for homicide.

Gideon drove the huge van. It had three full rows of seating so that the babies could ride in the back, Finn and I in the middle, and he and Eris up front. Two black SUVs followed with Gamma Lucien and Diane amongst the other warriors Gideon had brought to protect the babies.

I couldn't stop thinking about Mary. She was meek. I'd witnessed the fear on her face. To go in and rip Royce's throat out just didn't make sense.

"Mary must've been tougher than we thought," I said to the back of Eris' head. "Even after you talked to her again yesterday, I didn't think she would ever..."

My voice trailed off as everything clicked in my head. I should've said it in the link, but I couldn't stop the blurt.

"Eris! It was you!"

Gideon stiffened, and his head whipped to his wife. "Eris! Tell me that's not true."

"Well, I don't want to lie," she said, staring out the window.

He whispered fiercely, "If anyone finds out about this, you'll be arrested!"

"No one will find out. Mary and I worked it all out."

"Mary left to make it look like she did it," Finn said.

"Yes. She and Natasha should be on a white sandy beach somewhere soon, sipping margaritas and enjoying the rest of their lives. Besides, who's going to suspect a woman that gave birth less than a week ago?"

I put my hands on my cheeks. "He could have killed you!"

"Please. He didn't even know what was happening until it was over," she said, chuckling under her breath.

Finn laughed out loud, and leaned up, extending his hand for a high-five, which she gave.

"This is serious!" Gideon growled, and Finn sat back, snickering like a reprimanded child. "Eris! I told you I would banish him from the realm since I'm technically his Alpha now. Or was, at least."

"Out to the human world so he could terrorize them? Unacceptable."

Gideon was quiet, but ran his hand through his hair, like, twenty times in like two minutes.

"Gideon," she said, taking his hand. "I brought a daughter into this world three days ago. There was no place for Royce Caine on the planet with her. I did what had to be done."

He rubbed her thumb with his while their eyes glazed, continuing the conversation in the privacy of their heads.

When he focused, he looked in the mirror at Finn and me, commanding in his Alpha tone, "This information is never discussed again with anyone else."

We nodded. I wouldn't have told anyone anyway, but I felt the command set into my brain like stone.

Finn looked at me, eyebrows raised and a boyish little smile turning his lips.

'Well, I guess that takes care of that,' I said through the link.

'Sure does! Eris Royceslayer.'

I snickered at the twist of her nickname.

CHAPTER 43

FINN

WHEN WE GOT BACK to the pack house, Gideon linked Enid and asked her to come to the office. We had decided it was best for her to stay with the artifact today.

Gideon, Eris, Kat, and I walked to his office. Gideon carried Henry and Eris carried Ceres, both still asleep in their car seats.

When we opened the door, Cass was sitting at Gideon's desk. His bare feet were up on the desk, and he was chatting with someone on the phone.

"Oh, yeah, I'll let him know you called. Yeah, you take care, too. Mm-hm. Buh-bye," he said, and then hung up the phone.

He laced his fingers behind his head and remained reclined in Gideon's chair. "Oh, hey, guys. You're back."

Gideon looked like someone had insulted his mother. "Excuse me? What are you doing?"

"Well, Enid called and said you guys were leaving and that I should come help guard the artifact while you were gone. You know, help keep things running smoothly."

"Why are you in my office?"

"Because this is the doorway to the artifact, right? I'm just doing what I came here to do."

Gideon hissed in a breath. "And how do you know that?"

Cass chuckled, looking over at where the trapdoor was supposed to be expertly hidden. "Uh, I'm a dragon. I can sense the magic coming off of that thing from five miles away."

We all glanced at each other.

He arched his eyebrow. "Wait, you guys can't feel that? Wow, not the most perceptive species, are you? Barely better than humans, my gods."

Gideon glanced around, his face scrunched as if he smelled something vile. "What have you done to my office?"

I looked at the desk and side table. All the loose papers that had been strewn about were gone. Things were organized in perfect stacks, pens were in the holder, and every stray paper clip had found its way back to the little magnetic dish. I'd never seen it so tidy.

"I cleaned it. You're welcome," Cass answered, holding his arms out. "I don't know how you keep this pack running with all of that chaos."

"I like my chaos," Gideon snapped, walking over and shoving Cass' bare feet off of his desk.

Gideon searched the penholder. "Where's my favorite pen? See, you've ruined everything! It's going to take weeks for me to get everything back in order. Get out of my damn chair. And why aren't you wearing shoes?"

"Why are you wearing shoes?" Cass asked. "We're shifters. It's such an inconvenience to tie and untie your shoes all the time."

"Get some flip-flops or something."

"Hm. No."

"And don't ever answer my phone," Gideon scolded, pointing an angry finger at Cass. "As a matter of fact, don't come in here when I'm not here. You don't just go into a man's office and move stuff! Gods, were you raised in a barn?"

Cass thought about that, still reclining comfortably in Gideon's desk chair. "No. I was raised in a dungeon."

Enid walked through the door with Leo. "Cass! We've been looking everywhere for you."

I didn't miss my younger brother's eye roll as he set a glare towards the dragon.

"Enid. You invited this guy here?" Gideon asked.

"Well, yeah, he's part of the group now. You're the leader, Eris is the healer, and so on. Cass is..." She thought for a moment and then grinned. "He's our lovable rogue."

"Aw, thanks, little witch, that's nice. I don't think anyone has ever called me lovable before," Cass said, pulling a cigarette out of his pocket and putting it in his mouth.

Enid blushed, and Leo rolled his eyes again, crossing his arms.

Gideon shook his head. "Cass. My kids are in here."

Cass looked around as if he didn't know what to do and then waved at the car seats. "Hi, baby wolves!" He blew a small flame to light the cigarette.

"No! You are not smoking again in my office! And get out of my chair!"

Cass pinched the cigarette out and then stood, bowing and presenting the chair to him like a throne.

I laughed, looking over at Kat.

"Would you like to eat with us, Cass?" Eris asked.

Gideon's eyes widened, and he subtly shook his head at his wife.

Cass grinned. "That sounds nice. It's better than going back to the keep. I took over Xeron's place. Had to kill some vampires, but it's empty now." He sighed, reiterating, "So big and so empty."

"You should just move in here," Enid chimed.

I'd never seen my brothers look so much alike, both Leo and Gideon turning to her with wide eyes. Gideon's glazed, and it was obvious he was scolding her through the link.

It was an awkward thirty seconds while they argued. I could see Eris was also in on the conversation. Gideon sighed. Outvoted again, it seemed.

"Fine," he hissed through clenched teeth. "But you're not staying at the pack house. There's an empty guard tower on the edge of the northern forest. You can have it. You dragons like tall, menacing buildings, right?"

Cass smirked. "Yeah. They're fun to jump off of." He rubbed his hands together. "This is great! A new place with a pack." He looked at me. "You look like a man who knows. Where do I find the women? I've never had a wolf shifter before."

"Pike's Bar." Gideon glared at me and I shrugged. "What? It is."

"Don't tell him that!"

Eris said, "Welcome to our packlands, Cass. Let's go to lunch. I am starving!"

She and Gideon each took a car seat and led the way. Everyone else filed out behind them. I held my arm out to Kat, but she pulled her phone out of her pocket.

She stared at it. "Go ahead. There's something I need to do."

KAT

I took a deep breath and dialed the number. The ring trilled in one ear, and my heart pounded in the other. Hopefully, she would answer. Or, hopefully not. I couldn't decide.

"Hello?"

"Mom?" I asked, even though I knew it was her.

There was a beat of silence before she said, "Katarina? Why are you calling here? I thought we made it very clear—"

"I know, Mom. I know," I said, cutting her off. "I just had something I felt like you needed to know."

She said nothing, waiting for me to continue.

"I wanted you to know that I'm here in the supernatural realm, and I found my biological father. The man who assaulted you."

A sharp intake of breath and a clatter on the other end of the line.

"I just wanted you to know that he was... executed last night for his crimes. So he's gone. You don't have to worry anymore."

We were both quiet for a long while before she finally said, "Thank you for telling me. Is there anything else?"

My heart sank. "No, Mom, that's it."

"Well then, I better let you go."

"Okay."

The line was quiet again for a long second, and I brought the phone down, thinking she'd hung up.

She said, "Katarina?"

I whipped the phone back up to my ear. "Yeah?"

"I'm so sorry I couldn't do better for you." Her voice broke, and my bottom lip quivered, an instant tear rolling down my cheek. "Just... take care of yourself, okay?"

"It's okay, Mom. And I will," I whispered.

The line clicked dead, and I looked at my phone, which confirmed the call had ended. Wiping my eyes, I wondered if that was it. If that was the last time that I would ever speak to my mother in my life.

I am sorry it is this way,' Rieka said, and Hana whined in agreement.

There was a knock on the doorframe, and I looked up to see that Finn had waited for me, of course. He held out his arms, and I walked into them, crying into the soft cotton of his t-shirt. When I finally calmed myself, I was determined to be done crying over my parents for good.

"We can have lunch in the room," he offered. "If you don't want to be around everyone else."

"No, thank you. That's okay." I grinned and grabbed his hand, pulling him with me. "I want to go be with our family. Plus, watching Cass annoy Gideon is quickly becoming one of my favorite hobbies."

CHAPTER 44

FINN

I GLANCED OVER AT Kat in the passenger seat. She was staring blankly out the window, wiping at her face when a stray tear escaped and ran down her cheek.

We were in my car. I'd suggested we go for a drive after we'd ended a conference call with the lab in Sweden. We'd flown there earlier in the month, and, after extensive testing, they'd contacted us today with the unfortunate conclusion that Kat couldn't have a child of her own.

There weren't any absolutes, but they'd thrown a lot of technical words at us, like homologous chromosome pairs. They'd said, simply, that her DNA was "a mess," and they weren't even sure how she was conceived. She was a miracle in herself. Aside from that, a hybrid like Kat was so rare that they didn't have any previous data to draw on.

The doctor threw around a lot of "probably impossibles" and "most likely nots." They had suggested we try an egg donor and possibly surrogacy, but I don't think either of us had really been listening at that point. Maybe someday we would be ready to hear those things.

Her feelings in the bond were bitter and sharp. I was trying to keep my emotions under control, but I would be a liar if I said I wasn't upset, too. Disappointed that I might never get to experience those things with her.

Shaw was worried about her. *'Our poor mate. She's been through so much.'*

Her parents treated her like an invisible person her entire life. Celia was killed. Her biological father was a total creep and threatened her more than once. Not to mention being held captive at the dragon's keep, something she never talked about. I hadn't heard her mention it even once in the year we'd been together, besides when she was crying at Celia's grave. Maybe someday she'd want to talk about it. Maybe not. I'd be here, either way.

She grabbed my hand, and I brought her knuckles to my lips, kissing them softly while I pushed my love to her through the bond.

"I don't understand why I'm so upset," she whispered. "It's like, I knew. I always knew. But hearing it today, for sure, is so much harder than I expected." She got choked up, and sniffled. "And I'm sorry for you, Finn. That I can't give you the family you should have."

"It's not hopeless. They didn't give us zero chance. There's so much we don't know, Kat. And even if it doesn't happen, there are pups in this world that need parents. Even if fate has denied us the ability to have our own pup, that doesn't mean we can't raise beautiful children. But I understand why you're sad, and that's okay. I'm sad, too. It's hard news to hear, but like I said before, I don't love you any less, and I'm ready to face whatever the future brings us."

We pulled into the garage, and she took a deep breath, trying to steady herself. I reached over and dug into the glove box, finding a napkin and handing it to her.

"I just feel so bad," she whispered. "Like you're stuck with me. This broken person."

"Shut up, Kat," I said, and her lips curled. "Because I don't feel that way at all. I want to be with you forever, no matter what. I want to marry you."

"Is this you asking me?"

I shrugged. "I should probably do something more romantic than this. But I certainly would marry you. Right now, if you want to."

"No big, fancy wedding?"

"Whatever you want. I'll marry you in front of everyone or no one."

"I'll have to think about it."

"But for the honeymoon," I said, grinning, "I know where there's a perfect little bodega on the beach in Rio."

She smiled and leaned across the console to kiss me, then laid her head on my shoulder.

We sat in silence, letting our hearts ache and love together.

I laid my head back against the seat and closed my eyes. "Do you want to go for a run? It's been so long since I've gone for a run for no reason."

It had been a quiet few months since the battle at Diamond Moon. Now it was just waiting. Waiting for our enemy to make the next move.

Cass insisted they would come for the athame, but also said they would exercise great patience to get what they want. After losing two of their own at Diamond Moon, including Cass' father, who was their leader, they would take some time to regroup, but they'd be back.

Kat's door opened, and she started undressing, getting ready to shift. I grinned and got out. By the time I got around to her side, she was naked.

She grinned. "Are you coming?"

Unable to resist, I said, "Not yet," my lips curling until a smile cracked across my face.

She rolled her eyes. "A race to the other side of the lake, then? It's pretty private."

"To the other side of the lake," I agreed, pulling my shirt off over my head and tossing it into the car where her clothes were piled.

She shifted to Hana and stared up at me with intense golden eyes. "Hana? That's not fair!"

She yipped, so I reached down and stroked her soft, white fur. When she leaned into my hand, I said, "Told you I'd win you over, little fox."

Kat shouted, *'Go!'* in my head and took off, rounding the corner before I was even undressed.

'Cheater!' I answered, working desperately at my shoelaces before I finally used a claw to cut through them.

Maybe Cass had a point on that one.

I shifted, deciding to sacrifice my pants and boxers instead of taking the time to undress. Shaw barked after her and broke into a run, but we both knew she'd already won. I heard her giggle through the bond and picked up my pace. Goddess, she was fast.

And beautiful.

And wonderful.

And all mine. Forever.

Epilogue

Edana

I STARED ACROSS THE table at my two remaining companions. Their faces were drawn, pale with the realization of what we'd just lost.

"How could this happen?" Nox hissed.

I didn't know whether he meant it as a question to be answered or not. It was not a task I felt equal to, so I stayed quiet.

Tirich answered, shaking his head. "Typhon was a fool to underestimate the Pythonissam Viridi."

"You two abandoned him! Cowards!" Nox growled. "You could've helped him!"

I scoffed, spreading my fingers on the table. "And faced the Green Witch and her pack of dogs ourselves? They're smarter than we give them credit for. They've used Dragonsbane to make arrows. That's how they killed Semele. The Green Witch herself hasn't actually killed a dragon yet. Others have executed the finishing blows with her help."

"You're always the first to run. We know that, Edana! I should've had you take the artifact. I wouldn't venture to be such a coward," Nox said, baring his teeth at me.

I snarled at him but knew I would not win this fight if it turned physical.

"Typhon should've just come with us," Tirich defended. "There was no reason to stay aside from his own stubborn pride."

"And he wanted to kill that traitor," I added.

My companion's faces darkened, and Tirich hissed, "Cassian. That half-breed runt. I cannot wait to flay the flesh from his bones when I get my hands on him. He is the cause of this loss. We should've killed him when we had the chance."

Nox huffed and slumped back in his chair, unimpressed with our arguments.

I put my hands up. "Now what do we do? Not only have we lost Typhon and Semele, but my horde of vampires was decimated."

"As was mine," Nox agreed.

Tirich nodded, picking a gold coin off the table and flicking it, then catching it. "It will take us years to build up enough of an army to take the athame by force. And we'll have to face the Green Witch to do it."

I would never admit to the small blossom of fear that erupted in my chest at the name.

"That is true, and this is why we will not take it by force," Nox said, smirking.

Tirich and I looked at him, grinning. Nox was brilliant. Our most cunning ally.

"What have you planned now?" I asked.

"We're going to send one person in. They will retrieve the athame and bring it out to us. Easy."

Tirich's smile dipped into a frown. "Those wolf shifters may not be the most perceptive species, but I'm sure they'll notice a vampire among their ranks."

"I'm not sending a vampire," Nox said, enjoying our confusion when Tirich and I exchanged glances. "I'm sending a wolf."

"A wolf?" I asked, and jumped when Nox yelled, "Morga! Bring her!"

Morga was Nox's pet crone. She was so ugly that I found it hard to look at her. She must've been as old as we were, but unlike us, her appearance reflected her age. A hunched old hag, with her upper back curving almost impossibly; it looked incredibly painful. Her stringy gray hair hung in greasy tendrils around her wrinkled face and cloudy white eyes. It may appear she suffered from blindness, but she didn't seem to have any trouble seeing.

Morga hurried in, limping. "My Lord," she said, grinning and bowing. She had only three of her front teeth left, and they barely clung to her sickly black gums.

Ugly as she was, we owed everything to her. She was our champion, working for over two hundred years to free us from our tomb. Morga was not to be underestimated. She was a powerful and cunning witch.

"Come, pet," Nox coaxed, flashing a devilish smile to the young girl following the witch.

Her tight shoulders slackened, and she hurried over, sitting in his lap with a smug grin. Nox was a handsome man, his soft features rendering him less threatening than most dragons when he was in his human form.

His long brown hair hung to his shoulders, framing a face with deliciously plump lips and a light dusting of freckles. One might even think he looked innocent. The face of a cherub to hide the soul of a monster.

Nox stroked the woman's long, black hair. "Can you believe I found this poor, beautiful shewolf wandering in the forest outside of the realm, nearly starved to death? She was destined to be Luna of Gold Moon, but the cruel Maiden, Eris, took everything from her."

The wolf practically purred in his lap, intoxicated with being favored by one of the most powerful beings on the planet. The pets were often like that—in the beginning, anyway.

"She wants to help us," Nox said, kissing her cheek. "And in exchange, I've promised her a special place by my throne when we've regained our positions of power."

Tirich and I exchanged knowing glances, smirking. In the days of old, we always kept our favorites chained to our throne. Our playthings.

"My sweet Sophia," Nox cooed. "Our salvation."

THE LION AND THE WITCH TEASER

―――――◆◦◆―――――

Prologue

ENID

ERIS TWIRLED HER SWORD, already a master at fifteen. She was weightless on her feet, dancing around like she was made of air as she sparred with Father. He beamed at her footwork, keeping his grin as he attempted to outmaneuver her and failed. I dreaded my turn. Sword practice was worse than arithmetic, and I hated arithmetic.

I sighed. It was overly dramatic, causing my mother to peek over the top of her book. Her amber eyes studied me beneath thick lashes, and she tucked a strand of her buttery hair behind her ear.

"What's wrong, little dove?"

I tossed my hand up. "Eris is so good. Everyone already talks about how she'll be an amazing Alpha. I'm not a good fighter, and that means I'm a bad wolf."

Mother frowned and opened her mouth to reply, but Father's voice boomed across the exercise field.

"Enid, chin up. It's your turn!"

I sighed again, and Mother offered me a tenderhearted smile. "You're such a good girl, Enid, always doing as you're asked without complaint."

I nodded and trudged over to the sparring circle. As expected, I was still better at arithmetic than I was at sword practice. Always slow on the block and weak of the wrist. Father bested me several times.

"Light on your feet, Enid. Footwork! Where is your footwork? Sword at the ready. At the ready! Do not drop that sword down. Punch into the block; don't absorb it. Steady, quick blows when you are attacking! Move your feet. Your feet!"

When we finished, he said, "You are improving leaps and bounds every day, dove. Very good."

"What? I'm awful." I looked up into his round face and watched his forest-green eyes crinkle with a smile.

"You worked hard. That's all I ask of you, and all that matters."

"Are you busy or can we go again, Father?" Eris asked, stepping up beside me and taking the wooden sword from my hand.

His smile broadened. "Aye. And I'm not going easy on you this time!"

I shuffled back to Mother with tears in my eyes. She took my hand, and we walked in silence towards the library. Thad, Mother's personal guard, followed closely behind; the gentle, quiet shadow that was always with us.

Mother and I loved the library. The librarian always had a puzzle set out for us. We would work on it, sometimes for hours, until we finished it. Other times, we played chess. I hadn't beaten her yet. Someday I would.

I chose the puzzle table while Mother returned her now-finished book to the counter. The pieces presented two easy matches right away, and I smiled, clicking them into place.

Mother sat down and studied the puzzle, watching me find three more in quick succession.

"Enid," she said, pulling my eyes up to hers. "I don't like when you insult yourself by comparing your worth to others, especially Eris. Everyone is special in their own way."

I ran my finger over the small notch of the puzzle piece in my hand. "But Eris is so strong."

"She is older than you and has years more practice. That girl picked up a sword when she was a toddler and never put it down again. That's why we have a rule about no weapons at the supper table!" Mother laughed, shaking her head. "Eris' passion lies in being an Alpha. It's what's expected of her. She is a strong-willed woman and is going to make an excellent ruler someday."

"So I've heard," I said dryly. It felt like that was all anyone ever talked about.

Mother chuckled and grabbed a few strands of my hair, braiding it. "Well, I'm not a good fighter. Why do you think I need Thad?" I snickered, glancing at him, and he winked. Mother continued, her brow knitting with solemnity. "Maybe you should count yourself lucky."

"Why?"

"Eris' destiny has been chosen for her already. You are free to walk your own path. I think you're more like me, my lovey dovey. Your passion lies in art and beauty. We appreciate the small things. The sweet beauty of watching the tiny seedlings in the garden find their roots and blossom into flowers. The grace of the spider as she weaves her intricate web." Her eyes filled with tears. "Sometimes I think you're much too lovely for this dark world."

My cheeks warmed. There was no one in the world I'd rather be like than my mother. Maybe I was getting too big for it, but I wiggled into her lap and hugged her. She'd been in the stables. Her scratchy wool sweater still held the musk of her horses, and it mixed with her woodsy scent, the tinge of sharp pine tickling my nose.

"As you grow older, I hope you remember one thing."

"What, Mother?"

"Compassion is not weakness. Never, ever be ashamed of having a gentle heart."

She stroked my hair and hummed one of our lullabies while we both quietly clicked pieces of the puzzle into place. I hummed along, feeling better.

When she finished the song she added, with a soft curl at the edge of her lips, "I have a feeling, my sweet girl, that you will be the most special of all."

www.ingramcontent.com/pod-product-compliance
Lightning Source LLC
Chambersburg PA
CBHW050027180626
46810CB00002B/614